KT-418-132

Despite two national newspaper reports to the contrary, Kerry Wilkinson is male. Honestly.

His debut, *Locked In*, the first title in the Detective Jessica Daniel series, was written as a challenge to himself but became a UK Number One Kindle bestseller within three months of release.

His three initial Jessica Daniel books made him Amazon UK's top-selling author for the final quarter of 2011. When *Think of the Children* followed in 2013, he became the first formerly self-published British author to have an ebook Number One and reach the top 20 of the UK paperback chart.

Following *Playing with Fire*, *Thicker than Water* is the sixth title in the Jessica Daniel series.

Kerry has a degree in journalism, plays cricket badly and complains about the weather a lot. He was born in Somerset but now lives in Lancashire, thus explaining the climate gripes.

For more information about Kerry and his books visit:

Website: www.kerrywilkinson.com
or www.panmacmillan.com
Twitter: http://twitter.com/kerrywk
Facebook: http://www.facebook.com/JessicaDanielBooks

Or you can email Kerry at

kerryawilkinson@googlemail.com

By Kerry Wilkinson

LOCKED IN

VIGILANTE

THE WOMAN IN BLACK

THINK OF THE CHILDREN

PLAYING WITH FIRE

THICKER THAN WATER

KERRY WILKINSON

THICKER THAN WATER

PAN BOOKS

First published 2013 by Pan Books
an imprint of Pan Macmillan, a division of Macmillan Publishers Limited
Pan Macmillan, 20 New Wharf Road, London N1 9RR
Basingstoke and Oxford
Associated companies throughout the world
www.panmacmillan.com

ISBN 978-1-4472-2342-9

3 5 7 9 8 6 4 2

A CIP catalogue record for this book is available from the British Library.

Typeset by Ellipsis Digital Limited, Glasgow
Printed and bound by CPI Group (UK) Ltd, Croydon, CR0 4YY

Visit **www.panmacmillan.com** to read more about all our books
and to buy them. You will also find features, author interviews and
news of any author events, and you can sign up for e-newsletters
so that you're always first to hear about our new releases.

THICKER THAN WATER

1

Cameron Sexton's finger hovered over the standby button on the television remote control. He thought about calling upstairs to see if his wife was almost ready but figured if he kept quiet he might at least be able to watch the kick-off before having to leave the house.

He glanced at the teenager fidgeting nervously in the armchair across the room.

'Are you all right, Ollie?' Cameron asked.

The young man looked up from the television, nodding a little too enthusiastically. 'Yes, Mr Sexton,' he said. 'Thanks for calling me.'

'It's Cameron and thank *you*. It's always nice to have a reliable babysitter. How are your mum and dad doing?'

Oliver nodded, offering a vague 'all right', which Cameron thought could mean either 'they're absolutely wonderful, never been better', or 'they've split up and are living at opposite ends of the country', depending on which way the teenager's hormones were raging.

The sound of a whistle and an overly excited commentator took Cameron's eyes back towards the television screen. If he had remembered that the football was on, he would have suggested a different night to go out for a meal with his wife.

Cameron leant back into his seat as the commentator's

voice plus the oohs and aahs of the crowd broke the uneasy silence between him and Oliver. He tried to focus on the screen, resisting the urge to tug his suit trousers into a more comfortable position. They were feeling a little tight around his waist, although he tried to tell himself it was because they must have shrunk slightly at the cleaners, as opposed to his forty-something stomach being less forgiving nowadays.

The match was dull and Cameron felt his mind wandering. It was strange to be leaving your child at home in the hands of someone else, especially a person you didn't know that well and who wasn't technically an adult. Using Oliver had been his wife's idea. Eleanor knew his mother and, because he was about as polite and sensible as a teenager could be, they had asked him to look after Lara for an evening a few months ago while they went to the pub around the corner for a meal.

That had now become a monthly event that was both enjoyable and tentative. If anything, Cameron would have thought his wife would be the one nervous about leaving Lara – but she kept saying they were going to have to get used to it, which was true but also a bit of a shame.

Cameron squinted so he could read the match time in the top left corner of the screen and was surprised to see the game had already been going for five minutes. He stifled a sigh before standing and reaching across to hand the remote to Oliver.

'Here, you take this. We should be off out any minute. Well, whenever Eleanor is ready. You've got all this to come with girls and the like . . .'

Oliver took the control, shuffling in his seat, clearly uncomfortable with the topic. Cameron didn't know if the teenager had a girlfriend, or possibly even a boyfriend. The young man didn't seem overly confident but Cameron knew from his own experiences of being that age that very few seventeen-year-old lads had the bravado to talk to girls first. The ones that did were usually the biggest prats going, covered in gel and too much deodorant, not realising they were a couple of years away from ending up in some dead-end job for the rest of their lives.

Wondering when exactly he'd stopped knowing how to talk to the younger generation, Cameron offered a weak-sounding 'you can watch what you want', before adding: 'I'll go see where she is.'

He headed out of the room, moving quietly up the stairs until he saw his wife standing in the doorway of their daughter's room, her outline silhouetted by the night light from inside. Cameron stepped towards her, placing his hands on her hips and pulling her tightly as she gave a yelp of surprise.

'You scared me,' Eleanor said with a smile, playfully slapping his chest.

Cameron waggled his fingers in her face. 'Oooh, yes, I'm really scary.'

Eleanor giggled and turned around, pressing her back into him and resting her head on his breastbone. They stood silently in the doorway, watching their daughter's chest rise and fall, her eyelids twitching. Cameron found himself breathing in time with the young girl before his wife spoke softly.

'She's okay, isn't she?' Eleanor said.

'Well, she has got my genes. Let's just hope she ends up with my looks, intelligence, charm and charisma.'

Eleanor suppressed a laugh, spinning around, snaking an arm around her husband's waist and butting his shoulder gently with her head. 'As long as she doesn't have your head size.'

Cameron hugged his wife with one arm, using the other to pull the bedroom door until it was almost closed. 'And are you okay?' he asked.

'I can't believe she starts school in September. It only seems like yesterday we were in the hospital. Tomorrow she'll be dyeing her hair black and refusing to speak to us.'

As he smoothed down his wife's hair, Cameron tried not to laugh. 'Is that what you were like as a teenager?'

'I never dyed my hair but basically, yes.'

'At least we'll know where she gets it from then.' Cameron loosened his grip, kissing his wife on the top of the head. 'Come on, let's get going, or we'll never leave.'

Eleanor peered up at him wearily. She looked as tired as Cameron felt. When they had talked about having a regular 'date night', they'd agreed that regardless of his job, or how exhausted either of them felt, they would ensure they had one night a month for each other.

'Is Ollie all right?' Eleanor asked.

'I left him in charge of the TV and he knows where everything is. I made sure the baby monitor was working earlier, so he's all set. I even put a pizza in the oven for him.'

'Wow, my hero,' she mocked with a grin. 'Let's hope

Lara grows up to have your culinary skills as well as your giant head.'

Cameron glanced at his watch as discreetly as he could, not wanting to let on that he was in any way concerned about the time.

'How long ago did we order?' Eleanor asked.

Realising he had been caught, Cameron tried to reply in a way that didn't betray how annoyed he was. 'Around forty-five minutes,' he replied, knowing it was over an hour.

'I'm tempted just to say "sod it" and get a burger on the way home.'

Cameron failed to suppress a grin. 'Classy.'

Eleanor was trying to stop herself smiling too. 'You're the one checking the time.'

'I was checking out the back of my hand actually.'

She rolled her eyes. 'They're still hairy and clumsy, if that's what you're worried about.'

Before Cameron could respond, a waiter appeared over his wife's shoulder. 'Risotto?' he asked, before placing the plate in front of Eleanor and offering the steak to Cameron. 'Any sauces?'

Cameron couldn't avoid his wife's disapproving stare. 'No, fine, thanks,' he said, before waiting for the man to walk away. 'What?' he added innocently, looking at her, even though he knew exactly what she was thinking.

'You don't ask for ketchup in a restaurant,' Eleanor said.

'I didn't.'

'No but you were thinking about it.'

Cameron shook his head but could not stop himself smiling. 'What are you, the thought police?'

'When it comes to you, yes.'

Cameron cut into the meat, feeling his stomach rumble as a small amount of juice oozed onto the plate. Despite the time it had taken, he did have to admit the steak looked perfectly cooked and he had no doubt the thick, chunky, skin-on chips would be excellent too.

'Is it nice?' he asked his wife, nodding towards her bowl.

Eleanor chewed with her mouth tightly shut but nodded.

'Worth the wait?' Cameron added as he put a forkful of meat into his mouth.

She swallowed, taking a sip from her glass. 'Maybe.'

'What is a risotto anyway?'

He looked up to see Eleanor narrowing her eyes in the way that made the top of her nose crinkle. A strand of blonde hair fell across her face. Cameron thought she looked as gorgeous as ever as she moved it away. 'How old are you?' she asked.

'Forty . . . ish. What's that got to do with anything?'

Eleanor swallowed another mouthful. 'It's a rice dish. How can you not know that?'

'I don't know, I've never had it.' Cameron picked up a slice of steak with his fork and held it in the air. 'I eat man food.'

His wife smirked. 'Is that why your trousers are too tight?'

Cameron pulled a face of mock indignation, trying to think of something funny to respond with.

'Forty . . . ish,' Eleanor reminded him.

As they ate and chatted, Cameron risked another glance at his watch. They weren't running late as such but neither he nor his wife wanted to stay out any longer than they had to. He remembered the first time they had left Lara with Oliver, they had wolfed down a main course and then rushed home barely an hour later to find their daughter sleeping peacefully and the babysitter watching a film.

They had stayed out progressively longer on each subsequent date night. Somewhere at the back of his mind, Cameron expected to arrive home each time with the house a mess and Lara nowhere to be seen. It wasn't that he distrusted Oliver in any way, just that the irrational voice in his head always seemed to have more prominence than it should. They never went to the cinema because neither of them wanted to have their mobile phones on silent just in case they missed something. Even when they went to have something to eat, Cameron would make sure there was good phone reception and ensure Oliver had the restaurant's landline number just in case. He knew it was overdoing it but nothing would stop that little niggle that told him he should not leave his daughter.

He drifted back to the present as Eleanor put her fork down, picking up her napkin before starting to dab at her mouth. 'Are you okay?' she asked, apparently noticing his distraction.

'Fine, just thinking about dessert.'

Eleanor clearly wasn't taken in. 'She'll be fine.'

'I know.'

She tilted her head to one side, smiling widely. It was the exact expression that had made Cameron fall in love with her. She had a way of both grinning and chiding at the same time, one eye twinkling, the other attentive. 'I'll go phone the house while you look at the puddings,' she said, standing up. 'I'm not letting your trousers out for next time though.'

Cameron watched her walk away, her hips swaying, wondering if she would still be awake by the time he had managed to give Oliver a lift home. With those thoughts in mind, he was considering if dessert was a good idea after all. It wasn't often he saw his wife dressed up nowadays; the months of maternity wear, sensible shoes and breast pumps had become a necessary – albeit not too appealing – part of their lives.

As he took a cursory glance at the back of the menu, Cameron kept an eye fixed on the direction Eleanor had gone in. He had expected her to be barely a minute or two but began to feel something building in his stomach completely unrelated to what he had just eaten. Putting down the menu, Cameron watched the doorway. After a few minutes more, Eleanor finally emerged but he could see immediately that something was wrong. The smile from a few minutes before had disappeared as she walked quickly, the sway absent from her stride as she stared at her mobile phone. She didn't sit as she arrived back at the table.

'What's wrong?' Cameron asked, standing himself.

'No one's answering.'

'Did you try the house phone?'

'Of course.'

'What about Oliver's mobile?'

'That too – no answer.'

Cameron started patting his pockets, wondering which one he had put his car keys in. 'Shall we call the neighbours?'

Eleanor spoke with a forced calmness. 'No, let's just go. I'm sure everything is fine.'

The wait to pay was excruciating and Cameron could barely tolerate the silence during the car journey home. Each red traffic light and delay to give way at a roundabout seemed to occur in slow motion. He cursed any driver in front of him who was not going at least 10 m.p.h. over the speed limit. He could sense Eleanor in the passenger seat holding her breath as she tried to call the house. Each time, he could hear the phone ringing without being answered until his wife would hang up before trying again.

Neither of them spoke.

When they first moved in, Cameron had spent months struggling to reverse his car onto their driveway each time he arrived home. The thick brick pillars on either side seemed to have been placed deliberately to make life difficult and Eleanor would make jokes about his parking ability. Without even thinking, he drove in front first and switched off the engine, opening the door in one fluid movement. Eleanor was out of the car before it had stopped, heels clip-clopping across the tarmac as Cameron watched her climb the steps two at a time to their front door. He reached the bottom as she got to the top, a small cry escaping her lips.

'What?' Cameron asked, louder than he intended.

Eleanor was standing still as he joined her on the top step. She didn't have to say anything because he could see it himself – the front door was unlocked and open. Cameron looked at the fear in his wife's eyes. He was too scared to speak, in case saying it out loud would make it more real.

Gently, he eased the front door open, not knowing what he would see on the other side. Cameron realised he had been holding his breath and exhaled loudly as he stared into the hallway to see everything exactly as it should be. Eleanor's bright pink coat, which he so hated, was still hanging from the row of hooks on the right-hand wall. Lara's wellington boots and trainers were neatly placed on the floor underneath.

Cameron felt Eleanor pushing past him, heading for the stairs. Lara's bedroom was the natural place to visit first but, for some reason, he felt drawn to the living room. As he heard his wife's shoes ascending the wooden steps, Cameron slowly opened the front-room door, peering around it.

The room was bathed in a bluish haze with the glow from the television creeping into the darkened corners. Cameron stood for a few moments, staring at the screen, before remembering where he was. He blinked rapidly, glancing around the empty room which was, apart from the absence of Oliver, exactly as he had left it. Cameron noticed the house phone undisturbed on the side table, before he picked up the remote control and switched the set off, allowing darkness to engulf him.

He turned to walk back into the hallway but his foot brushed across the top of something hard. He bent down and picked up a mobile phone, examined it and put it in his pocket, stepping into the hallway. Cameron felt his stomach gurgling uncomfortably as he rested one hand on the banister at the bottom of the stairs. His house had a different aura about it in a way that was difficult to describe. He remembered when the new-born Lara was first brought home, and Eleanor spent the best part of two days sleeping. Owning a property wasn't about the bricks and tiles, it was about those memories, and now they suddenly seemed tarnished.

Cameron held on to the banister, eyes tightly closed as he slowly started climbing the stairs. He winced at every creak, listening out for the scream of anguish he knew would soon be coming from above.

As he neared the top, Cameron opened his eyes one at a time. He fully expected to see his daughter's bedroom door flung open with a pile of clothes or toys on the floor. Instead, Eleanor was standing in the doorframe staring inwards, illuminated by the night light in an almost identical fashion to a few hours previously.

'Ellie?' he said softly.

His words echoed around the hallway, unanswered. Cameron stepped closer to his wife until he was standing directly behind her. He peered over her shoulder until he could see the room clearly. He blinked rapidly, wanting his eyes to confirm it was true.

Even from the doorway, he could see Lara's chest rising and falling as she slept soundlessly.

'She's okay,' Eleanor said gently as Cameron pressed into her back. He felt his wife push into him before relaxing her muscles so he was supporting her weight. 'I thought . . .'

'I know.'

They stood in silence watching their daughter breathe. Cameron would have been happy standing there for the rest of the night but his wife turned and nestled her head into his shoulder. 'Where's Oliver?' she asked.

'I don't know. He's not downstairs.'

'He wouldn't have just gone home . . . would he?'

Cameron rubbed the bottom of the woman's back soothingly. 'His mobile phone was on the floor.'

Eleanor pulled away and met her husband's eyes for the first time since they had left the restaurant. She asked the question they were both thinking. 'So where is he?'

2

Detective Sergeant Jessica Daniel finished chewing the chip she was eating and scowled at her friend across the canteen table in disapproval.

'I'm not rising to it,' she said.

Detective Constable Isobel Diamond laughed. 'You always rise to it. There's no way you're going to let it go.'

Jessica picked up another chip and put it in her mouth, shaking her head. 'I'm a changed woman.'

Izzy laughed again. 'Not that changed if you're still talking with your mouth full.'

Jessica swallowed. 'That was just a treat for you. Anyway, I'm not rising to it.'

'I'm just asking if you're ever going to take Adam's last name.'

'Yes but you're not really asking, are you? You're stirring.'

Izzy giggled further. 'I am a bit, yeah.'

Jessica looked across the canteen table at Detective Constable David Rowlands. 'What's up with you anyway? Nothing funny to say?'

The constable had been swishing his cup of tea with a teaspoon absent-mindedly for around five minutes. 'Jessica Compton would make you sound like a farmer's daughter,' he concluded, not looking up from his mug.

Jessica raised her eyebrows and met Izzy's surprised stare. 'That's a bit rude,' Izzy replied.

Dave shrugged, picking up his tea and downing what was left. He offered a half-smirk as he raised his gaze to their eyes. 'It does sound a bit *farmy* though, doesn't it? It's like you should be working somewhere in Alabama throwing hay bales around.'

'Have you ever been to Alabama?' Jessica asked.

'No, you?'

'Surprisingly no, but I doubt they throw hay bales around.'

'Anyway,' Izzy said. 'Are you changing your name or not?'

Instead of replying, Jessica picked up another chip and chewed it deliberately slowly. 'It's your first day back, Iz,' she eventually said. 'You've returned earlier than anyone expected. Haven't you got more important things to be getting on with?'

'Not really, no. Everyone's being particularly nice and offering to carry stuff or take work off my hands. I might have a few more children if this is what everyone's reaction is like.'

She raised her eyebrows in a silent suggestion.

'Don't even say it,' Jessica replied. 'You either,' she added, turning to Rowlands.

Izzy snorted with laughter. 'It's going to happen, Jess. You're married. It's kids, grandkids, great-grandkids, the lot from now on.'

'My mum's been dropping hints,' Jessica confessed.

'After she got over us flying to Vegas, she started talking about us figuring out somewhere more permanent to live so we can "sort out the spare room".'

Izzy giggled knowingly as Dave kept a straight face. 'Are you still living at your mate's flat?' he asked.

The house Jessica had lived in with her boyfriend Adam had burned down and they had been staying in an apartment owned by Jessica's oldest friend. 'For now,' she replied. 'We're looking for places but it's bloody boring . . .'

'. . . And you wouldn't know which name to write on the mortgage,' Izzy interrupted.

Jessica tried to stop herself smiling but Izzy's mood was infectious. 'There's nothing wrong with keeping your own name,' she insisted.

'Adam could take yours,' Dave suggested unhelpfully. 'Adam Daniel.'

'I did mention that but it didn't go down well.'

Izzy swished her long red hair behind her and tied it tightly. 'I've missed all of this.'

'What, winding me up?' Jessica said.

'Pretty much, yes.'

Jessica grinned. 'At least you're honest. How is Amber?'

Whether it was deliberate or not, Izzy shuffled in her seat until she was sitting up straighter. Her smile widened. 'I'm missing her. I know her grandparents are looking after her fine but you get used to spending every day together.'

'When I saw you last, it didn't look as if you'd slept in a week,' Jessica pointed out.

Izzy shrugged. 'Amber's sleeping a bit better now and doesn't wake up so often in the night. You get used to it.' She paused for a moment, before adding with a wink: '*You'll* get used to it.'

Jessica ignored her. 'My mum reckons she used to give me a tiny amount of whisky on my dummy whenever I couldn't sleep. You should try that.'

'I'm not giving my baby alcohol to make her sleep.'

'It didn't do me any harm.'

'Aside from the chronic wine intake nowadays, you mean.'

Jessica ignored the dig. 'Are you sure it's not just a massive scam to get extra presents? Not only do you get gifts for Christmas and birthdays, you now get Mother's Day stuff as well. It's one big cycle of getting free stuff.'

'Yeah, you're right,' Izzy replied sarcastically. 'That was my first thought when I found out I was pregnant.'

Jessica grinned. 'You're quiet,' she said to the other constable.

Rowlands, who was fiddling with his empty mug, shrugged dismissively. As Jessica took another chip, he locked eyes with Izzy. There was an awkward silence as Jessica glanced up and caught them.

'What?' she demanded, wondering what she was missing. Dave quickly looked back at the table. 'Are you two up to something?' Jessica persisted, although neither of the constables replied.

'So are you going for Jason's job or not?' Izzy asked.

Jessica paused for a moment, wondering whether to let the obvious subject change go. After a very deliberate pause to let her friends know she was onto them, even though she wasn't, Jessica replied. 'I've been asked to apply but I don't think it's for me.'

Both constables groaned together. 'Jess, you'd be perfect,' Izzy said. 'You practically do the job already.'

Jessica shrugged dismissively, although she knew it was true. Ever since Detective Inspector Jason Reynolds had been suspended for leaking sensitive information to the media a few months earlier, his workload had been spread out among his colleagues – with Jessica and Detective Sergeant Louise Cornish taking the brunt.

Their bosses had already been looking for an additional inspector but whoever got that position would end up doing it in place of DI Reynolds instead of alongside him. That was until the results of his disciplinary were through, which would be months, if not longer.

'They're interviewing over the next few weeks,' Jessica said. 'But I don't want to end up sitting around here all day. I'd rather be out there annoying people.'

'You are very good at being annoying,' Rowlands replied.

Jessica wiped up the remaining brown sauce with her final chip and bit it in half. 'Thanks, I'll take that as a compliment.'

'So you're definitely not going for it?' Izzy continued.

As she finished the final part of her lunch, Jessica pushed the plate away. 'Nope. I'd be jealous if anyone else got to order Dave around. That's my job.'

'It's not because you're thinking about the pitter-patter of tiny feet, is it?' Izzy asked with a smile.

Jessica rolled her eyes. 'You're not going to let it go, are you?'

Before Izzy could reply, Jessica saw Detective Chief Inspector Jack Cole striding into the canteen. He didn't need to speak before she was on her feet. 'What's up?' she asked.

He was biting his bottom lip, unsure how to phrase his words. 'I'm not sure,' he finally admitted. All three officers were now standing. 'It's good to have you back,' he added, turning towards DC Diamond.

'Thanks, Sir.'

'What do you need?' Jessica asked.

The chief inspector cleared his throat. 'You know the usual policy on missing persons is to wait a day but we've had something this morning that is a little different . . .'

Jessica kept one eye on the road as she tried to glance sideways to see Izzy's expression. 'Are you going to tell me?' she asked.

'What?'

'What's going on with you and Dave? Or, more importantly, what's going on with Dave? He's been moping around for ages now.'

Izzy sighed slightly. 'You should probably ask him.'

'I have, he gives that blokey "nothing" reply, then carries on sulking.'

'It's probably just the Chloe thing. Ever since he split up with her, he hasn't quite been himself.'

Dave had broken up with his girlfriend a few months

18

previously but Jessica hadn't had much of a chance to talk to him about it because she had been dealing with her house fire at the same time. She flicked on the indicator and turned left, impressed by the fact she knew where she was going.

'Didn't he break up with her?'

'Yes.'

'So what's the problem?'

Izzy replied after a short pause. 'I don't know.'

Jessica didn't think it sounded too convincing but didn't want to push her friend so soon after her return from maternity leave. She manoeuvred her way through a selection of side streets, pulling up outside the address Cole had given her. With the absence of anywhere to park, she blocked in whoever was on the driveway and then, with Izzy a few steps behind, walked up the small set of steps before ringing the doorbell.

Almost instantly, a man opened the door. He was tall, with slightly greying hair tucked behind his ears. He was attractive in the way some men were when they reached a certain age, his delicate wrinkles displaying a wisdom and kindness as he stood hesitantly on the top step. He pushed himself up onto tip-toes looking over the officers towards the road and then, eventually, inviting them in.

Jessica had been on many call-outs with Izzy in the past and, given the woman's bright red hair and good looks, she was almost always eyed – even briefly – by the men they visited. After confirming his identity as Cameron Sexton, Jessica knew instantly something strange had happened because he barely gave the constable a second glance. Instead, he invited them into the living room, pointing them towards the sofa and continuing to pace.

'Are you all right, Mr Sexton?' Jessica asked.

He was wearing a jumper over a shirt, which was half-untucked from his jeans. He fiddled with his sleeve for a moment before stopping and sitting in an armchair opposite, fixing Jessica with a stare. 'I don't know if we should be angry or worried,' he said.

Cameron went on to explain that he and his wife had come home from an evening out to find their front door open and the babysitter missing.

'I understand your child is fine?' Jessica asked.

Cameron nodded. 'She slept through it all last night. We took her to the hospital this morning, just in case, but everything is fine.'

'How long have you been using Oliver Gordon as a babysitter?' Jessica asked.

'Six or seven months? He would come over once a month or so and we would pop out for something to eat. It wasn't even necessarily for us to have an evening away, more so that Lara could get used to being with other people and also, I suppose, to get Eleanor used to not being with her all the time.'

'Why Oliver?' Izzy asked, before adding: 'I mean, why not a relative?'

Jessica wondered if the constable was thinking about her own child and how she had left Amber with her parents-in-law.

Cameron continued to tug nervously at his clothes. 'No reason really. Ellie's parents aren't around any more and mine live quite a distance away. Oliver is the son of one of Ellie's friends so we've known him a bit as he's grown up. It was just one of those things.'

Izzy nodded, apparently satisfied.

'Is it always Oliver that you use?' Jessica asked.

Cameron responded with another nod and then continued, 'We phoned his parents last night to see if he had gone home but obviously he hadn't. That's when they called you.'

'And you found Oliver's mobile phone?'

Cameron stood and walked around to the doorway to show the two officers exactly where it had been left on the floor, then took the device out of a drawer underneath the television and handed it across before sitting back down. Jessica put it in a plastic bag just in case but the fact it had already been picked up and handled meant it was unlikely they would be able to get anything useful from it.

'I was really angry last night,' Cameron said. 'At first we thought he had just left and gone home. Then, when we called his parents, we realised he wasn't there. They said to call his mobile but I had already found it here. Then they started panicking.'

'Is he usually reliable?' Jessica asked.

'Always. I mean, he's like most people that age; he's a bit quiet but that's just being a teenager, isn't it? He gets here early and there have never been any problems in the past. Plus Lara always liked him. She can't say his name properly and giggles about it. She calls him "Dolly". We keep saying it's "Ollie" but she can't seem to say the word without putting a "D" at the front.'

Jessica already had the briefest details of Oliver's past but he had no record of anything, other than being born and attending a private school just outside the city.

'Have you spoken to his parents?' Cameron added.

'Officers have been there,' Jessica replied. 'We're heading there next. We wanted to visit you first to establish exactly what happened. What was the house like when you got home?'

Cameron shook his head, as if not wanting to remember. 'It's hard to describe. It looked normal but it didn't feel right. Have you ever walked into a room and thought, "Something's gone on here"? It was like that. As soon as I got in the front door, I had this feeling.'

Jessica had an inkling of what he meant.

Cameron shivered, perhaps recalling the moment, before continuing: 'After I saw Lara sleeping upstairs, I didn't know what to think. I was angry, then worried. Then I thought maybe someone had broken in.'

'Did you check to see if anything was missing?'

'We went all around the house. All the obvious stuff is here: the televisions, our stereo, things like that. Then we checked the drawers in our bedroom to see if any of Ellie's jewellery had gone. None of it is expensive anyway but there's no reason for a burglar or someone else to know that. I can't say for certain nothing's missing but, if it is, we don't know what's gone.'

'Did you check his phone when you found it?'

Cameron tugged at his eyebrow guiltily. 'I . . .'

'You're not going to be in trouble if you did,' Jessica

assured him. She was hoping there might be an easy solution.

'I had a look, that's all, but I couldn't even get to the keypad bit because it had this lock screen thing. I thought he might have called someone or something like that.'

Jessica knew their experts would be able to check but it did seem strange that Oliver had left his phone behind when leaving the house.

'Does anyone else have a key for the property?' she asked.

Cameron shook his head. 'Just me and Ellie. We don't even keep a spare with the neighbours or hidden in the garden. I guess that's pretty stupid in some ways, if we ever were to lose ours. We're not that friendly with the neighbours but would be able to call them in an emergency. It's not that we don't get on, we just don't talk that much.' He pointed to one side, then the other. 'They moved in about six months ago, while they've been here for years. You wave to say hello but that's about it.'

Jessica knew it was pretty much the same everywhere. After she had moved into her old flat, her father had told her during one of their almost-regular phone conversations to go and meet the neighbours. He had then told her off when she admitted two weeks later that she hadn't bothered. 'That's why the country's going to the dogs,' he insisted. Jessica didn't necessarily disagree but, dogs or not, she still couldn't be bothered with saying hello to complete strangers.

After checking they had the correct details for all the

timings, the officers said their goodbyes and indicated they would be in contact when they had news.

Back in the car, any awkwardness had disappeared. 'What do you reckon?' Izzy asked as Jessica drove.

Jessica began to speak then stopped herself. 'You tell me. First day back, let's see how much you've forgotten.'

Izzy laughed. 'Well, I believe him for a start. He didn't look shifty as such, just uncomfortable.'

'They've probably chopped him up and buried him under the patio,' Jessica replied, joking.

Izzy didn't laugh. 'Why send us? Why not uniform?'

'I don't know but I can guess it's the usual reason – covering our arses. There's no point in sending a Scene of Crime team because, as far as we can tell, no crime has taken place. Nothing's been taken, the child is still there. On the surface, it's just a teenager who has disappeared – and he's not even been gone that long. The only problem is, if something major has happened and we hadn't looked into this stuff now, we'd get huge stick in the future. If Oliver turns up tomorrow and he's just stormed out after an argument with his girlfriend, then no harm done.'

'Is that what you think has happened?'

Jessica didn't speak for a moment, not because she didn't know her own mind, simply because saying it out loud made it seem more real.

'I think someone's taken him.'

3

Jessica had no firm reasons for thinking someone had taken Oliver but had worked on enough cases, and interviewed enough people, to recognise the high likelihood that something bad had happened. Without knowing much about the teenager, she could guess his type simply because of who Cameron and Eleanor were. They weren't the sort of people who would dump their daughter with anyone, which meant Oliver must at least appear to be conscientious and mature. Still, some people probably thought that about her, so that in itself didn't prove much.

When she had been younger, she could vaguely remember the daughter of their old next-door neighbours coming to keep an eye on her every now and then. Usually, it involved the babysitter letting her stay up slightly later 'as long as you don't tell your mum and dad' and then, presumably, the girl sitting downstairs watching television and drinking copious amounts of alcohol before hiding the evidence. Regardless of the small amount of work involved, it was still a position of trust and, while some parents might be happy to leave their children unsupervised or with someone unsuitable, the Sextons certainly did not fall into that category.

Oliver's parents were everything Jessica expected them to be. Their semi-detached house was immaculately kept with a nearly new car on the driveway. Owen Gordon was dressed in almost identical clothes to Cameron and his wife Gabrielle was the epitome of middle-class with dyed hair, perfectly manicured nails and the vague air that she could be worked up into a moral outrage about pretty much anything.

After the two officers were invited into the Gordons' house, Jessica eyed the surroundings. She could guess from the walls that Oliver was an only child – and a spoiled one at that. There were photos of him at every age all over the hallway, with nothing of anyone else.

In the living room, after confirming much of what she had already been told by Cameron, Jessica moved the topic from the events of the previous evening to Oliver himself. Both of his parents insisted he had been acting normally over the past few days.

They were sitting closely together on the sofa, with Owen holding an arm around his wife's shoulders. She was close to tears. He clutched a tissue in one hand, nervously brushing at seemingly invisible flecks of dust on the armrest with the other.

'Has he ever not returned home in the past?' Jessica asked.

'Never,' Owen replied. 'He isn't late for anything.'

Jessica had expected as much. She had no reason to believe there was anything untoward from the response – but her parents never knew about the odd occasion she bunked off college with her friend Caroline when they were younger. Teenagers always kept some things back from their parents.

'Does he have many friends who might know where he's gone?' she added.

Oliver's parents could only offer two names between them. 'We called them last night and this morning,' Owen said. 'Ollie was always good about leaving details just in case.'

After confirming the young man had no particular after-school interests and no part-time job, Jessica was left wondering what he actually did when he wasn't studying or in his bedroom. From what she had been able to gather, Oliver only had two close friends and rarely left the house. Her standard questions about whether he had ever run away before, or whether they had fallen out recently, were all met with firm denials.

If everything was as claimed, Oliver had been an angelic child since birth who never got into trouble.

'Does he have a girlfriend?' Jessica persisted, desperately trying to hear something she could work with.

'He's focused on his studying,' Gabrielle insisted, leaving Jessica to wonder if the woman remembered being a teenager herself. Admittedly Jessica hadn't been a young male but, from her recollection, seventeen-year-old boys usually only had one thing on their minds – and it certainly wasn't college work.

Although it wasn't something she would usually push, Jessica wanted to see if she could get a reaction. 'Boyfriend?' she asked, making sure she met both parents' eyes. She saw a second or two of panic in Owen's face before he stumbled over a reply.

27

'I don't think he's into that,' he said, before clarifying quickly, 'not that it would be a problem.'

'I'm just trying to establish something that may have made him upset,' Jessica said, trying to stay empathetic. 'Usually when teenagers disappear, it might be because they've fallen out with someone, maybe a friend or a parent. Or perhaps they are worried about something?'

Both parents looked on blankly.

'Do you mind if we have a look around his room?' Jessica asked. 'I know you've probably checked already. We're looking for anything that could help.'

Owen untangled his arm from his wife and stood, pointing towards the door, before leading them up a flight of stairs. More photos of Oliver lined the walls: there he was on the beach, in a park, in the garden. Always by himself, always smiling. As they reached the top, the man must have noticed Jessica's interest because he answered the question she hadn't asked.

'There were complications when he was born,' Owen said. 'Gabby couldn't have any more children after Oliver. I know you probably think we're a bit over-protective but he's our only child.' He tailed off before adding: 'He's all we have.'

Jessica felt Izzy's hand touch her gently on the back. No one spoke for a few moments before Owen turned and pointed to a doorway.

'It's that room there,' he said.

The two officers entered and then waited until they had heard the man reach the bottom of the stairs.

'Are you all right?' Jessica asked.

Izzy pressed herself up against the back of the door. 'It's hard to describe. It's probably because I've been off for so long but, before, it was easier to take a step back and see everything as a case. Now, everyone is someone else's child.' She ran her hands through her hair and shook her head dismissively, as if telling herself not to be so stupid. 'What are we looking for?'

They both knew the question was rhetorical and Jessica didn't reply. Instead, she stood in the corner and took in the room.

The walls were clear, except for two posters; one that seemed to relate to a video game, the other a print of a Salvador Dalí painting. Oliver had a king-size bed to himself, which was facing a flatscreen television on top of a wide dresser with a games console next to it. A few hardback books were on a bookcase in the opposite corner with a small telescope, but it was mainly occupied by stacks of films as well as a few computer games.

'Tidy, isn't it?' Izzy said.

'My personal hell,' Jessica replied. 'I don't know what kind of person can put everything away neatly. It's unnatural.'

As if to emphasise the point, she slid back the door on a wardrobe to reveal orderly rows of shoes and trainers underneath lines of shirts that had been ironed and hung.

'Anything?' Izzy asked as she poked through a drawer underneath the television.

'No – everything's on a computer or phone nowadays. If he's still missing in a day or two, we'll have to get the tech guys in.'

'We're wasting our time, aren't we?'

Jessica sat on the bed, almost bouncing because of the softness of the mattress. 'Maybe; at least we've got a good idea of what he's like. I reckon his mum still cleans his room, so I doubt he'd leave anything dodgy around. Also, look at the movies, they all have safe age ratings. There's the odd fifteen or eighteen, but they are mainly things which wouldn't offend.' Jessica stopped to feel under the pillow and run her hand along the length of the mattress. 'I don't know the kid but it all seems a bit too homely.'

Izzy had turned around to face Jessica and was leaning against the dresser. 'You're very cynical,' she said. Whether it was deliberate or not, Jessica thought her friend's tone sounded a little harsher than usual.

Before she could reply, the constable apologised. 'I didn't mean it like that. I just thought that, maybe, it's nothing to do with Oliver at all. Say he is a bit naive, maybe that's what attracts other people who might want to harm him? Or use him for something? We don't know if he left the Sextons' house voluntarily, if he was taken, or if something else happened.'

'Actually, that's exactly what I was thinking too.'

'Really? I know what you said in the car but I thought that, with the questions downstairs, plus the room, it sounded like you were saying he couldn't be *that* sheltered. I thought you were hinting that Oliver was up to something?'

Jessica shrugged. 'Maybe he is but I doubt it. I think that's why Jack sent us out here.'

Izzy picked up a snow globe from next to the television

and tipped it upside down, before turning it over. 'Adam's changed you,' she said with a smirk.

'Bollocks he has.'

The constable laughed. 'Before you would've been annoyed at Jack, wondering why he was sending you out to a missing persons case after less than a day. Then you would have been suspicious of Cameron, wondering if he or his wife had somehow killed Oliver – not just joking, really speculating about it. Or thinking it was a big set-up. Then you would have come here and kicked up a stink. Now you take a step back and absorb it all.'

Jessica felt defensive. 'Are you saying I've lost my instinct?'

Izzy put the snow globe back down and paced across to the window. 'The opposite, actually. I'm saying it's better because, instead of barrelling in, you're a little more . . . *refined.*'

Arching her eyebrows, Jessica replied: 'Refined means boring.'

The constable laughed again. 'Only you could think that. Maybe you haven't changed after all.'

Jessica patted the corners of the sheets back into the bed to ensure she hadn't made too much of a mess. She had a look underneath but there wasn't even a rogue pair of shoes, let alone a stack of animal porn or snuff videos. She didn't want to rummage too deeply through the teenager's possessions but a quick glance through the dresser and the rest of the wardrobe revealed nothing interesting, aside from the fact that he folded his boxer shorts too neatly.

Izzy was in the process of checking each of the film cases individually when Jessica stopped her. 'We may as well go. There's not much we can do here. We'll have to talk to his friends and then check whatever CCTV we have from the streets near the other house to see if he was caught anywhere.'

'His poor parents.'

Jessica let the words hang for a few moments. 'What's it like being a mum?' she asked.

Izzy grinned, although her eyes looked tired. 'It's great. I never thought I'd want kids, it was always Mal. But now, I can't think of a world without Amber.'

'Why did you come back to work then?'

The constable pulled a face and, for a moment, Jessica thought her friend had taken offence. 'Because I don't want to be defined by it.'

It wasn't the first time Jessica felt as if someone else was the adult in the room as she somehow struggled to keep up.

'I love being a mum but I don't want to just be "Izzy, the mother". I want to be "Detective Constable Isobel Diamond, the police officer", "Mrs Diamond, the wife" – all those things and more. I love Amber and I love being with her but I didn't want to become someone who spends so long being at home that I'm incapable of doing anything else.'

It was clear to Jessica her friend had been bottling up her speech for a while. 'You'll always be "Izzy the wind-up merchant" to me,' she assured her.

'Isn't that why you're not taking Adam's name? Because

you don't just want to be "Jessica Compton, the wife"? You want to do your own thing?'

Jessica stared at her friend. 'There is another reason . . .'

Before she could say anything else, her mobile phone began to ring. She took it out of her jacket pocket, sighing for Izzy's benefit as she saw the caller's identity.

'Well, well, well,' she answered. 'Look who it is.'

She was slightly dismayed to hear that Garry Ashford's voice did not waver as he replied. He was a journalist that she knew she could intimidate and certainly annoy. In the past they had helped each other with various things and, although she'd never tell him, he was one of the few people she trusted.

'How's married life?' he shot back.

'Is that a tiny hint of jealousy?'

'Jealous I didn't get to see you squirming in a dress. I heard you went to Vegas to avoid everyone?'

'Well, if you will listen to Dave Rowlands as a source, then you will be fed misinformation. Anyway, if you've been caught flashing in a park again, then no, I'm not going to ask about having the charges dropped.'

She heard the man suppressing what she assumed for the benefit of her own ego was a snigger. 'Have you got a few minutes to come to the office?' he asked.

Jessica swirled her hand in the air to apologise to Izzy for taking so long on the call. 'Can't you just tell me on the phone?'

'It's serious.'

'You've not locked yourself in a toilet cubicle again, have you?'

'Jess . . .'

Jessica changed her tone. 'All right, we'll come over but we're supposed to be on the way back to the station, so you'll have to give me something.'

Garry took a deep breath as if wondering how to phrase things. 'We took a call this morning from someone who said her son is missing.'

Jessica involuntarily let out a gasp, somehow knowing the woman sat in the living room below was the person who had made the call. She wondered why Oliver's mother hadn't told them she had phoned the media. Garry didn't seem to notice as he continued. 'You know what missing persons cases are like – you won't do anything for a day or so and we don't run anything unless we've heard from you, otherwise we'd be printing a new story every time someone had an argument and stormed out for the night.'

For a reason she wasn't sure of, Jessica didn't want to let on that she knew anything about Oliver Gordon, let alone that she was standing in his parents' house. She gave a non-committal 'uh-huh'.

'Anyway, we have this new guy who started two weeks ago. He's straight out of uni and you know the type. They're keen but don't really have a clue what they're doing. We've been giving him the shit jobs to see what he's like . . .'

'Wow, what a boss you are.'

'Honestly, Jess, if I wind you up, just wait until you meet him, he . . .' Garry sounded as if he was about to go off on a rant before he stopped himself mid-sentence.

'Either way, we put this call onto him just to shut him up for half an hour. It's not that we're unsympathetic but you don't know if there's actually a story, or just some over-protective mum who's had a shouting match with her lad.'

'What happened?'

'We put this guy on the births, deaths and marriages page a few days ago. It's a lot of work for not much reward and everyone here is always dodging it. He did a decent job but noticed one thing after taking all the details down about the missing lad. Can I run a name past you?'

'Who?'

'Have you heard anything about an "Oliver Gordon"?'

Jessica felt a tingle run along her back, her suspicions confirmed. 'What about him?'

'We had his mum phoning in this morning to say he went missing last night – but we already ran an obituary for him two days ago.'

4

Jessica dropped Izzy back at Longsight Police Station where they worked, asking her if she could start double-checking Oliver Gordon's background and also look into his friends. She then left her car and took a marked police vehicle. The *Manchester Morning Herald*'s offices were in the centre of the city and she had no intention of driving around looking for a parking space. Instead, she left the car half on the pavement, half on the road on a side street just off Deansgate and then walked the short distance to the cafe where Garry Ashford had suggested meeting.

The small coffee shop was in an area surrounded by swanky new glass-fronted buildings, looking as if it had been dropped into the wrong century. A bell tinkled over the door as Jessica walked in. The smell of exotic teas was both pleasant but strange as she immediately spotted Garry sitting in the corner drinking from an espresso cup, one leg crossed over the other. The walls were brown, almost as if stained by the fumes, and Garry's outfit blended perfectly as he was wearing a pair of brown corduroy trousers, with a matching jacket over the top of a white shirt. His hair had grown since she had last seen him, scraggily hanging below his ears.

He was jabbing at his phone screen but looked up when Jessica scraped back the chair opposite him and sat.

'Still not got a mirror in your house then,' she said.

They had met in this exact cafe a few years ago. Back then, Garry would have squirmed awkwardly but instead he grinned. 'It's good to see you, Jess.'

'You too but your girlfriend can't seriously be happy about going out in public with you wearing stuff like that? And what's going on with the tiny cup? Can't you drink a proper mug of coffee?'

Garry finished the espresso and put the cup on the table. 'Ever the good mood.'

Jessica ignored him. 'Let's hear it then.'

Garry pocketed his phone and leant forward, reaching into a bag on the floor and taking out a copy of the *Morning Herald*. He flicked through the pages then laid it flat on the table, which wobbled as he put pressure on it. 'This is from two days back,' he explained, pointing to a square box towards the bottom of the page. Jessica leant in to read.

'REST IN PEACE OLIVER GORDON
BELOVED SON AND FRIEND'

The notice concluded with a date and 'taken too young'.

'How often do you run these?' Jessica asked.

'Twice a week.'

'How does it work?'

'It used to be something you would pay for but that stopped a few years ago because there were so many places people would put notices for free on the Internet. The bosses figured they would rather have people buying the paper to read the notices and make some money than make more or less nothing because people weren't paying for the spots and the pages were relatively empty.'

'How popular are the pages? I've never looked at one.'

There was an awkward smile on Garry's face. 'It's not really for people like you. You've not got kids. For people who have children, this is something they'll keep plus, because they're often involved in other activities with other new parents, they all look out for each other's too. You're only going to put a marriage notice in if you want it to be seen by others, which doesn't sound like you at all, and then you have the death notices. Although you do get the odd younger person, it's the page that is most read by the older folk because they aren't generally looking for these things on the Internet. They check for names of people they might know who have passed away.'

It sounded pretty morbid to Jessica. 'These are the most popular pages?'

Garry shook his head. 'Actually, that's the crossword.'

'Seriously?'

'God forbid you ever get a clue wrong. Once we printed the wrong grid and we were taking calls for three days about it. People were going crazy, phoning up and saying, "I'm never buying your rag again" and so on. We got this letter handwritten in green ink saying they were going to fire-bomb the building.'

'Over a crossword?'

Garry laughed, seeing the senselessness in his description. 'I know.'

'So if people only ever buy the paper for the crossword

and the births, deaths and marriages bit, why even bother with all the news?'

Jessica was trying to wind him up but he answered seriously. 'Half our managers think the same thing. I wouldn't mind but, if we get a detail in a story wrong, no one bothers us.'

Trying to bring him back around to the subject, Jessica pointed to the death notice. 'Do people email these in?'

'They can but this was phoned in.'

'Have you got any way of checking who calls you?'

'Not directly. You'd have to check with the phone company. I can get you the details.'

'Do you usually take the name of the person who has placed the notice?'

'Initially but the paper doesn't keep the information long-term because we don't take any payments and have no real need. We used to have vast filing cabinets full of it all but it was getting ridiculous, then some management guy had this big thing about data protection and so on, so we shred it. I had a look for a name before I called you but there's nothing on the spike. We have these recycling people that come around, so I guess it went out with that.'

Jessica nodded in reluctant acceptance. 'So you've just got this new guy who took the call?'

'Yes, Ian. I'll take you up to meet him.'

Garry shuffled nervously in his seat, so Jessica spoke the words for him. 'He's Sebastian's replacement.'

'Yes.'

Sebastian was a journalist who had become too

involved with his stories, creating incidents to report on and then getting carried away.

Jessica thought Garry was going to apologise so she stood before he had the opportunity, reaching into her pocket and dropping a few pound coins onto the saucer next to the espresso cup. 'I'll get this but I'm taking that paper. Let's go.'

The offices of the *Morning Herald* were only a few hundred metres away from the cafe. Garry used a security pass to swipe them through the front door and they headed for the lifts. They were in one of the tallest buildings in the city and, while Jessica knew that was where the paper was based, she had never visited before.

'Impressive,' she said, examining the various company names on the walls before the lift doors opened with a hum.

'We're only on one of the floors. It used to be two but they crammed us all into one to save on rent. You won't think it's that impressive when we get up there.'

Garry wasn't wrong about that. As modern as the building seemed, the floor he worked on looked as if a paper-bomb had gone off on it. Entire rainforests had been sacrificed, simply so the office could be covered by an apparently endless onslaught of rubbish. As soon as she stepped out of the door, her eyes were assaulted by the clutter. Boxes of white printer paper were stacked immediately on her right, next to a whirring photocopier. On her left, there was a wall filled with framed newspapers. At one point they would have been neat and lavish, but the frames were hanging at awkward angles and two of them were cracked. Ahead of her was a mass of desks, each with a computer and seemingly another stack or two of paper. Jessica wasn't tidy herself but this was taking things to a new level.

They walked side by side, Jessica following Garry's lead as he weaved through a bank of desks towards the far side of the room. 'Why is it so messy?' she asked.

'No idea. It's always been like this.'

Although it wasn't overwhelming, there was a hum of noise; a mixture of fingers tapping at keyboards and journalists chatting either to each other or on the phone.

They soon reached a glass-walled office with 'Garry Ashford, News Editor' written on the door. In other circumstances, that might have been impressive but the impact was dampened by the fact it had been printed on a sheet of A4 paper and Blu-Tacked to the glass. Garry held the door open for her and then closed it once they were both inside.

'It's not that funny,' he said as Jessica made no attempt to stifle her giggles.

'That is the shittiest sign I have ever seen.'

'Someone's coming to do it properly,' Garry insisted.

'Still can't spell your own name, either.'

Garry walked around the desk and sat as Jessica took the chair across from him. From what she could tell, Garry's office was one of the few clutter-free spaces on the floor. The walls were a faded yellow and clearly hadn't been decorated in a while but his desk was clear except for a computer. The only other piece of furniture was a filing cabinet in the corner.

'I don't even use that,' Garry said, indicating the cabinet as he noticed Jessica looking at it.

'How come you get your own office?'

'Dunno really. The news editor has always had one, so I ended up inheriting it when I got the job. I spend most of my time on the floor anyway.'

'Where's this Ian guy?'

'I'll get him but, if you're going to shout, just remember these glass walls aren't that thick.'

'Why would I be shouting at him?'

'You've not met him yet . . .'

'Why are you so convinced I won't like him?'

Garry grinned knowingly. 'Let's just say I don't think he's your type. His dad is on the board of directors, which is why we had to hire him. He's not as bad as I thought he might be but . . . well, you'll see.' He stood and walked back towards the door.

Jessica might not have met him but she knew exactly what Garry was warning her about when he returned a few minutes later with a man who looked as if he had somehow been created solely to annoy her. Ian walked with a swagger that he had neither the looks nor natural charisma to pull off. As he offered his hand for Jessica to shake, he eyed her up and down, before offering a posh-sounding: 'I didn't realise police officers could be so attractive.'

If Jessica could have summed him up in one word, it would be 'floppy'. He had light brown hair with a blonde tint, which Jessica guessed was artificial, that was parted along the centre and then drooped bouncily on either side. His face was slightly shiny, as if he had spent his lunch-break moisturising, and he wore a suit which was probably more expensive than any single piece of equipment in the room.

Jessica rolled her eyes and accepted his handshake, refusing to grimace as he deliberately squeezed tightly and smiled. 'You must be Ian,' she said, sitting back in the chair.

The man perched on the edge of Garry's desk, so that he was peering down at her. Garry said he would leave them to it, suppressing a smile as he left the room and closing the door behind him.

'I am, what's your name?'

'Detective Sergeant Daniel.'

'Do you have a first name?'

Ian was smiling in what Jessica guessed he thought was an appealing way. In reality, it made his face seem crooked, his pointed nose angled to the side and his too-thin lips slanted into what was closer to a sneer.

'Do you want to take a seat?' Jessica said, ignoring his request and indicating Garry's chair.

Ian slid off the desk, walking around it before sitting down with his legs splayed wide.

Jessica could feel her patience being pushed. He had that smug look about him, like he'd eaten the last of the biscuits and didn't care that anyone knew. 'I understand it was you who took the phone call for the death announce-ment relating to Oliver Gordon?'

'Indeed.'

The fact he couldn't even answer 'yes' or 'no' to a yes or no question was infuriating. She asked him to elaborate on exactly what the job entailed although, from the way he described it, working on the births, deaths and marriages page was somehow equivalent to an undercover journalistic operation that was exposing corruption at the heart of government. Seemingly, without him, the paper would come crashing down.

Jessica eventually steered the conversation around to the information she needed. She wondered if Garry had told her not to shout at Ian specifically because he knew she would be desperate to after spending five minutes alone with him.

'Tell me about the caller,' Jessica asked.

'It was male,' Ian said.

'Older, younger?'

The man ran his hand through his hair. 'I don't remember completely but he definitely sounded like an adult.'

Jessica had taken one of the notepads from the top of the filing cabinet and was making notes. 'So over thirty?'

'Perhaps a bit younger.'

'So are you saying it was a young adult, between eighteen and thirty?'

'Maybe. He could have been older.'

Jessica realised she was pushing the pen into the pad with increasing pressure. 'How much older?'

'I'm not sure. Maybe between eighteen and fifty?'

Jessica bit into the skin on the inside of her mouth to stop herself swearing. 'That's a broad age range.'

Ian had leant back in the chair, resting his foot on the opposite knee. 'I didn't realise it would be relevant at the time. I only remembered the name because I had to ask the guy to spell it out.'

'You had to ask him how to spell Oliver?'

'It might have had a double "L".'

Jessica tried to suppress a sigh. 'Fine, anyway, you asked the man how to spell it. And what did he sound like? Was he unhappy? Frustrated? In a hurry?'

Ian looked back blankly at her and Jessica realised she wasn't going to get anything of use. Aside from the actual notice in the paper, the trip had been a waste of time. Although they would be able to get the phone records through at some point, it didn't necessarily mean it would give them any answers. Pre-pay mobile phones could be used without credit cards, so they could be put in anyone's name, while phone boxes, although rarer now, could still offer anonymity. Assuming whoever had called in the notice knew what they were doing, there wouldn't be an easy way to track it. Ian's description had narrowed the person down to one gender but, given his lack of awareness of the age of the person involved, she wouldn't be certain he had got the sex right either.

Jessica tried again. 'Do you remember anything other than the fact that it was a male who sounded somewhere between the ages of eighteen and fifty? Did you write the name down?'

Ian brushed his eyebrow with his finger, smoothing it. He clearly wasn't interested in the rest of the conversation. 'Sorry, I can't recall.'

Jessica ripped the top page from the pad, although her notes consisted of little other than '18–50', then 'knob-head' written in capital letters. She folded it over and put it in her jacket pocket, then stood. She had been going to hand him a business card before thinking better of it. 'If you remember anything else, ask Garry to give me a call.'

Ian got out of the chair and put his hands in his pockets, standing with his hips thrust forward. 'Are you not going to leave me your number?'

'I'm not sure there's anything more you can tell me.'

'Maybe I could take it for non-professional reasons?' Jessica couldn't be sure but she thought Ian winked.

'I'm all right, thanks.'

'If you're sure.'

Jessica opened the door and walked out before Ian could add anything else. Garry was standing a few desks away talking to one of the staff but she managed to catch his eye as she headed towards the lift. He caught up with her as she pressed the button to go down. 'You'll need my pass to get out,' he said.

'How do you put up with that guy?' Jessica replied.

The lift pinged into place and they both stepped inside. 'I don't really. I put him in a corner and let other people give him work. He's only here because of his dad.'

'He'll probably be running the place in eighteen months.'

'Don't even joke. Still, it was him who noticed the name match-up.'

'At least he's an observant idiot and not just an idiot.'

As the lift opened onto the ground floor, Jessica and Garry stepped outside. He used his card to swipe her through the security check and then waited by the door with her. 'If he thinks of anything else, I'll drop you a line.' After a short pause, he added: 'What's going on with this kid? Is he missing? Dead?'

'Who are you asking as? Journalist or interested bystander?'

Garry grinned sheepishly. 'A bit of both.'

'I guess it doesn't matter seeing as his parents have been on to you. Either way, he's missing. We don't know any more than that yet.'

'What do you think?'

'I think that if someone was calling your paper predicting his death a few days ago, then we have a pretty serious problem.'

5

Kayleigh Pritchard picked up the carrier bags from the foot well on the passenger's side of her car. The handles strained as she lifted, the thin plastic vulnerable against the weight of the groceries inside. She wondered what the point was of having 'bags for life' if she never remembered to take them out of her car boot. Instead, she was building up an ever-larger collection of plastic bags in the cupboard underneath her sink, and the ones in her car certainly would last for life, seeing as she never used them. She carried the shopping to her front door and put it on the doorstep while fumbling with her keys thinking, not for the first time, that she really should clear it out.

Because it rarely seemed to stop raining, her wooden front door was permanently swollen and always needed a hard shove.

Kayleigh practically fell over the threshold as she shoul-dered the door inwards and, after retrieving her bags, fought the door back into place before pausing for breath. The daily battle with the door had been going on for a few years and wasn't getting any easier.

She stifled a shiver as a draught breezed through her. Hoping she hadn't left the bedroom window open again, Kayleigh carried her bags into the kitchen, where the actual reason became obvious. As she entered, her eyes were drawn to the broken glass scattered across the floor. Kayleigh put her shopping down and tiptoed to the back door, careful to avoid the shards.

The bottom half of the back door was wooden but the top was made from translucent bobbled glass, which now had a jagged hole in the centre. Kayleigh stared at the keyhole and cursed herself for being so lazy. Because she struggled to find her keys, she always left the back-door key in the lock. Kayleigh tried the handle to see if it would open, wincing as she heard glass splintering under her shoes. The door required as much of a yank as the front one had, but the fact it was unlocked proved someone had smashed the glass and then used the key to open it. The key was still resting in the keyhole.

Kayleigh pushed the door closed and leant against the fridge, closing her eyes in frustration. She remembered the previous time she had been broken into a few years ago, when she had carelessly left a window open and gone out for the day. Back then, she had promised herself she would learn her lesson. Over time, she had simply become lazy, constantly misplacing keys, leaving curtains open and, as was now apparent, carelessly leaving keys in locks. Although Ordsall didn't have the best of reputations, Kayleigh had rarely experienced problems in the area since the initial break-in.

Looking around the kitchen, apart from the glass, Kayleigh struggled to see anything that was out of place. She weaved around the glass and her shopping, making her way into the living room. She didn't own much of value but what she did have was in the main room of the house. Fully expecting to see the television gone, Kayleigh was surprised to see it on top of the cabinet exactly where it had been that morning. Next to it was her stereo which, while not worth that much, would surely be worth taking if someone had broken in. As with the kitchen, Kayleigh could not see anything out of place, with an empty glass still on the armrest of the sofa exactly where she had left it the previous evening. She stepped across to the cabinet underneath the television and opened the drawer, taking out her laptop almost so she could believe it was still there.

She was full of relief, not just because the computer hadn't been stolen – but more because she didn't want to lose the photos she had on it.

Realising that someone who had broken in might assume she had something valuable upstairs, Kayleigh checked her bedroom. It was still untidy but that was nothing to do with the break-in and everything to do with her own messiness. The duvet cover was half on the floor, with shoes scattered across the carpet. Kayleigh checked the side table next to her bed where she kept the spare house keys, but everything was as it should be.

The landing and spare bedroom were equally clear, so Kayleigh walked back down the stairs into the hallway, feeling confused and wondering if it was just kids who had been playing around.

She returned to the kitchen, approaching the sink and staring out of the back window. A lane ran along the rear of the property and she had long known the rotting wooden fence inherited from the previous owner offered little privacy from whoever chose to walk past. There were local gangs but Kayleigh hadn't had a run-in with any of them and pretty much kept herself to herself.

After putting the frozen items of food in the freezer, Kayleigh wondered if she should sweep up. If anything, calling the police could bring her more attention and, with the fact that apparently nothing had been taken, Kayleigh considered whether she would be better tidying up and then getting a glazier to come out. The excess on her insurance would surely be as much as it would cost to repair the door anyway, so the hassle of standing around while a police officer took photos and left a crime number didn't seem worth it. Then there would be the forms to fill in and the endless things to sign. As if being broken into wasn't bad enough, they then tried to kill you off with paperwork.

Kayleigh pulled the dustpan and brush out from underneath the mass of carrier bags in the cupboard below the sink and crouched, swishing the fragments of glass into the pan, while being careful not to kneel on any. The hole in the window wasn't that big but Kayleigh found small slivers of glass in far-flung corners of the room. When she was finished, she emptied the pan into the large wheelie bin outside the back door and then found the phone book in the living room, before calling the first glazier on the list.

With everything sorted as best it could be, Kayleigh filled up the kettle with water and set it to boil, wondering why life couldn't be easy. She went to sit in the living room, where she could watch through the living-room window for the work van to arrive, but instead felt the all too familiar pressure on her bladder, so headed upstairs.

As soon as she opened the bathroom door, she realised something wasn't right. The hole in the back door had made the air fresh downstairs but the bathroom smelled of something that reminded her of a summer a few years ago when the bin men had gone on strike. Rubbish had been left to rot for three weeks and the lane at the back of her house where everyone put their bins reeked of rotting, decaying waste. Kayleigh flashed back to that summer as she stepped into the room, eyes drawn to the bath. She had taken a shower that morning and always left the curtain half-stretched along one side of the tub so it could drip dry.

It was then she knew someone had been in her house.

The curtain was pulled the entire way around the bath, shielding her from whatever was inside.

She crept forward until she had one hand on the shower curtain but the smell was finding a way to seep through her senses even though she was holding her breath. The stench almost made her gag. Feeling the need to breathe in, Kayleigh closed her eyes and quickly pulled at the thin sheet. She heard the plastic rings at the top clattering into each other and then slowly opened her eyes.

Kayleigh felt strangely calm. She had watched television shows and films where people would go running and screaming and, although her head was telling her to close the door and call the police, her first thought was that she wouldn't be able to take a shower any time soon.

And then she finally breathed in, her senses taking control of her body.

Kayleigh closed her eyes to take away the scene but this offered no protection from what was now etched in her memory. Even in the semi-darkness, she could see everything clearly.

It wasn't the young man's body which had been dumped in her bath that terrified her as much as the way his eyelids were hanging open, exposing small red blotches in the whites of his eyes in a way she knew she would never forget.

6

In the days it had taken for Oliver Gordon's disappearance to become an official case, Jessica had guessed it would only be a matter of time before his body turned up. They had decided not to publicise the fact the boy's death had been predicted in the pages of the *Herald* and no one else had apparently noticed. As soon as the call came through that a woman had found a body in her bathtub following some sort of break-in, Jessica knew it would be Oliver.

With Reynolds still suspended and DCI Cole busy trying to manage more than his own workload, Jessica grabbed Izzy and headed out to the address in Ordsall. If she had been at home, it would have been a ten-minute walk at most from Salford Quays but, instead, Manchester was its usual static self. Jessica skipped through as many side streets as she could remember before finally emerging into the network of terraced redbrick houses where the flashing blue lights of an ambulance and two police cars were already waiting.

Now that she was back at work Izzy seemed determined to throw herself back into the job as much as she could. That didn't stop Jessica from regretting bringing her when she saw the state the body was in. The Scene of Crime team had already attended the house and taken what they needed and Jessica had only managed a quick look at the corpse before it was covered and taken out. It would have to be identified formally but, seeing as she had spent the past few days staring at photos of Oliver, she had no doubt it was him.

'Any idea what happened?' Jessica asked the Scene of Crime officer.

The man was clearly in a hurry but stopped for a few moments to talk to them. 'I wouldn't want to say a hundred per cent but probably some sort of asphyxia. I'm sure you'll hear for sure in a day or two.'

Everyone who investigated crimes was used to dealing with knife attacks and Jessica had seen various horrific aftermaths, where people had been left with parts of the body hanging out. Gun crime had been increasing in the city in recent years too, especially as their Longsight base was in the middle of a known gang area. Despite that, there was always something she found more brutal about crimes involving suffocation.

Jessica could vividly remember being shown a public awareness video at school. It was during an assembly and she had spent the first few minutes giggling and messing around. But her eyes had soon been drawn to the screen, where the tape showed two young girls playing with a plastic bag. It warned of the danger of playing around with such a dangerous object and, even though it was completely overblown, large parts of it remained in the back of Jessica's mind even now.

She still remembered interviewing a woman who had reported her husband for domestic abuse after he had punched and kicked her, then slammed her up against a wall and throttled her. As the woman tried to talk about the events, her voice drifted between being audible and not, while Jessica could not stop looking at the purple and black mark around her throat.

Stabbing or shooting someone could be an instinctive act but actually choking them to death, however you did it, was a fierce, savage choice.

After the body had been taken away, Jessica and Izzy were led into the living room by a support officer, who introduced her to the house owner.

Kayleigh Pritchard acknowledged the detectives with a blank nod. Jessica would have guessed her to be somewhere in her early forties. She was still wearing a uniform from a local supermarket, her dyed black hair hanging limply around her shoulders. The woman was cradling a mug in her hands, her legs wrapped underneath her as she sat in what looked like an uncomfortable position in an armchair.

Kayleigh seemed unwilling to meet Jessica or Izzy's eyes, instead staring into whatever was left at the bottom of her mug.

'I know you've had quite the shock,' Jessica began. 'But, if it's okay, we would just like to run through your afternoon with you.'

Kayleigh talked them through how she had arrived home from work and found a hole in the glass of her back door. She spoke about how she had been burgled in the past but, because nothing seemed to have been taken, she assumed it was just kids messing around.

'I was worried about my laptop,' Kayleigh added. 'I've

got all these photos from nights out. There are pictures from when I was younger too. All sorts of stuff I didn't want to lose. When I saw the broken window, I assumed my computer and television and everything would have been taken. It was a relief when they were still there but then . . .'

Jessica could see the parallels to what had happened at the Sextons' property, although that scene had taken on a different light because they now knew Oliver's fate. They would have to look at whether someone had knocked on the door and then attacked the babysitter. Although they had found no signs of a struggle, Oliver didn't have the largest of physiques and could easily have been over-powered, especially if he had been surprised. Jessica was struggling to concentrate on Kayleigh's story, and had to stop her mind wandering back to the previous scene.

Kayleigh lived alone and had been in the house for around five years. After checking the necessary details such as her workplace, Jessica asked the woman to show her the back door. The Scene of Crime team would have already been through the house but Jessica didn't like relying on photographs, preferring her own memory.

She could not stop herself shivering as they entered the kitchen. Kayleigh instantly apologised. 'I'm sorry, I cleaned up. I know I shouldn't have but I thought it was kids at the time. I didn't think it was worth getting you involved.'

'Did you tell the crime scene team that?'

'Yes. They took all the glass and everything and used that powder stuff on the door handle but I had already touched that too.'

'I'm sure they've got everything they need,' Jessica replied as reassuringly as she could.

As Jessica had been checking the door, Izzy had been pacing around the kitchen. 'Was there any stone or brick or something like that inside?' she asked.

Kayleigh shook her head. 'I don't remember, your people asked the same thing but I've not cleaned up anything like that.'

Jessica had been thinking along the same lines. It meant whoever had broken in had likely planned what they were going to do. Along with the brutality of the method of killing Oliver, she was concerned at the way the perpetrator had made it hard for themselves to leave the body. Dumping it in the canal, leaving it in a ditch or even burying it in a shallow grave somewhere were all relatively easy ways to dispose of a body, but someone had gone out of their way to ensure it would be found – and, apparently, left it specifically in this house. Jessica wondered if Kayleigh realised the implication.

'Is there anyone you know could have a grudge against you?' Jessica asked, not wanting to spell it out exactly.

Kayleigh had clearly thought it through already and shook her head. 'I've been trying to think. It's not the best neighbourhood, but there's no one around here I've had a problem with.'

'Any upset ex-boyfriends or anything like that?'

'No, I've been single for a while. I keep myself to myself, go to work, come home. Sometimes I'll go out with the girls from work but we never get in any trouble. Every now and then we get a bit of noise at night time but I don't even complain about that. You never know how people are going to react.'

Although Jessica had suspected that would be the answer, she also thought there must be something which related either to Kayleigh or the house itself which had invited this. Until she could get a team of people looking into things, she held her tongue.

Jessica indicated towards the woman's uniform and asked what she did at the supermarket. Kayleigh worked in the bakery section and appeared enthusiastic as she spoke about it. That type of day-in, day-out familiarity would have driven Jessica crazy but she had always held a curious admiration for people who were quite happy to do that. Adam was the opposite. He had recently moved from being with the forensic science service to working at the university. He did small amounts of teaching, while generally helping out with the research projects and he enjoyed the routine of having certain days and times when he was working.

Because Jessica knew the name of the victim, even though it wasn't official, she decided to try a new tack. 'Do you know someone named Oliver Gordon?' she asked.

Kayleigh didn't seem to realise that the name could be the identity of the victim. She stuck out her bottom lip, shaking her head slowly. 'I don't think so.'

'How about an Owen or Gabrielle Gordon?'

The woman thought for a few moments, then shook her head again. 'I've never heard of them. Should I have?'

'No, it's fine,' Jessica assured her. 'Can we see upstairs?'

Kayleigh led them back through the house and up the

stairs. The Scene of Crime team had taken their time examining the area before removing the body and although there would be photos of how things had been left for Jessica to see, she thought it would be best if she had some idea of what the area looked like.

Cole had asked Jessica to hold off on instantly attending the crime scene when they had received news through of the body find. They knew the house would be cramped with the paramedics, uniformed officers and Scene of Crime team, while recent force policy had been shifting more power into the hands of the science team and away from CID, partly due to one of their colleagues in the Northern division, who had accidentally trampled across a scene, destroying evidence in the process. It was the type of thing everyone who didn't work in his division found partially funny, relieved it hadn't happened to them.

'I opened the window,' Kayleigh said, holding the bathroom door open for them. 'Your people took all sorts but it still smelled of . . . *it*.' She spoke the final word reluctantly, before adding: 'He was in the bath.'

Jessica and Izzy entered but Kayleigh refused to move past the doorframe. As happened frequently, Jessica was struck by how normal everything appeared. There were rows of shampoo bottles on a shelf next to the window and a green flannel in the shape of a frog was sitting on a shelf close to the shower head. Jessica could guess the curtain had been taken by the team but, if it wasn't for that and the faint odour she wished she didn't recognise, she would not have known anything was untoward.

Jessica and Izzy went through the motions of checking around the enclosed area, although they knew the Scene of Crime team would have already done the same.

As they left the room, Kayleigh was leaning on the banisters at the top of the stairs, nervously biting her lip. 'Are you all right?' Izzy asked, placing a hand on the woman's arm.

Kayleigh stared straight into Jessica's eyes. 'How do you do this?' she asked, before clarifying: 'You can't un-see things, can you?'

Jessica felt uncomfortable, as if the woman was asking something she had long not wanted to query herself. It was as true a thing as anyone could have said.

'We have people you can talk to if you want,' Jessica replied.

Kayleigh nodded but didn't want to let it go there. 'How do *you* cope though?'

Jessica could feel Izzy watching her too and suddenly felt self-conscious. She mumbled something about having 'special training', although she wasn't convincing herself, let alone anyone else. The truth was, you dealt with it in the only way you could: you got on with it. Some would use alcohol to help, others leant heavily on their partners. Jessica knew DCI Cole made sure he didn't take work home, instead protecting his family time as far as possible. Jessica's own way was to immerse herself in work; it was all she knew.

They started to descend the stairs together, with Jessica at the rear. 'Are you going to be all right here tonight?' Jessica asked. 'A support officer will stay with you for a while but we should be able to help if you want to find somewhere else for the night.'

'I'll be okay,' Kayleigh replied, leading them to the front door. She opened it, adding: 'What happens now?'

'We've got another stop-off, then we're heading back to the station,' Jessica said, taking a card from her jacket pocket and handing it over. 'I'll call you later if you want. Feel free to contact me.'

Kayleigh turned the card over in her hands, smiling weakly.

'Are we off to the Sextons?' Izzy asked as she walked through the door. It was exactly where Jessica was planning to go but, before she could follow her colleague, she heard Kayleigh begin to say something, before stopping herself.

'Are you all right?' Jessica asked.

Kayleigh smiled wearily. 'Yes, it's just I used to know someone with the last name Sexton.'

It dawned on Jessica that, although she had asked the woman if she knew Owen and Gabrielle, she hadn't asked about the family whose house the body had disappeared from. 'What was the first name?'

She already knew the reply before it came.

'I used to know an Ellie Sexton.'

7

Jessica knew there was no particular reason to have asked about the Sextons but was still annoyed with herself for not doing so. Izzy had stopped and turned and they both realised they had been seconds away from missing something obvious.

'How do you know Eleanor Sexton?' Jessica asked.

Kayleigh seemed confused for a few moments, before it dawned on her who this was. 'Ellie's involved?' she said, her eyes widening in surprise.

'We can go through that at another time,' Jessica replied. 'We need to make sure we're talking about the same person.'

Kayleigh said that Eleanor was married to someone called Cameron; she also knew the woman's maiden name. 'We used to work together,' she added, waving the two women back into the house and closing the door behind them. 'It was years ago though.'

'Can you remember how long?' Jessica asked, leaning against the front door.

Kayleigh took the cue that Jessica was keen to get her answers and go, and didn't move towards the living room. She shook her head. 'I don't know. Maybe twenty, twenty-five years back? A long time.'

Kayleigh was only forty-three, so that meant half a lifetime ago.

'Where did you work?'

Jessica thought she saw the woman wince slightly but it could have been a shiver because of how cold it was. 'There was this casino thing in the centre. It's not there any more. We worked on the floor, serving drinks and looking pretty, trying to get customers to stay for longer.' She smiled wryly. 'I was a bit younger back then.'

'Were you good friends?'

'I guess, I mean as close as you can be with work people. We didn't hang around much outside of work but we got each other through the days.'

'How long ago did you leave that job?'

Kayleigh sighed and started counting on her fingers. 'I only worked there for around a year. I started when I was twenty-one, so I guess that's twenty-one years?' She looked towards Jessica to check that her maths was correct.

'Did you stay in contact much after that?'

She nodded. 'Sort of. It wasn't as easy back then of course, we didn't have mobiles and computers and the like. I lived in this flat and didn't have a phone, while she was living with her parents. She would write me letters a couple of times a year but I was never very good with that kind of thing. We lived on opposite sides of the city but met for coffee once or twice a year.'

'Have you been in contact recently?'

'No, we drifted apart. She started going out with Cameron and her priorities changed.' Before anyone could speak, she quickly clarified her remark. 'It wasn't a problem, I know these things go in cycles. Sometimes you're really close, sometimes you grow apart.'

'How long ago was that?' Jessica asked.

'Not long after they got married, so maybe ten years ago? I went to the evening thing but you know what it's like; there are so many people around, you don't get time to speak to each other. We hadn't really been friends for a few years and I think she only invited me because we'd once been close. The last time I saw her was on her wedding night.' She paused for a moment and then added: 'Is she okay?'

Jessica nodded, wanting to offer reassurance without giving much away. 'Why did you leave the casino?'

Kayleigh shrugged. 'I don't know. I guess it wasn't what I wanted to do. It was only ever about the money – and even that wasn't so good.'

'Did you leave at the same time?'

Kayleigh stopped looking at her, instead glancing towards the wall and then the floor. 'More or less. We're both around the same age and wanted to do something else.'

'Did you have another job lined up?'

'Not at the time. I've done a few things since.'

'You've not worked with Eleanor since, though?'

'El-ea-nor . . .' Kayleigh rolled the word around her tongue as if it felt uncomfortable. 'She was always "Ellie" when I knew her . . .' She tailed off before remembering what she had been asked. 'Sorry, no, we've not worked together since.'

Jessica nodded and took a few final details before

reaching around to reopen the door. 'Okay, well, if you think of anything else, don't hesitate to get in contact.'

The two officers made their way back to the car in silence. Once the doors were closed, Izzy asked what they were going to do next.

Jessica didn't know if she should defer upwards but could guess the response would be along the lines of getting on with things as there were no officers free. 'I'll take you back to Longsight. There's not much point in going to see Eleanor – Ellie – until we know some facts. Have a good look into this casino place, let's find out who ran it and why it shut down, then see if you can find anything else to link these two women together, or to Oliver or his family. Check Eleanor's maiden name and see if anything else pops up through that. Get Dave involved if you can stop him moping for five minutes. Call me if you find anything.'

'What are you going to do?'

'I'm going off to be annoyed by teenage boys.'

Izzy seemed slightly confused but laughed anyway. 'Fair enough.' After a pause as if weighing up whether she should ask, she added: 'Do you want to finish telling me what you were going to say about there being another reason for you not taking Adam's name?'

Jessica switched on the engine and kept her eyes facing the front. 'Let's go.'

Oliver had attended a private school in Worsley on the far west of the city. Jessica had to jump through a couple of hoops in order to be able to speak to the two main friends his parents had told her about. First, she needed their parents' permission, which had been granted on the condition any interview took place on school property. Because of that, she then had to gain additional permission from the school. If either of the boys had been suspected of anything, it would have been far easier but Jessica was simply trying to get some background from them.

As she drove onto the school's grounds, Jessica couldn't help but be impressed. The first thing she noticed was how much green there was. Her school had one playing field at the back that was on a slight slope. Each winter, someone painted the markings of a football pitch while after the Easter term break, they would return to find it had become an athletics track.

Everything around her was a world away from that. She could see a pair of tennis courts on one side, a cricket pitch on the other and what she thought was a running track with a proper synthetic surface beyond that.

She followed the signs until reaching a small car park at the back of a large mock-Tudor building. It was bright white, with black-painted beams running the length and height of it and baskets of bright flowers hanging down. Jessica got out of the car and took a step back to survey everything. It was so far away from her own experiences of education, let alone the comprehensive schools she had visited at various points around the city, that they were barely comparable. Some places had an almost menacing aura about them, where it would have been no surprise to find out there was a murky underworld, even among young teenagers. Here, it felt like an environment where people would be free to learn.

As Jessica well knew, that didn't mean there wasn't something under the surface.

She walked into the main reception, where she was met by posters advertising ski trips, formal dances and a weekend visit to see an opera in London. She remembered one of her own school trips to a former cotton mill. It wasn't even a current working one, instead half an empty warehouse, half a museum. Quite a difference.

Her thoughts were interrupted by the receptionist asking if she could help. After having her identification checked – which included a phone call to the station, a lot of foot-tapping, finger-drumming and plenty of general hanging around – Jessica was finally led through to meet the head teacher.

Although the man was friendly, Jessica could see straight away that he had a presence that intimidated even her, let alone students. His voice was the sort that boomed across playgrounds, scaring the shite out of anyone even thinking about getting up to no good, while he wore a suit which fitted him perfectly and showed off a trim physique despite his grey hair. Of everything, it was the man's gaze that showed his authority. Jessica knew eye contact could be an important factor when she was interviewing people, but the head took that to the extreme, locking himself into a stare with her and forcing her to look away first.

Despite the intensity, there didn't seem to be anything untoward about his manner. He spoke of the entire school's shock at Oliver's death and explained there had already been a special assembly after he went missing. That would be followed by a second when it came to the young man's funeral. He told Jessica how the school catered for children of all ages from nursery all the way up to eighteen-year-olds, with the emphasis on creating responsible adults. Still, that's what they all said. Blah, blah, blah 'social awareness'-this, blah, blah, blah 'effective policy'-that. One day, Jessica would stumble across a broken head teacher who admitted, head-in-hands, the kids in their school were sodding awful.

After his own interrogation, he took Jessica through to an empty office and then left, before returning a few minutes later with two young men.

There didn't appear to be a formal uniform for sixth-form students but both were dressed in smart black trousers, with a dark jumper over the top of a shirt. They sat next to each other, shuffling nervously and not looking up from their smart, highly polished, black leather shoes. Jessica already knew their names but had to clarify which one was 'Terry' and who was 'Richard'.

'I'm Richard, miss,' one of them replied.

Jessica tried not to wince at the word 'miss'. It made her feel old. She didn't know if she should be correcting them, so let it go. His voice was clearly local but he had lost some of the twang that could make a simple 'How are you today?' sound like a threat depending on the strength of the Mancunian accent.

'I'd like to get a bit of an insight into what Oliver was like,' Jessica said. 'I've spoken to his parents and the head but I'm guessing you guys know him a little differently than everyone else?'

The two half-shrugged, half-nodded almost in unison and Jessica knew she was going to struggle. She thought it might have helped to bring Rowlands with her. Even though he'd had the hump since breaking up with Chloe, he could still turn on the matey-charm thing with other young men, banging on about 'the footy at the weekend' or some stupid video he'd seen on the Internet.

'How long have each of you known Oliver?' Jessica asked.

They were both sitting up straight, hands in their laps, with Richard slightly the taller of the two. His brown hair was neatly side-parted, his skin showing a few acne scars. Regardless of upbringing, there was no escaping certain aspects of being a teenager. He peered towards Jessica but stared at a spot just to her right. 'We've been coming here since we were thirteen, so five years.'

'Is that the same for you?' Jessica asked Terry.

The second boy had sandier-coloured hair but a posture which perfectly matched his friend's. 'I've been here since I was nine,' he said. 'We became friends not long after Rich and Ollie started, so five years too.'

They both spoke in a considered fashion and Jessica couldn't quite work out if it was because they had been trained in the same way they had clearly been taught how to sit, or if it was because they were both in some sort of shock. Still, if that headmaster bellowed at her to sit up straight and pronounce her words properly, she'd probably do it.

She nodded towards Richard, waiting for him to look towards her. 'How about you start? Just tell me about what Oliver was like.'

'How do you mean?'

'What type of things did you do together?'

The young man shrugged dismissively before responding and Jessica was pleased to see not every aspect of being a teenager had been coached out of him. 'He liked scientific things, he was interested in the stars and constellations. He was talking about doing astronomy at university.'

'He was pretty good at art too,' Terry added. 'But I'm not sure that's what he wanted to do, even though he could.'

'I noticed a few computer games at his house . . .'

For the first time, Jessica saw the two boys interact. They looked sideways at each other, sharing a grin. 'We used to go to Ollie's to play games,' Richard said. 'My mum and dad wouldn't let me have any and Terry lives too far away.'

Jessica nodded. 'What about girls? Was there anyone Ollie was seeing?'

The smiles vanished almost instantly, both young men's gazes returning to the floor. Jessica suspected their awkward behaviour was simply because they weren't used to being in a room on their own with a woman.

'He wasn't going out with anyone,' Richard said.

'Do you know that for sure?'

'Definitely, we would have known. He was more interested in other things.'

From everything she had seen, Jessica had no reason to doubt that. 'Were you into anything else? There seems to be a lot on offer around here: sports, trips, visits and so on.'

'None of us really do sports,' Terry replied. 'It's sort of encouraged around here but it's not our thing.'

'What about the trips?'

'We've gone on a few,' Terry replied. 'It's no big deal. Some people get involved in everything around here. They're in every club and go on every visit.'

'You don't, though?'

'Nope.'

For the first time, Jessica had an inkling that, although the trio might well be uncomfortable around girls and perhaps a little naive, they weren't as perfect as everyone made out. Terry's pronunciation had sounded carefully coached until the 'nope', when it had slipped back into his local accent.

Jessica slouched slightly in her chair. 'So what do you get up to away from school? Come on, I know what it's like being a teenager, you can't just sit around playing games all day? You must have a laugh somehow? I got up to all sorts of stupid things when I was your age.'

Instead of getting the chummy reply she was hoping for, both young men sunk backwards. She could see any forced confidence they had drain away. Terry started to speak but, as the other boy's body language tensed, he stopped and turned it into a cough.

Jessica looked from one to the other. 'We're talking privately,' she assured them.

The silence told her the moment was lost. She had missed something but wasn't entirely sure what.

Richard glanced at his watch, then at Jessica, this time looking directly at her. 'We're going to be late for a class . . .'

He stood before she could reply but Jessica knew there was little else she could ask anyway.

'Let me leave you my number,' she said. 'If you think of anything, you can call any time. Even if you think it's not important it might be helpful.'

She gave each of them her card and, even though it wasn't something she would usually give out to teenage boys, wrote her mobile number on the back. If she started getting calls consisting only of heavy breathing, then at least she would know where they were coming from.

The pair shuffled out but Jessica saw them transform almost instantly as they entered the corridor. Their backs straightened again and they stood tall as they walked towards reception. Jessica closed the door and sat back in the seat. She took out her mobile phone, hoping she had missed a call from Izzy while it had been on silent. The screen was blank, so Jessica flipped through the contacts and called her friend instead.

'How's it going?' she asked.

'"Hi" to you too. We've got a few things on the go but you're not going to like them.'

'What have you found?'

'We know who the casino owner was but Jack told me not to tell you everything today. He said we'll talk tomorrow.'

Jessica checked her watch. It was the end of her shift but she was still confused. 'Why?'

'Let's just say it's complicated.'

8

Jessica was tired of living in someone else's property. First it was Adam's house, which never felt like home, now it was her friend Caroline Morrison's flat. Adam was dealing with the insurance company and they knew that, at some point, they would be house-hunting. The house they used to live in had been seriously damaged by the fire and even if they were given the money to repair it, neither of them was keen to return. Jessica's problem was that she had no inclination to spend her days off traipsing around other people's houses as if she knew what she was doing.

When she'd been looking for a flat, before she knew Adam, her dad had advised her to 'check for damp'. Jessica had no idea what that meant, other than physically touching the walls to see if they were wet. He had laughed for almost fifteen minutes on the phone when she told him what she had done. If it had a roof, some walls, an indoor toilet that flushed and no holes where there shouldn't be, she would have declared everything 'fine' – which was likely why a career in surveying was never going to be on the cards. Knowledge-wise, it did rank her above a fair percentage of estate agents, though.

Adam seemed to have some idea of what he was doing, so Jessica was more than happy for him to 'pick somewhere'. He wasn't as enthused about making such a big decision on his own, which only annoyed her more.

The one aspect of Caroline's flat Jessica would miss when they eventually left was the view. If there was nothing they liked on television, which was most of the time, Jessica and Adam would sit on the balcony watching the whole of Salford Quays beneath them. Even if it was cold, they would wrap up in coats and jumpers, put their feet up on the railings and play I-spy. It might seem childish but Jessica had as much fun doing that for free as she had paying for all sorts of other things.

The evening wasn't too cold for the time of year, but Jessica was still wearing the heavy coat she had 'liberated' from the station's uniform store a few years ago. Adam was wearing a T-shirt, which annoyed her as he kept insisting he wasn't cold, even though he had only just got out of the shower. He was wearing a bobble hat, with small strands of his damp, long black hair poking out of the bottom of it, and he still hadn't had a shave, leaving dark wisps of hair on his chin. He glanced over the rail in an exaggerated way, then turned to Jessica and grinned. 'I spy with my little eye something beginning with B.'

Jessica rolled her eyes. 'You're not peering through some woman's bedroom window again, are you?'

Adam laughed. 'Not while you're around.'

'You shouldn't be looking whether I'm here or not.' Jessica paused while looking over the rail and then leant back into her seat. 'I don't know, bin?'

'Nope.' Jessica gave an overstated 'um'. 'You can talk about work if you want,' Adam offered.

Although he hadn't asked her to, Jessica had been making an effort to try to keep office matters at the station. Largely she was succeeding but Adam must have noticed how distracted she seemed. 'It's fine,' she said.

'What about Jason? Is he still suspended?'

Jessica paused to think, wondering if it was a good idea to bring work home. She sighed. 'I spoke to him last week and he's not coming back. Even if they find in his favour, he's done.'

'Because he gave information to the papers?'

The exact ins and outs were more complicated than that but, at its core, that was exactly why the inspector had been asked to stop coming to work. The fact he had been right to do it, certainly in her mind, didn't really matter when it came to the wrath of their bosses. You could be as incompetent as you wanted – as long as you didn't make them look bad.

'Something like that. He's going to sit it out on full pay and then quit before he gets pushed. He hasn't told anyone else yet.'

'What's happening with you, then?'

Jessica thought for a few moments before responding: 'Building.'

'Huh?'

'I-spy.'

'Oh right, no.'

'Buggy?'

Adam leant forward. 'Where's a buggy?'

'I don't know, it begins with B.'

'All right, no, not a buggy.'

Jessica nodded at the bottle by his foot. 'Beer?'

'Nope.'

Taking a deep breath, Jessica put her feet down and picked up the bottle by her own feet, taking a swig. 'I don't know if I want to go for the job. It's a bit more money but it's a lot more faffing. I don't think I can be arsed.'

'You can't want to be a sergeant forever?'

'Bird?'

'Nope.'

Jessica swilled the liquid around and had another drink. 'I don't know if I want to do this at all forever. Do you want to be in a lab all your life?'

'I don't know,' Adam said. 'Maybe. I've not really thought about it.'

Jessica wished she could be like that. 'Blonde?' she said, nodding towards a tower block across the way from them. She could clearly see the woman's hair colour as she shook a rug over the railing.

'Nope but thanks for pointing her out.'

Jessica whacked him playfully with the back of her hand. 'We'll see. They want to interview me.' It was a conversation they'd had before and Jessica didn't know if he was asking to see if she had changed her mind or because he thought she should go for it.

Adam picked up his own beer. 'How's Izzy?'

'She's just Izzy. Happy being a mum, happy being at work. Now she's had the baby, she's back to having bright red hair and scaring some of the higher-ups. It's good to see her around.'

Jessica clinked her empty bottle on the railing and

turned to face Adam, raising her eyebrows. 'I'm not getting up,' he said, reluctantly passing across his half-full bottle.

Jessica took it and grinned. 'I knew you'd give me yours.' She took a swig, adding: 'Balloon,' nodding towards the horizon where a hot-air balloon was taking off.

'No, that wasn't there before.'

'Bus?'

'Nope. How's Dave?'

'Still being annoying. He's trying to sort us all going to see Hugo later in the month. He has this residence thing at a comedy club. Are you up for that?'

'Definitely.'

'Breeze?'

'You can't see the breeze.'

'Yeah but I can't think of anything else beginning with B.'

Adam pulled his hat down over his ears and Jessica wondered if he was going to finally admit he was cold. She could see the goosebumps on his arms. 'Have you told any of them yet?' he asked.

'I almost told Izzy but not yet. They were all so busy congratulating me on the wedding and everything that I didn't have the heart to tell them.'

'That doesn't sound like you.'

Jessica finished the beer, then picked up her original bottle and stood. 'Come on, let's go inside before you turn blue while still insisting you're not cold.'

'I'm not cold.'

Jessica rubbed his arm. 'What are these, then? Anyway, what's your B?'

Adam pointed towards a flat on the building next to theirs where the washing was hanging over the rail. 'Bra.'

Jessica opened the door and stepped inside. 'Predictable.'

'You didn't get it.'

'That's because I'm not a perv.'

After sliding the door closed, Jessica took off her coat and hung it over the handle. She walked into the kitchen and opened the cupboard under the sink, dropping the two empty bottles inside. As she was about to close it, Jessica noticed a cardboard envelope which had been ripped in half. She took the pieces out and held them together, seeing Adam's name and his work address written in black felt-tip.

'What's this?' she called across the open-plan room.

Adam was looking at his phone but, when he peered up, Jessica could see his surprise, even from the opposite side of the room. 'Er, nothing. Just work stuff. I don't know why I brought it home.' Jessica took another look at the envelope and was about to put it back in the bin when Adam offered another guilty-sounding: 'It's nothing.'

Although he had been nervous around her when they had first met, it had been quite some time since he had stuttered his way through a conversation, let alone been openly evasive.

Jessica crossed the room and sat next to him on the sofa. 'What's going on?'

Adam put his phone in his pocket. 'Nothing, it was just a letter, I was in a hurry so I brought it home. It's uni stuff.'

Jessica had no reason to think anything different, despite his odd behaviour. 'You were a bit of a geek at school, weren't you?' she said.

Adam seemed grateful for the change of subject. 'Well, I wouldn't put it like that . . .'

'But you were . . .'

'Liking science doesn't make you a geek.'

'What does it make you, then?'

'I don't know, someone who likes science.'

Jessica snorted. 'Whatever. Anyway, what types of things did you get up to with your mates when you weren't being scared of girls or trying to steal their underwear?'

Adam took off his hat and ruffled his wet hair. 'I don't know. We just hung around. We watched rubbish old horror movies and thought about making our own. One of my mates had a games console which we used to play on. I wasn't very good but we'd play a bit of football in this other guy's garden. I did my homework too, unlike some people.'

He dug Jessica playfully in the ribs and she squealed. 'Get off.'

'Why are you asking?'

At first, Jessica wasn't going to say but she figured Adam could only help. 'There's this kid we're looking into. Everyone says he's just normal. He likes astronomy, he plays games, hangs around with his mates and watches television. Everything normal that you'd expect. But then he went missing, before turning up dead. No one seems to have a clue why him.'

Adam rested a hand on her back. 'Could it just be he was in the wrong place at the wrong time?'

'It probably is. I guess I just want to think there's something more to it than that.'

Adam kissed the top of her head and then stood. 'I'm going to go dry off and then sort some clothes out for tomorrow.'

Jessica watched him walk into the bedroom, wondering what she should do with the evening. Izzy had refused to give her any further details on the casino owner, saying they had to check a few additional things and that there was going to be a team briefing in the morning. Whatever it was, it didn't bode well.

She reached under the sofa but couldn't find what she was looking for, so checked the cabinet underneath the television. At a loss, Jessica walked through to the bedroom, where Adam was leaning into their joint wardrobe. 'Where's the laptop?' she asked.

Adam poked his head around the door and nodded towards the dresser at the bottom of the bed. 'I was using it in here earlier.'

'I'm going to email my mum while I've got nothing else on. She keeps going on about how I never call her – but then when I do I can't get off the phone because she's busy telling me about how Gladys in the village is finally having her hip fixed or how she saw someone making a quiche on TV, or something like that. She'll try to talk me through it and then it's onto whether or not I'm eating properly, how you are, how I am, how Dad's doing. By the time I get off, it's a week later. Emailing's easier.'

'Have you at least told them that we're not . . .'

'Not yet.' Adam rolled his eyes. 'It's easier like this for now,' Jessica added. 'I'll tell them when the time's right.'

'You can't leave them thinking it for too much longer.'

Jessica picked up the laptop and walked back to the door. 'I know. I'll sort it.' She walked through to the living room and plugged it in, waiting for the device to boot up, as she wandered back to the glass balcony door and stared into the darkness. She had long since regretted making the phone call from the airport to tell her parents and Izzy that she was flying out to get married. They had all understood at the time but Jessica didn't have the heart to tell them what had happened.

As her mind began to drift, Jessica heard the computer beeping. Each time it did something she didn't expect, her first instinct was to whack as many keys as she could to see if it helped. Her second instinct was to call Adam. The printer's not working – 'ADAM!'. The screen's gone blue – 'ADAM!'. Someone's asking me to send my bank details to Nigeria – 'ADAM!'. If all else failed, violence – or at least the threat of it – often did the trick.

Usually the laptop would have booted straight onto a screen from where she knew she could load the Internet browser. Instead, it had stopped at a password screen and was asking for a username.

'ADAM!'

He came into the room holding two shirts. One was bright blue, the other grey. 'Which one?' he asked.

Jessica pointed to the grey one. 'What's going on with this?'

Adam hung both shirts over the doorframe and walked to the sofa. 'I had to set us up separate logins. I've got all this stuff from the university which is confidential and sensitive. I couldn't risk you accidentally deleting it or anything like that.' He laughed as if it was a joke but Jessica could tell he was lying.

'I don't even look at all that stuff. I only ever use the Internet.'

'It's more of a just in case thing. It just means you'll have access to your own files now.'

Adam typed in a username for her, adding: 'You can pick your own password.'

'I don't want to pick my own password – I'll never remember it. I just want it to login like it used to.'

Adam squirmed awkwardly, shuffling from one foot to the other. 'Sorry.'

Jessica typed in a password and then watched the main screen appear. As Adam picked up his shirts and went into the bedroom, she checked the empty Internet browser history and wondered what he was up to.

9

Although Adam had been keen to act as if nothing was wrong, Jessica had made it clear she wasn't happy. She was still in a mood the next morning as she made her way into DCI Cole's glass-walled office for a senior briefing before the chief inspector talked to the rest of the team.

Cole was sitting behind his desk, with Jessica, DS Cornish and DC Diamond in a semicircle around him. Jessica had never known Izzy sit in on a senior team briefing in the past, so she knew her friend must have something important to share.

When she first started attending briefings, Jessica had felt herself itching to get away. She couldn't see the point in sitting around talking when you could be out doing something instead. Recently, she had begun to realise it was more of a way to offer ideas and share opinions.

'I do have something for you,' Cole began, picking up a printout from his desk. 'As we thought, Oliver Gordon was killed by asphyxiation. As far as we can tell, there was no strangulation – his neck wasn't bruised and his hyoid bone is also intact.'

Jessica was waiting to hear whatever the news was about the casino Kayleigh and Eleanor had worked in but knew the chief inspector would get to it when he was ready. Although she didn't have any great depth of knowledge of anatomy, she had only been in uniform for a few months when she found out the hyoid bone was at the top of the neck, almost directly under the chin. She had been working late shifts and been told to attend a 999 call at a local petrol station. A worker had been robbed but his attacker had also beaten him around the chest and body with an axe handle. The man could barely breathe but had somehow managed to call the police. When Jessica arrived, she could see the dark purple marks on his neck and the man croakily said at least two of the blows had caught him under the chin. When they were alone, the more experienced officer she had attended the scene with said he thought the man had broken his hyoid bone, adding that Jessica would recognise it herself if she ever had a case that involved strangulation.

'Were there any major chest injuries?' Jessica asked now.

The chief inspector shook his head. 'He was likely killed by a plastic bag or something similar wrapped tightly around his face. He took at least one hard blow to the face, probably a punch, which may even have knocked him out before the bag was wrapped around him. There are a few minor marks on his back, which could have come from someone digging an elbow in, or pushing a knee into him if they were on the ground.'

'Was there anything else at the scene?'

Jessica had not seen much when she'd been at the house but other members of the force would have been examining the Sextons' property as well.

Cole shook his head again. 'The homeowner found

86

Oliver's phone but we've not come up with anything untoward in the records. The hallway had various household things already in it – coats, shoes and the like – but they were apparently untouched.'

Cornish had been taking notes but stopped to interrupt. 'Do we have any idea what happened then?'

Jessica had been wondering the same thing since first attending the scene. Cole took a large breath, shaking his head. 'We still don't know if Oliver was killed at the Sextons' house or if he was taken off-site. It might have been that there was a knock on the door and he opened it, only to be punched in the face and then suffocated. We haven't found anything in the house and can't find anything that says he was in contact with anyone else, or that he left the property either voluntarily or not. His computer is clean too and none of the neighbours saw anything. Checking the traffic cameras nearby is needle in a haystack stuff so we just don't know.'

Jessica knew DS Cornish had definitely gone for the inspector role and, assuming they hired internally, Jessica thought her office mate would get the job. She certainly had the drive and efficiency to do it, although Jessica didn't know how she felt about the prospect of Louise potentially outranking her. Although they got on, they had little in common and rarely talked about anything other than work.

The sergeant said nothing but started writing.

'I didn't get anything from his parents or friends either,' Jessica said. 'We can maybe leave it a few days, then try talking to them again, but everything pretty much adds up to the fact that Oliver was a relatively normal kid.'

'Normal' was a word most members of CID hated. What they didn't want was the situation they had – where no one had a bad word to say about the victim. 'Yeah, sure, I saw him taking part in that drug-fuelled Wizard of Oz-themed orgy' they could cope with. 'All he did was sit in his bedroom watching movies' was a struggle.

'How are we going with the newspaper obit?' Jessica asked. She had been slightly out of the loop since bringing back the details and handing them over.

'Isobel,' the DCI said.

Izzy glanced at her notes, then looked back up and spoke confidently. 'We've been in contact with the phone company to try to trace whoever made the call to place the notice. Considering we had the paper's full cooperation, we thought it would be easy, but it's taken them this long to come back to us with a payphone in the city centre. It's only a few hundred yards away from the newspaper office.'

'Do people only use payphones to make nuisance calls?' Jessica asked, only half in jest.

Izzy continued: 'Because of the length of time this has all taken, any CCTV we may have had of the area is gone. All we have to work with is the description of the caller.' She looked towards Jessica and this time she smiled. 'I think it's fair to say that's left us with quite a wide scope.'

'A man who is eighteen to bloody fifty,' Jessica exclaimed in disgust. 'How many teenagers do you know that sound like a fifty-year-old? Or vice versa?'

'What are we going to do about this?' Cornish asked.

Cole caught Jessica's eye and she guessed the answer before he spoke. It was the only thing they could realistically do. 'For now, we're going to put it to one side. Apart from the staff at the paper, no one else knows. If any readers saw the notice on the day, then they didn't clock it and no one else has come forward to point it out.'

'It can only have been done for attention,' Jessica said, picking up the point. 'Assuming it was our killer, they wanted us or whoever to see it. Obviously we have but there's not much benefit at the moment to sharing it with the public. If the killer wants us to notice them, we're better off keeping it quiet and hoping they try to get our attention again – hopefully without murdering anyone.'

Cole nodded a short acknowledgement. Jessica knew the danger was that whoever was responsible could try to get their attention by killing someone else – but that was a risk anyway. The body had been left for them to find, the newspaper notice deliberately placed. If the perpetrator was trying to show off by pre-announcing their crimes, it could likely happen again. If the team could spot it in time, they might be able to do something about it.

'We've been in dialogue with the paper,' Cole added. 'They've agreed to keep everything quiet for now, although we may end up having to give them something at the end of all this. They're now taking more details of callers and people who email in for any obituary notices but that doesn't mean the same thing will happen again.'

'How are we doing with Kayleigh?' Jessica asked, trying to hide her impatience.

The chief inspector nodded towards Izzy, who

answered. 'Kayleigh's been in the house for five years and there were only two other sets of owners in the previous twenty-five years. The ones from furthest back have both died while we can't find any connection from the most recent ones to Oliver or his family, or to Cameron and Eleanor. I managed to speak to them last night but they have moved out of the area and don't appear to have any link to anything.'

'So was whoever left the body targeting Kayleigh, or was it random?' DS Cornish asked.

Cole was scratching nervously at his head. His hair had been receding rapidly over the past year or so and Jessica wondered if he realised how much the job was ageing him. 'It's hard to know,' he said, nodding to Jessica, who took up the conversation.

'It could be random but it would be *very* random. Firstly, they could have left the body anywhere. Secondly, there must have been easier houses to get into if that's what they wanted: places with windows left open and so on. It was only a single pane of glass to break at the back of Kayleigh's house but the guys reckon it was smashed with one brute-force strike. They'd have had to protect their hand but it could even be something like a punch.'

'How would they have known about the key being left in the back door?' Izzy asked.

Jessica shrugged. 'It could be someone Kayleigh knows, or that could have just been good or bad luck depending on which way you're looking at it. If they went equipped to break in, they would have probably found a way in any case.'

The constable nodded in agreement. 'We spoke to Eleanor Sexton yesterday. She was a bit surprised to hear Kayleigh's name but pretty much confirmed everything we had already been told – they worked together at a casino in the city but left around twenty years ago. They stayed in intermittent contact but nothing in the past decade or so. Neither of them seem to have been in any sort of trouble in the past and we can't see anything else that would connect them. If Kayleigh hadn't told us she knew Eleanor, we wouldn't have known.'

The constable glanced up at Jessica as if to say the information she had been waiting for was finally on its way. She then turned to the chief inspector, who picked up a grey file from his desk and opened the cardboard cover.

He looked at Jessica specifically as he spoke. 'Have you heard of Nicholas Long?'

Some local criminals were notorious, their faces and names known to pretty much everyone in uniform, but this wasn't a name that instantly rang any bells for Jessica. 'He sounds familiar,' she replied, not knowing if it was because he was some sort of crook she should recognise, or if he was someone else semi-famous.

Cole held up an enlarged photograph for them to see. It showed a man somewhere in his early fifties smoking a cigar, grinning broadly. His skin was rubbery, his cheeks red and sagging, and his forehead covered in wrinkles, with strands of hair combed across his scalp in a way that fooled nobody.

Jessica shook her head slowly. 'I've definitely seen him before . . .'

'He's a little before your time,' Cole said. 'Nicholas Long is a businessman in the strictest sense of the word. He currently runs a club in the city centre but that's a vast scaling back of his operations. Twenty years ago, he ran the casino that both Kayleigh Pritchard and Eleanor James, now Eleanor Sexton, worked at. In between times he has run various businesses, including employment agencies, pubs, and a snooker club.'

'What type of club does he run now?' Cornish asked.

'It's a gentlemen's establishment,' the chief inspector said, raising his eyebrows towards Jessica, who didn't know why he simply didn't call it a 'strip club'.

Jessica was beginning to fill in the gaps but didn't interrupt as Cole spelled it out. 'Throughout all of this time, he's been suspected of various criminal offences, drugs being the main one, but prostitution and people-trafficking as well. They've been trying to pin illegal weapon possession on him for some time but have never been able to find anything. Apart from GBH charges when he was a teenager, he's somehow managed to keep a clean record. To all intents and purposes, he is a legitimate above-board businessman.'

He paused as if waiting for the question that didn't come, then flicked through the file and took out another sheaf of papers. 'What he may not know, although I suspect he does, is that the Serious Crime Division have been looking into him for the past two years. They've been checking his books and employment records.' He fixed Jessica with a stare. 'This means that we have to tread very carefully indeed.'

Jessica broke the gaze and looked towards Izzy. 'Have we got anything else on him?'

The constable glanced sideways at their supervisor for assurance before referring to her own notes. 'Nicholas Long is fifty-five years old and is married to Tia Long.' She held up a photo of a young woman with tanned perfect skin and flowing dark hair. She couldn't have been any older than thirty at the most.

'I wonder what attracted her,' Jessica said.

'He has a teenage son, also called Nicholas, with a former wife called Ruby. He comes from Moss Side where our records are a little sketchy. What is clear is that he does still have some sort of high respect in the area.'

She passed across a photocopy of a newspaper article from a few years ago with Nicholas Long standing outside a building grinning at the camera. Jessica skimmed the first few paragraphs before handing the page to DS Cornish.

'As well as the boxing club he paid for mentioned in that article,' Izzy added, 'he also owns one of the main pubs in the area plus paid for recent renovations to a community centre on the estate.'

'He can't live there, though?' Jessica queried, knowing that a man who had that kind of wealth would probably not choose to reside in one of the most deprived areas of the city – even if he was seemingly happy to spend money there.

Izzy shook her head. 'He's got a few properties but the main one seems to be a bit further south, close to the golf course in Didsbury.'

'Nice area,' Jessica said.

'Clearly things are very sensitive,' Cole said. 'I spoke to the superintendent and the SCD yesterday and everyone is keen for us not to do anything that may interfere with their investigation. They are looking into things like the boxing club as they figure it was a way to siphon away illegitimate money he may have made and then create something that makes that cash harder to find – and makes him a sort of hero at the same time. This guy is not stupid.'

Jessica knew he was talking directly to her, even though he had been subtle enough to look at all three of them while speaking.

'What would you like me to do?' Jessica asked, refusing to take the bait.

The chief inspector picked up his pen and started drumming it on the table. She could tell he wished DI Reynolds was around. 'You can go speak to him to find out if he knows either of the two women who used to work for him, just . . . be careful with it.'

Jessica nodded as her supervisor gave them a brief rundown of what else would be going on, then sent them on their way. He and DS Cornish would lead the main briefing downstairs, leaving Jessica clear.

Izzy and Jessica descended the stairs together. 'Are you going to go on your own?' the constable asked.

'I'm going to grab Dave and force the moody git to smile at least once.'

'I'll call you if I find out anything but our records are awful when we start going back that far.'

As they reached the bottom they paused before heading off in different directions.

'What are you going to do?' Izzy added, quietly enough so that only Jessica could hear.

Jessica didn't hesitate in her reply. 'What I always do – go piss someone off.'

10

Despite being told by her boss to take a week off, Kayleigh desperately wanted to go back to work. The back door had been fixed and the police officers had finished whatever they were doing, generally getting in the way. Although she had never minded living alone, now she felt trapped in a house that no longer seemed like hers.

Kayleigh lay in bed staring at the flaking paint on the ceiling, wondering if whoever had dumped the body in her bath had entered her bedroom. Had they looked themselves up and down in her full-length mirror? Had they gone through her things? Was it someone she knew? She closed her eyes tightly and focused on her breathing, remembering the yoga classes she had gone to and wanting to believe that it would help calm her enough to make everything go away. Of course it wouldn't: you spent so much time thinking that you weren't breathing correctly that focusing on anything other than your breathing was impossible.

In the days since her find, Kayleigh's friends had offered her rooms to stay in but, although she had been tempted, it also felt like to accept would have been giving in. That didn't make her feel any more comfortable in the house, however. It was easy to show bravado on the phone, not quite so simple in an empty home when everything was dark and quiet outside. Kayleigh hadn't been scared of the dark since she was a child, when she would jump at the pipes clanging around her parents' old house, or worry about what might be in her wardrobe. Since finding Oliver's body, she had slept with the light on every night, struggling to drift off and instead dozing in twenty-minute bursts which made her feel more tired than if she had simply stayed awake.

The outside sounds didn't help either. In an area where people worked shifts and others arrived home in the early hours from the pub, there was frequently some sort of noise in the vicinity. Kayleigh would strain her ears, trying to hear if anyone sounded close to her front door.

Feeling more tired than she had when she went to bed, Kayleigh rubbed her stinging eyes. One part of her wanted to spend the day trying to sleep but the other was urging her to get out and do something.

Forcing herself to clamber out of bed, she ran a hand through her greasy and lifeless hair. She stepped close to the mirror, staring into her eyes, before examining the skin on her face which looked pale and puffy. With a sigh, she took off her nightie and picked up yesterday's clothes from the floor. The effort of hunting through her wardrobe, where the intruder might have touched the contents, felt like too much to deal with. Shivering slightly as she finished dressing, Kayleigh turned and left the room without a final look in the mirror.

Despite the window having been fixed, Kayleigh's kitchen still seemed cold, even when she kept the central heating on. She stifled another shiver while opening the fridge, the bright white light hurting her eyes. Although she didn't feel hungry, Kayleigh had been forcing herself to eat in the mornings in an effort to try to keep some sort of routine going. As she hadn't left the house in days, the fridge was looking decidedly empty, with only a dribble at the bottom of the milk bottle and a few salad items that could barely make a snack between them, let alone a proper breakfast. Who wanted green stuff at a time like this anyway? If ever there was a time where you could feel justified in polishing off a packet of muffins, this was surely it.

Because she worked in a supermarket, Kayleigh was used to picking up whatever she needed at the end of her shift, and so actually going food shopping was something she had only done once or twice in the past year.

Kayleigh first checked the back door was locked, even though she had done it the night before, and then walked around the ground floor, ensuring each of the windows was also secure. Twist one way, then the other. Rattle, rattle. Tug it, push it. Definitely closed.

After going back upstairs to take her house keys out of the bedside cabinet, she re-checked each possible point of entry a second time, before hunting through the cupboard under the stairs to find her warmest coat.

As she left the house, Kayleigh locked the door, lifting the handle half-a-dozen times before finally admitting to herself that it was secure. She knew she was becoming obsessed but that didn't mean she could stop herself. If she had been that conscientious before, the events of the past week might never have happened.

Kayleigh turned, surveying the street in front of her. Although she had lived there for a few years, it now seemed alien. A woman pushed a buggy along the pavement at the end of her pathway, which somehow made her want to go back into the house. Her enthusiasm to get back to work feeling misplaced, she wondered if the person with the buggy might be connected to whatever had gone on. Perhaps they used the buggy to keep stolen goods in and now they were coming back to re-examine the scene? It was the perfect cover.

Taking deep breaths to calm down, Kayleigh slowly assured herself it was simply someone on their way home from dropping their children off at school.

She breathed in through her nose, focusing on letting the air out through her mouth. Maybe those yoga classes weren't so bad after all? When that seemed to work, Kayleigh walked to the end of her drive before setting off towards the local shop. Each time anyone passed her on the pavement, she felt edgy and kept her hands firmly in the pockets of her coat. It only took her five minutes to make the journey to the main road, where there was an express version of a supermarket. She bought bread, milk and some fruit, ignoring the worker's small talk, avoiding the allure of the cakes, biscuits and chocolate, and quickly exiting. As someone who worked in a similar environment, Kayleigh felt guilty about snubbing the checkout girl as she always hated it when customers refused to talk to her. Some of them wouldn't even look at her, presumably thinking they were too good to be interacting with someone who worked in a supermarket.

As she walked through the sliding doors at the front of the shop, she jumped as a man reached out and touched her on the arm.

If she hadn't been so shocked, she would have yelped but he spoke before she could say anything. 'Do you know the time?'

Kayleigh stumbled over a reply but he continued. 'My phone's out of battery and there are no clocks anywhere. I'm supposed to be going for an interview but I don't know where it is. My bus was late and now I think I'm late.'

Kayleigh noticed the shoulders on the man's suit were far too big for him and he was nervously glancing from side to side. He was at least six inches taller than her and smelled of cheap aftershave, like one of her ex-boyfriends. The one who 'stayed late' at work a lot. Kayleigh struggled to speak and he offered a 'sorry' before entering the shop. She didn't know if it was her expression or his haste which had made him walk away.

Realising she could feel her heart beating hard, Kayleigh turned and walked back the way she had come, keeping her head down and moving as quickly as she could without breaking into a run. As she reached her front door, she half expected it to be open and tried the handle before digging into her pocket to take out the key. She almost fell inside, shoving the door with a bang behind her, and leaning against the inside of the frame trying to catch her breath.

Kayleigh scanned the hallway, looking to see if everything was as it had been when she had left. It took a while but after convincing herself no one had been in the house during her absence, she crept through to the kitchen and put the shopping bag on the floor before peering through the window to see if anything in the back garden was out of place. She hated the feelings of unease but could not stop herself and wondered how long it would be before she could leave the house without double-checking every door and window. Or how long it would be before she could see a stranger without thinking they might be out to harm her.

As someone who had previously been confident and relatively outgoing, Kayleigh hated the person she knew she was becoming, detesting even more the person who had put her in this position by breaking into her house.

Resolving that the best way to start pulling herself together was to clean herself up a bit, Kayleigh put the shopping away and made her way upstairs to the bedroom where she picked up a fresh towel. She knew the reason she hadn't been keeping on top of things was because she dreaded going into the bathroom. The police team had spent days testing everything and taking samples but she couldn't see past finding Oliver's distorted body.

After undressing, Kayleigh wrapped the towel around herself and carefully entered the bathroom. One of the police team had ended up cleaning things for her and, in that sense, the room looked and smelled better than it had in years. That didn't stop her remembering the odour from before.

She turned on the warm water before realising that she no longer had a shower curtain. It had been taken for evidence but she had somehow switched off from the fact that it would need to be replaced. Kayleigh couldn't stop picturing Oliver in the bath, even as she stood under the cascading water that half-sloshed onto the floor, trying to wash everything away.

After finishing, she stood and looked at her face in the bathroom mirror. Somehow the water had washed away some trace of the bags under her eyes, but her skin was still a sallow white. Her hair at least felt a little more normal, and she reached onto the nearby shelf to pick up her hair-brush. Realising it wasn't in the spot where it usually was, she checked the shelf above, then the bathroom cabinet. She couldn't think of a reason why anyone from the police team would have taken it – and hadn't seen the brush on the list of things they had taken. She had another in the drawer next to the mirror downstairs but didn't fancy going all that way.

Kayleigh re-wrapped the towel around herself and walked through to the bedroom where she checked her bedside table, even though she never left her brush anywhere but the bathroom.

She sat on the bed, gently towelling her hair dry and wondering where she could have possibly put it.

11

'Cheer up, Dave, we're going to one of your favourite hangouts.'

Jessica was determined to get her colleague to offer something other than a sullen grunt of acknowledgement. She glanced sideways from the driver's seat to Rowlands, who simply stared ahead. 'Kid there,' he said, nodding to the side of the road.

'I can see him,' Jessica protested, even though she hadn't. Her reputation around the station as a bad driver had begun to die down over the past year or so but some people, chiefly Dave, perpetuated it.

'Cyclist too,' he added.

Jessica swerved exaggeratedly around the man on a bicycle. 'Are you going to do this the whole journey?'

'What?'

'Point out potential hazards on the road.'

The constable laughed. 'Maybe.'

'At least you're laughing.'

Dave didn't reply, so Jessica thought she would push it while they were alone. 'Come on, you can tell me what's up. I know it isn't just breaking up with Chloe – that was ages ago.'

'It's nothing,' he snapped.

'We're supposed to be mates. I know you've told Izzy what's going on.'

'I haven't actually because there's nothing to tell.'

Jessica sighed noisily. 'Why are all the men in my life acting mental at the moment?'

Rowlands shuffled in his seat. 'Problems in paradise?'

Jessica couldn't tell if he was being sarcastic, so she took the question seriously. 'Not really. Adam's just being . . . man-like. You know, all "nothing's wrong" and so on.'

'That's what you're like.'

Jessica stayed quiet, watching the road, knowing the constable was right. She thought of all the times he, Izzy, Caroline, Adam and everyone else had asked her if she was 'all right', only to be met with her grumpy-sounding 'I'm fine', even when she wasn't. She was more worried by the fact she had recognised that than anything else.

'Either way, in all seriousness, have you been to this strip club?' Jessica asked.

The constable sounded indignant. 'Why would I have?'

'I don't know, before Chloe you were always going on about raucous nights out. I figured this would be the type of place you might be familiar with.'

'Well, it's not.'

'All right. You're not under caution. I believe you.'

Nicholas Long's club was along a side street not far from Albert Square. The front was completely blacked out, with silver writing declaring it 'Manchester's Premier Gentlemen's Establishment'.

Because they were only looking to talk to Nicholas in an unofficial way, they had contacted him and asked to arrange a meeting. They told him it was to discuss some of his former employees and hadn't offered any further information. Given the choice of him coming to the station, or them visiting his house, he had reminded them he was 'a very busy man' and invited them to his club instead. Jessica didn't know if he had done that to put them off but had accepted anyway, not even balking at the fact he wanted to talk in the evening. Cole had told her twice in their briefing to be careful, so she figured meeting on his terms was a good way to start.

From the times on the front window, Jessica knew the club had been open for less than five minutes. Before entering, she rested against the glass, leaning in closely to talk to Rowlands. 'When we're inside, just go with it.'

'How do you mean?'

'You'll see.'

Before Rowlands had a chance to reply, Jessica pushed open the door, entering a darkened hallway. She led the way towards the light, where there was a man standing behind a counter sucking his little finger. He stopped as he noticed them approaching and stood taller, eyeing them up and down from a distance. He was tall but not particularly imposing and, on first impression, looked too young to be working in such a place. He had short brown hair that was gelled and spiked and it was only when Jessica got closer that she saw the beginnings of crinkles around his eyes that indicated an age somewhere in the early twenties, as opposed to the teens.

'All right, Scott?' Jessica said, noticing the man's name tag. At first he seemed taken aback, partly by having his name mentioned but also, Jessica assumed, because they didn't get too many female visitors.

He seemed almost annoyed when he realised how she had found out his name. 'Are you members?' he asked tersely, picking up a tissue from the counter and throwing it into a bin in the corner.

'We're here to see Nicholas,' Jessica said. 'You might want to work on your welcoming strategy, by the way. Sucking your fingers and keeping snotty tissues on the counter surely can't be good for business.'

Scott scowled as he picked up a phone from the desk and spoke too quietly for them to hear. 'You can wait there,' he said, putting the receiver down and pointing towards a sofa on the opposite side of the cramped entranceway.

The room could have only fitted two dozen people in if they were packed tightly. There was the door they had come through, then a second one which presumably led to the main part of the club. Next to that was a closed hatch with 'Cloak Room' written over the top. The decor was almost entirely red, with matching carpets and wallpaper and a beech-coloured wooden border running around the walls. A chandelier hung from the ceiling, with fake candles on each of the prongs, and Jessica could almost taste the air-freshener which had seemingly been emptied into the room at some point in the past few hours.

'Familiar setting this, Dave?' Jessica whispered.

'I told you, I've not been here before.'

'Maybe not to this one . . .'

Before she could wind her friend up any further, a brute

of a man stomped through the door opposite the one they had entered by. His head was shaven and his dark shirt was bulging from the muscles underneath. Jessica stood but still felt half the man's size as he stretched out sausage-like fingers to shake her hand. 'I'm Liam,' he said before Jessica could check his name tag. 'I'm the bar manager here. Nicholas is a little busy at this exact moment but I've been told I can offer you any drink you might like on the house while you wait.'

His tone was cheerful and didn't sound forced. Although it wasn't high-pitched as such, Jessica would have expected something much more booming from such a hulk of a man. He didn't even squeeze her hand tightly as they shook.

'I'm all right, thanks,' Jessica replied.

Liam glanced towards Rowlands, who offered a sheepish, 'I'm fine too.'

'We did have an appointment time,' Jessica said sternly, wanting to remind the man that they weren't simply people who had wandered in off the street.

Liam scratched his ear and Jessica realised he was wearing an earpiece. A small radio microphone was clipped to the lapel of his suit. She looked into the top corner of the room and saw a green light blinking underneath a CCTV camera that was pointing straight at them. The man said 'no worries' loudly, then turned and waved them towards the door.

The inside of the club was decorated in much the same way as the lobby: red carpets as far as she could see, and the same paint and wood effect around the walls. Liam led them past a row of empty bar stools but Jessica couldn't help but feel her eyes wander towards the half-dozen women sitting in the back corner. None of them was wearing very much but they spun almost in unison to stare at her. Jessica made sure not to turn away but her attention was taken as she heard a clatter behind her, where Rowlands was picking up a stool he had walked into. Jessica would have offered a 'look where you're going'-stare, if it wasn't for the fact Liam had stopped in front of a door just to the side of the bar.

He used his body to shield a keypad from Jessica's view and typed in a code before turning the handle and holding it open.

She took the hint, squeezing past him into a large corridor with Rowlands just behind. 'First one in front of you,' Liam called after them.

There were four doors, with a fire exit sign illuminated at the far end. In contrast to the rest of the building, the corridor was painted in pure white and felt cold. With Liam watching them, Jessica opened the first door without knocking.

Nicholas Long looked pretty much the same as he had in the photos Jessica had seen, although his skin was redder and his hair thinner. His cheeks sagged slightly over his jawbone as he put down a heavy-looking glass of whisky and stood up from a high-backed leather chair, walking towards her offering his hand. His grey suit looked expensive but it also clung to his portly frame, making him look enormous.

'Ms Daniel,' he said, 'I didn't realise from your voice

you would be quite so . . . appealing.' His eyes flickered up and down her figure, the words slithering from his lips. Whether he was coming on to her, or trying to creep her out, she wasn't sure. He was like the lecherous bore at the end of a Wetherspoon's bar, regaling anyone within hearing distance with stories about how great he was while tucking into a pint of bitter at ten in the morning.

Jessica glared into the man's eyes and shook his hand. 'I didn't realise you'd be quite so . . . *old*,' she shot back.

Nicholas paused for a moment and then laughed loudly, though his reply didn't sound genuine. 'Feisty too. I like that.'

The man's office was lined on one side entirely by filing cabinets, with two computers on the desk. Jessica noticed a rank of monitors, including one showing a black and white image from the entrance area they had been waiting in. He saw her glance towards the screen and laughed a second time. 'I've got to keep an eye on my empire,' he said, returning to his desk and sitting, while picking the glass up in one fluid movement and downing the contents.

'You're not driving home, are you?' Jessica asked, sitting in the seat opposite him, trying to make eye contact. She could feel Rowlands hovering nervously behind her.

'I thought this was a friendly visit?' Nicholas replied, reaching into a drawer under the desk and picking out a decanter.

'This *is* me being friendly,' Jessica replied.

The man poured himself a drink and then nodded towards her. 'Want one?'

Jessica didn't take her eyes from the man. 'Whisky's for old men.'

Nicholas's top lip began to curl but he stopped himself and nodded at Rowlands. 'You?'

'No thanks.'

There was a sofa at the back of the office behind the door and Jessica turned to see her colleague sitting down.

'Suit yourself,' Nicholas replied, putting the bottle back into the drawer. 'So, how can I help you?' His tone was exaggerated and far too sweet compared to the steely look in his eyes.

'Eleanor James and Kayleigh Pritchard,' Jessica said, watching for a reaction that didn't come.

Nicholas shrugged his shoulders dismissively and checked his watch. 'Who?'

'They're two women who used to work for you.'

He stuck out his bottom lip and shook his head, making the flabby skin of his cheeks wobble. 'I've never heard of them. When did they work for me?'

'In your casino around twenty years ago.'

Nicholas put the glass down and stared at Jessica before bursting into a forced laugh. 'Do you know how many businesses I've run in that time? How many people I've employed?'

'It must take a lot of experience to run a strip club,' Jessica said.

The man glared at her. 'I prefer the term "social club".'

'It *is* a strip club though.'

'I'm surprised a young woman such as yourself is so

against the empowerment of women to legitimately earn large amounts of money.'

Jessica didn't want to get into that particular argument. 'So you don't recognise the two names?'

'No.'

'How about faces?' Rowlands leant forward and passed Jessica two enlarged photos, which she held up for the man to see.

Nicholas smiled provocatively. 'The one on the left is pretty.'

'I thought you liked your women in their twenties? It is Tia, isn't it?' Jessica replied, wiping the grin from his face.

'What's my wife got to do with this?'

For the first time, Nicholas's tone was outright menacing, each syllable echoing around the room with a hiss. He was staring at her, trying to figure out what she was up to but Jessica knew what she was doing – or at least she thought she did. She could hear Cole's warnings ringing around her ears as she slid the two photographs across the desk.

'Do you recognise either of them?'

Nicholas didn't look at the pictures, instead picking up a cigar from the table and putting it into his mouth. He chewed on the end, peering at Jessica and smiling with his eyes. 'Nope.'

'You do realise it's illegal to light that in here,' Jessica said, picking up the photographs and nodding towards a half-full ashtray.

'I own this place.'

'It's also a workplace, meaning no smoking.'

Nicholas's eyes narrowed, his brow twitching angrily, before he composed himself and broke into a smile. He opened his top drawer and dropped the cigar into it. 'It's heartening to know we have such defenders of the law working for the state.'

Jessica held up the photographs for a second time. 'Look again.'

She saw his eyes dart from one photo to the other but if he recognised either of them, he didn't let on, shaking his head once again. 'If you leave me the names, I'll look into my records and see if I can find anything out for you. It's twenty-odd years ago; I don't know what you expect, I shut that casino down years ago.'

Jessica nodded, figuring it was as good an offer as she was going to get. She handed the photographs to Rowlands and then put on as sweet a voice as she could manage. 'You could let some of our people go through your records if it makes life easier . . . ?'

Nicholas's smile was fixed but Jessica could see a vein throbbing on his forehead. His skin had reddened further and he was nodding slightly. He barely moved his lips as he replied. 'No, thank you. I'll be in contact if I find anything.'

Jessica thought about standing to leave but couldn't resist. 'That's probably sensible. Who knows what they'd find . . . ?'

She knew instantly she had him. Nicholas glanced sideways at the bank of monitors, then the area around his Adam's apple began bobbing up and down. She couldn't see it clearly because of the overhanging flap of skin but he could evidently no longer contain his fury.

He thumped his hands onto the table. 'Who do you think you are?' His eyes were narrow with rage, his hands shaking. Jessica said nothing. 'Who do you fucking well think you are?'

Jessica reached into her pocket and took out a business card, sliding it across and speaking sweetly. 'Detective Sergeant Jessica Daniel. It's nice to meet you.'

Nicholas glared at her. 'Do you know what I've done for my community?' He waved his hands dramatically towards the wall, where there were framed photos and newspaper articles, including the one she had already seen outside the boxing club.

Jessica stood and walked across to them, taking a cursory glance. 'Very impressive. We've all been talking about how clever you are, haven't we, Dave?'

Rowlands followed her lead, although she would have preferred it if his voice hadn't faltered as he muttered a slightly unconvincing: 'Yeah, really clever.'

Nicholas stabbed a pudgy finger at the monitors. 'Do you know what I've done for these lads? Both Scott on reception and my bar manager, Liam, were unemployed kids. I gave them something from nothing. They came in on work experience and look at them now.'

'Bravo.'

'I don't know why you lot are always on to me. Don't think I haven't seen you sniffing around my businesses. I can smell you a mile off.'

Jessica walked across to where Rowlands was sitting and

took a final pair of photographs from him. She held up the first one, making sure Nicholas was looking at it before speaking. 'This is Oliver Gordon. Do you know him?'

Nicholas seemed slightly stunned by her change of tack. She saw at least some of the anger drain from his face. 'No.'

Jessica flipped the photos around until she was showing him the one of Oliver's dead body. 'How about this one?'

Nicholas didn't flinch but he didn't sound angry either. 'No.'

Jessica put the photos down and then reached across, picking up the card she had left as well as Nicholas's pen. She flipped it over and wrote 'Eleanor/Ellie James' and 'Kayleigh Pritchard' in clear capital letters, then offered him the card and pen. He took both but put the pen down, studying the names and downing the rest of his drink. She was convinced she saw some sort of recognition in his eyes. He didn't seem the type to forget names or faces of the women he employed.

'Give me a call when you find out more about them,' Jessica said.

She started walking towards the door but Nicholas clearly wanted the final word. 'Ms Daniel,' he said, his voice now under control again.

Jessica glanced over her shoulder with one hand on the doorknob. 'What?'

'If you want to return to see me, you best make sure you either have a warrant or an appointment.'

Jessica gave him her broadest smile. 'You were lucky

this time,' she replied. 'I'm not usually an appointment type of girl.'

With that, she left the room, clattering through the door that led into the club. Two men were sitting on stools at the bar and turned to watch as she stomped through the main area. She ignored Liam, offered a 'see you soon' to Scott, who was still sucking his finger, and then banged the front door on her way out into the cool evening air.

She was walking so quickly that it wasn't until she reached the main square that Rowlands caught her up. 'That went well,' he said.

Jessica couldn't help but laugh, although she didn't think Cole would agree.

12

Although she had not expected Nicholas Long to complain, Jessica spent the rest of the week waiting to be called into Cole's office for a telling off. When it never came, she realised she had judged the man perfectly. Some rich, well-connected local criminals would instantly get their lawyers on the case the moment the police did anything that wasn't quite by the book. Jessica knew Nicholas was nothing like that. For one, she suspected he resented paying a lawyer a penny of anything, let alone for something he would deem unnecessary. Secondly, he seemed the type who revelled in fighting his own battles. He wouldn't want someone in a smart suit throwing around accusations on his behalf, he would rather be at the centre of everything himself.

Jessica had no reason to believe he was involved in anything to do with Oliver's death but they didn't have an awful lot else to go on either. Both Eleanor and Kayleigh insisted there was nothing sinister to them leaving their casino jobs and Nicholas had not come back to them with any further information. She realised the dangers of winding him up, not only because the Serious Crime Division were looking into him but also there was a strong likelihood he was a very dangerous man. None of that would be obvious, of course, but the force wouldn't be putting that amount of time and expense into someone they thought might have been growing cannabis in a back bedroom. The suspicions of weapon trading in particular seemed strong, although nothing had been proven. She had the feeling people above her would settle for anything, even something tax-related, if it meant getting him off the streets.

With that in mind, she had made the decision to put herself in the thick of things. She hadn't needed to wind him up but had at least seen the real Nicholas Long up close. It wasn't a pleasant experience.

Jessica wanted to keep Izzy away from any direct contact and had asked her to concentrate on finding anything further that linked Nicholas to any of the Sextons, Gordons, or Kayleigh. She felt sure there must be something under the surface.

In the meantime, all of the test results were back from the scene of Oliver's disappearance at the Sextons' house and the break-in at Kayleigh's. They hadn't found anything in the way of fingerprints or DNA from either site that was useable. The only useful lead they had helped generate was the discovery of footprints in the back garden at Kayleigh's. Unfortunately, that had only led them back to a delivery driver who had left a parcel at the rear of the house a few days prior to Oliver's body being discovered. Kayleigh told them it was something that happened regularly on her estate.

In all, Jessica was not having the best of times at work and Adam was certainly acting strangely at home. It wasn't a massive deal but, in the past, he would regularly leave his mobile phone on the arm of the sofa when he did things like go to the toilet. Now he carried it with him everywhere. Jessica didn't need to use any of her skills to know something was going on but, at the same time, didn't want to accuse him of anything. In some ways it was worse because he acted perfectly fine with her and joked around in the same way he always did. He even arranged for them to have a house viewing and, as much as Jessica had been willing for something to come up at work to get her out of it, the active cases they were working on stayed frustratingly immobile.

For Jessica, buying a house – especially with another person – was perhaps the final aspect of admitting she was definitely old. Well, that and having kids, which was something that was certainly not on her agenda. She had always rented up until a few months ago when she moved into Adam's. Even though that never felt like her house, it did at least allow her to convince herself Adam was the grown-up, not her.

The estate agent was clearly annoyed to be working on a Sunday, which Jessica wouldn't have minded if he wasn't trying to disguise it with an over-the-top cheery voice. People who clearly hated their job she could take, happy people she could not – especially if they were putting it on.

Adam knew her well enough to realise her frustration and squeezed her hand as the estate agent fumbled with the front door and led them inside. The man's spiky hair reminded her of Rowlands from a few years ago and his breath smelled of mint, which Jessica told herself was to cover up the amount of alcohol he had no doubt had the night before.

'This is the living room,' he said enthusiastically, showing them into what was, quite obviously, a living room.

'I was wondering,' Jessica mumbled loudly enough for Adam to hear.

'As you can see, the room does need some work but obviously that's reflected in the price. How about I give you a few moments alone and then I'll show you the kitchen?'

Adam nodded an acceptance as the agent left the room while Jessica stared at the wall. '"Needs some work"? There's a bloody hole in the wall.'

'The ad did say, "needs modernising".'

Jessica crouched and put her hand into the gap in the brickwork where there was a small feathering of insulation. 'Did it say, "needs a bit of building"?'

Adam laughed. 'It's just an old fireplace that's been taken out. It's easy enough to fill in and re-paper.'

'Maybe I'm old-fashioned, but I generally prefer to buy houses that don't have large holes in them.'

'How many houses have you bought?'

Jessica couldn't stop herself from giggling. 'I don't know. I can't keep count, seven or eight? I've got a holiday home in Barbados.'

The rest of the tour went largely the same way, with a sink that was hanging off the bathroom wall by a pipe being described as 'in need of some plumbing work', and exposed electrical wires where there should have been a light fitting 'something that will need to be looked at'. Jessica would have been only half-surprised to find there was no roof, something the estate agent would surely have called 'a minor inconvenience'.

She wondered if they should get him involved with their own destroyed property. The fact large parts had burned down and others had collapsed would no doubt provide 'a unique living arrangement'.

As Adam offered a degree of interest, Jessica switched off from the tour. She was thinking of ways the agent could come and work for their press office, where he could call dead bodies 'life-impeded' and describe stab victims as 'vulnerable to pointed objects'.

Before she could come up with anything further, she found herself standing at the top of the stairs with both men staring at her. It was obvious one of them had just asked a question.

'Sorry?' Jessica said, looking from one to the other.

She saw the moment of recognition in the estate agent's eyes as he figured out her 'aah's and 'ooh's of the past ten minutes had not been genuine.

'I was simply wondering if this might interest you, Mrs Compton,' he repeated.

Jessica looked at Adam, then the man. She felt Adam squeezing her hand. 'It's not Mrs Compton.'

The agent stumbled over his reply. 'Oh, right, sorry, I just assumed . . .'

'We'll let you know,' Adam interjected before any further damage could be done.

Jessica didn't need to answer Adam's 'I take it you don't

fancy it?' question as they reached the end of the driveway – she couldn't think of too many worse ways to be spending a weekend.

Because it had been a nice-looking morning, Adam had convinced her to walk to the viewing. As they cut through a selection of alleyways, Jessica wanted to ask him what was really going on with his phone and their laptop but couldn't bring herself to completely believe there was a problem. Instead they walked in an uncomfortable silence until they reached the entrance to a park that linked the estate to their destination. The early morning sun had been replaced by the usual grey haze which so often seemed to hang over the city, a breeze whipping along the paths. Jessica was regretting not bringing her pilfered jacket and was about to suggest heading for a nearby shopping centre where they could catch a taxi, when she saw a boy leaning up against the fence.

Jessica had always been terrible with children's ages unless they were babies, and she barely knew the difference between a seven-year-old and a thirteen-year-old. In general, they were just small, probably annoying, people.

As they passed the child, he caught Jessica's eye and she could see that, although he wasn't crying, his eyes were red. There were dirty scuff marks on the palms of his hands and smears of mud on his arms.

'Are you all right . . . mate?' Jessica asked, not knowing how to approach a child. Was calling someone 'mate' considered grooming according to police guidelines? Probably – most things were. She remembered her mother constantly telling her when she was young not to talk to strangers. Now she was the stranger.

His brown hair was ruffled and dirty and Jessica could see an additional mark over one of his eyes as she crouched onto one knee. 'Where's your mum?'

'I don't know,' he replied, his eyes filling with tears.

Jessica was feeling more and more uncomfortable. 'Did you come here with someone?'

The boy nodded.

'Where did you last see them?'

He turned and pointed towards a small play park a few hundred metres away. 'I was playing there and Mummy said she would be waiting by the gates.'

Although Jessica felt confident dealing with most situations, the one thing that always panicked her was children. She looked at Adam, making sure the child couldn't see her, and pulled her best 'I don't know what to do' face, trying to raise her eyebrows in a 'have you noticed he's a kid?' way, just in case that wasn't apparent.

Adam took the hint and crouched next to her. 'What's your name, pal?' he asked. Was 'pal' more of a grooming word than 'mate'? Either way, Jessica thought it was a good question, something she certainly would have asked if he had been an adult. She wondered why it had eluded her.

'Corey.'

It didn't sound particularly Mancunian, but Jessica assumed at least one of his parents had picked it up from an American or Australian television show. It was one step away from 'Chad', 'Bubba', 'Buddy', or something with 'the Third' on the end of it.

'How old are you, Corey?' Adam continued.

'Seven.'

'Right, shall we go find your mummy?' Adam held out his hand for Corey to take and then started walking towards the play park.

Jessica felt a little embarrassed at not having thought of the obvious solution herself. As they walked across the grass, Adam kept the boy talking, asking what kinds of things he was interested in and whereabouts he lived. If he offered the kid sweets, she'd probably have to arrest him.

'What happened to your hands, Corey?' Jessica asked.

'I fell off the swings.'

'Is that when you went looking for your mum?'

The boy nodded, before Jessica realised Adam was trying to steer the conversation away from anything that could further upset him.

The play area wasn't full but there were a few dozen children running around. Adam walked around the edge with Corey, looking from side to side and asking if the boy could see his mother. After one lap, it became clear she wasn't there. The child had told them his mum had 'yellow' hair and was wearing a red coat. Adam suggested that one of them stay with Corey, while the other went off to check the car park and security office. For a moment, Jessica thought he was going to suggest that she stay but, maybe thanks to the panic on her face, he said he would wait.

Jessica first checked the car park but, aside from a group

of men in football kit changing their shoes, there was no one else around. The park's office was on the far side of the field, leaving her navigating around the wettest parts. To make matters worse, after she finally reached the other side, a large sign next to the door read 'Closed on Sundays' and the only person anywhere near her was a man walking a dog.

Jessica used the path to return to the park which was technically a longer route but took less time because she wasn't having to walk around the squelchy parts of the field.

Any hopes that things would already be resolved were dashed as she arrived back at the play park to see Adam waiting just inside the gate with Corey at his side. She gave a slight shake of her head as he noticed her but, unfortunately, the child saw it too. Jessica watched his face fall as Adam crouched and rested an arm on his shoulder.

'I'm sure she'll be along any minute,' Adam said as hopefully as he could.

Jessica wanted to ask him what to do next but didn't want to say it out loud. She could feel the wind getting stronger as a few parents passed her on their way out of the gate, clearly worried about the gathering clouds overhead. As Jessica turned to watch them go, she saw a woman with blonde hair and a red coat in the distance. She was strolling, chatting to a man who towered over her.

'Ad,' Jess said to get his attention, then nodded in the direction of the couple.

As soon as Corey noticed them, he let out a yelp and began running in their direction. Jessica and Adam followed at a distance and, by the time they had caught up, the child was busy hugging the woman's leg.

'Get off,' she said irritably.

'Are you all right, Corey?' Adam asked.

The boy let go with one arm but held on with the other and turned to face Adam, nodding enthusiastically.

'Who the fuck are you?' the woman said in a strong local accent, glaring at Jessica, even though it was Adam who had spoken. In some areas of Manchester, that was as polite a welcome as you'd get. She was holding a cigarette with one hand and the man had taken a step away.

Jessica was about to respond in kind but Adam got in first. 'We've been waiting with Corey because he fell over and couldn't find his mother.' His tone was steady and calm, definitely not the way Jessica would have replied.

The woman glanced down at her child, then returned to staring at Jessica. 'Are you all right, Core?' she asked, without a second look.

'My hands hurt,' Corey replied.

His mother still didn't look down. 'We'll have a look when we get home,' she said, before offering a far more aggressive, 'What?' in Jessica's direction.

Adam again jumped in ahead of her. 'Nothing, we're just glad he found you safely. You've got a lovely young man there.'

Finally the woman stopped looking at Jessica, turning towards Adam and sneering, 'Fuck off, you paedo prick. Is this what you do? Go around touching up kids?'

Jessica watched Corey bury his head further into his mum's leg, which she twitched to free herself.

The woman turned to leave with a final, 'And what have I told you about talking to strangers?' as she started to walk back the way she had come.

Jessica was about to step in but Adam placed one hand on her shoulder. 'Don't,' he said authoritatively. She was stunned not by the way he was holding her, or by what he said, but instead by the way he said it. She was used to him joking with her, even being jumpy on occasion, but had never heard him speak with such weight.

Once Corey and the two adults were around fifty metres ahead, Adam started following them, Jessica falling in step next to him. 'Where are we going?' she asked.

'I'm hoping she's going to get into a car and that we can get the number plate,' Adam said. 'With that and Corey's name, you should be able to get her name and we can get onto social services.'

'We're not supposed to use the system for that . . .'

'You can ask someone senior, though, after what we just saw?'

Adam's question sounded so matter-of-fact that Jessica couldn't help but answer positively. As they kept their distance from the couple, she added: 'How did you know what to do?'

'When?'

'With Corey when we first saw him.'

Adam didn't break stride, even though it started to spot with rain. 'I don't know. How do you know what to do in your job? How do you know what to say when you're with a suspect or a victim?'

'I don't know . . . I just do.'

'Exactly.'

'But he was just a child.'

Jessica glanced sideways and, even though there was a look of serious concentration on Adam's face, he still broke into a grin. 'He's still a person, Jess, just a little one. You treat them the same. What would you have done if it was a lost adult? You would have found a way.'

Although she started to protest, Jessica stopped herself. Somehow she had reached her mid-thirties without figuring that out. She tried to think of the children she'd had contact with in the past few years and realised it was only really Izzy's baby she'd spent even a small amount of time with – and she seemed to sleep a lot. Most of her immediate network of friends consisted of people who were childless.

Lost in her thoughts, Jessica bumped into the back of Adam as he stopped at the edge of the pathway which led into the car park. He went to move forward but Jessica stopped him. 'I'll go.'

Adam sat on the nearby bench as Jessica ducked behind a hatchback and edged around the tarmac. She could see Corey getting into the back seat of a car, his mother standing impatiently next to him holding the front seat forward. When he was in, she climbed in herself and blew a kiss to the man who had been with her as he got into the adjacent vehicle. Jessica could guess what was going on and typed both number plates into her phone, thinking she would do a bit of digging and if a social services query didn't get her anywhere, then there might be an anonymous letter or two ready to give someone a surprise.

Jessica double-checked she had the right digits as each car pulled away, then stood and walked back to Adam. She was momentarily confused as the bench he had been on was empty but then she saw him walking away from her towards the play park. Jessica followed quickly, then realised he was talking on his phone. She slowed her pace, although the pitter-patter of the rain was preventing her from hearing anything. As Adam turned and noticed her, his eyes wide with surprise, she heard him say abruptly, '. . . anyway, I can't talk now. I've got to go', before stabbing the phone to hang up and pocketing the device.

'Who was that?' Jessica asked, trying not to sound as if she was accusing him of anything.

'No one, just a marketing call.' Adam locked eyes with her and she knew he was lying. Before she could reply, he added breezily: 'Did you get the numbers?'

As Jessica stumbled over a response, he stretched out his hand for her to hold and they turned to head home.

13

The killer had endured a mixed week. What he hadn't expected was for Kayleigh to spend almost seven days indoors following the discovery of Oliver's body. He hadn't necessarily thought she would return to work straight away but his plans had been put back by the fact she seemingly did not answer the door either. A few days before, he had watched a postman ring the bell three times before resting on the glass to write out a card and then leaving that. The killer knew the woman was in, yet no one else would have realised that unless they were watching as closely as he had been.

The only time she had left was to go to the local shop. Even though he had watched her every move, there hadn't been a time when no other pedestrians were around. He had thought about simply smashing his way in for a second time but discounted it, assuming she would be far more alert. One quick mobile call from her would be enough to get her taken to safety and ensure he would not have his opportunity.

Instead, he watched and waited. His vantage point was a little unconventional, the long-closed public toilet block a few hundred metres from Kayleigh's house. Although it was uncomfortable, it did at least give him protection. Apart from the odd drunk looking for somewhere to stay when it was raining – and they soon disappeared when he told them what he would do to them if they didn't – the killer had the place to himself. Although he could not watch the house twenty-four hours a day, he knew there must soon come a time when Kayleigh went back to work, giving him the perfect opportunity.

Each morning, he would return to the block and watch until lunchtime. If she had not left by then, he assumed it would be one more day. Finally, she broke her isolation, the killer observing as she stepped nervously out of the house just as the sun was coming up. He could see her breath flitting into the air as she tested the front door handle half-a-dozen times after locking it. He didn't know exactly what shift she was working – but had found out where she worked by checking through her cupboards after leaving Oliver. The mass of carrier bags from one supermarket under the sink had given him a clue and the nametag she kept in her bedside cabinet almost confirmed it. The fact she wrote 'work earlies' or 'work lates' on a branded supermarket calendar, coupled with a spare uniform in her wardrobe, gave him as much verification as he could hope for. He had thought it would be harder, but hunting for payslips or anything more official hadn't been needed.

As she finally seemed to accept the door was locked, the killer quickly left the abandoned building and jogged out of sight towards the pavement. By the time she was back in his eye line, Kayleigh was hurrying away from him towards the main road. He walked as quickly as he could without drawing attention and gradually gained on her. As she turned a corner, he ran to catch up, slowing back down to a walk as he reached the point where she'd turned.

The distance was barely fifty metres as the killer pulled his hat down and then buried his hands in his pockets. This was about figuring out exactly what 'work earlies' entailed and discovering her method of transport.

Kayleigh checked nervously over her shoulder a few times but he kept his stride, making sure his matched hers and that he didn't gain, except for when he wanted to.

He followed her across the main road and, as she leant against the glass of a bus stop, the killer slowed his pace until he had no choice but to halt at the same place. Although he didn't think she would recognise him, he did at least have the cover of the other four people also waiting. While Kayleigh, second in line, was bobbing nervously from one foot to the other, he waited at the back and was soon joined by more people.

The killer took great pleasure watching the woman touching her ear and scratching her head nervously. She pulled her coat tighter and continued to stare at the ground until a bus pulled up next to them. After waiting until she had made a move, he slipped onto the bus, taking time to fumble with change to ensure Kayleigh had found a seat before he turned. She was sitting three rows from the back, staring at the rail in front and refusing to acknowledge anyone around her, or the surroundings outside the window.

Being careful not to risk any sort of possible recognition, he walked towards the back of the bus while looking

131

out of the opposite window and then slid into the seat behind her. He saw Kayleigh's body tense as she felt his presence. Her jumpy movements were so satisfying that he wanted to lean in and smell her. He could practically feel the fear in the air and took enormous delight from the fact he knew he had caused it. It had been quite an effort to find out where she lived, let alone Ellie Sexton, whose name change had not helped at all. Luckily, people's carelessness with social networks and open access to the electoral roll through the Internet had made things easier than he could have imagined. It had still taken plenty of work but had not been as impossible as he first thought it might be.

As the bus made its various stops, Kayleigh did not move until they were outside the neon glowing sign that matched her uniform. The killer waited until she was off and then stood, ringing the bell again to ensure the driver did not pull away. He stumbled along the aisle and muttered a 'thanks', before following Kayleigh, making sure there was a greater distance than before. He knew she was untouchable at work but that wasn't the point.

He first spent half an hour on a bench at the far end of the supermarket's car park, waiting for the sun to fully come up. After that, he had a cup of tea in their cafe, before spending time browsing the store as aimlessly as he could. He bought a couple of items, paying with cash, then left and returned to the bench. He knew it would be a long day, but then it was always going to be. You had to make some sacrifices for the greater good, and this was his.

He didn't know how long a shift Kayleigh might work

but he could guess it would either be six, eight, or ten hours. With the time he had wasted inside the store, over two of those had already passed.

Although he thought about leaving and instead going to wait near Kayleigh's home, he didn't want to risk her heading somewhere else, certainly without his knowledge. Instead he sat and waited until, finally, the woman emerged not long after lunchtime. The man dumped his coat in the bin and put on the one he had bought in the store, removing his hat. While it had been easy to stay relatively out of sight on the bench away from the store, he didn't want to be recognised by Kayleigh on the return journey.

He hurried across the car park, reaching the bus stop before the woman, and leaning on the shelter as he watched her stagger along the pavement with two shopping bags. He could sense the excitement building as he got on the bus, this time sitting on the very back set of seats, a few rows behind her. Each stop seemed to take an age as his mouth filled with anticipation.

Finally, the vehicle stopped close to Kayleigh's house and he filed into the queue to exit directly behind her. He allowed her to get a lead as he trailed her back through the estate, keeping a careful eye out for any potential bystanders. He knew it wasn't quite time for parents to start picking their children up from school and felt his heart soar as they turned the corner onto Kayleigh's road, which was empty apart from a handful of parked cars. He had been planning to wait but he might never get a better time than now to act.

He quickened his pace, ensuring he was close enough and then, as Kayleigh put her shopping bags down next to the front door, he took his hands out of his pocket and stepped onto her driveway.

14

Jessica lay in bed staring into the darkness, wondering why she couldn't bring herself to ask the simple question about why Adam was being so secretive. Given his parents had died when he was young, and his grandmother a couple of years ago, he didn't have any other family to be communicating with. Other than the people he worked with, he had never really had much in the way of friends, certainly not since they had been seeing each other, so Jessica had no clue. She hadn't challenged his 'no one' responses and was not used to being in such a position.

Usually, she would speak or act first and worry about the consequences later. If a suspect or witness had lied to her so blatantly, she never would have held back – and yet she could not bring herself to question Adam. She lay awake wondering why but could not come up with anything better than the fact she didn't really want to know the answer.

As she rubbed her tired eyes, Jessica heard her phone begin to vibrate on the floor. She let it ring for one extra time, hoping it would wake Adam, then pressed the button to answer. She was only half-surprised by the caller's information that something had happened at Kayleigh Pritchard's house and that she should get there quickly.

Jessica could never remember feeling as physically sick at a crime scene as she did after getting to Kayleigh's house. It wasn't anything she specifically saw, it was the reality of it all. In part it was because she had been sitting in the woman's living room a week or so before but also, although she tried to tell herself differently, she knew it was largely due to what was going on with Adam.

She had a quick glance around the hallway, then turned and dashed across the road into a small garden area where she hunched behind a hedge and threw up on the ground. She felt close to tears as she rose and walked back to the door, asking one of the officers who was smoking nearby if she could have some chewing gum.

The hallway was littered with items of shopping. Jessica could see a tin of beans that had rolled towards the stairs at the far end and a bottle of washing-up liquid on its side in the doorway that led into the living room. There was a box of cereal, two bottles of water lying in the middle of the hall and a packet of biscuits had crashed to the floor at some point, leaving crumbs across the carpet.

Jessica couldn't stop the thought going through her mind that it would be really difficult to clear up the broken bits.

'Wait there,' a voice said, as Jessica looked up to see a Scene of Crime officer walking carefully towards her. She recognised the woman's face from various scenes over the past few months but didn't know her name. Quite often, team members would move on to other roles, the late nights and short-notice calls taking their toll on people who were usually civilians anyway. Someone threw Jessica protective covers to go over her shoes and she steadily walked around the food until she was next to the other woman.

'Is the body gone?' Jessica asked, realising it was an obvious question, considering the lack of one in the hallway.

As it was, the answer was one she didn't expect. 'She was found in the bath upstairs. They took her about fifteen minutes ago but we've still got people up there.'

'Shite . . .'

Jessica couldn't think of anything more constructive to say. She looked around the hallway, realising she had missed a half-full carrier bag hidden behind the front door on her first look around. Something in the bottom was weighing it down but a bottle of shampoo had split and congealed into a blue pool.

Although she had her own ideas about what had happened, Jessica wanted to hear it from someone else, so asked what the woman thought. Seemingly grateful to be asked for her opinion, she pointed towards the objects on the floor. 'I'd say she was attacked from behind, presumably after opening the front door.' She indicated the positions of the carrier bags. 'Although the objects are spread across the floor, the bags themselves are directly below where she would have been standing, so it probably happened as soon as she stepped inside.'

'How did she die?'

Jessica could have guessed the reply before it came.

'Probably asphyxiation, she has all the signs, although it'll need to be confirmed.'

If how Oliver had died was anything to go by, then Jessica guessed the killer had surprised Kayleigh from behind, smothering her with a bag or something similar.

The woman turned towards the broken biscuits. 'It looks like she fell forwards, crushing those and possibly knocking these bottles as well.'

It sounded like a horrible way to die, face-down as someone pressed a knee into your back, pulling something tight around your mouth to stop you breathing.

'What happened then?' Jessica asked.

Pointing towards the stairs, the woman continued her theory. 'Somehow, she ended up in the bath upstairs. You're going to have to leave it with us for a day or two to find out if she was dragged or carried. We haven't found anything on the stairs yet, but we're going to rip the whole of this carpet out to test for shoe prints, hairs or blood.'

'What else have you found?'

The woman turned and crept back towards the front door, crouching and pointing to a spot on the wall. Jessica looked on from a distance, not wanting to accidentally interfere. 'It looks like a partial shoe print here,' she said. 'It's probably too small to be a man's, so may well be the victim's.'

'Was there . . . anything else?' Jessica didn't want to say the words but the woman took the hint.

'You'll have to wait for the autopsy but her clothing wasn't torn. She could have been re-dressed, of course . . .'

She nodded over Jessica's shoulder towards the man now standing in the doorway. Cole was wearing a large coat far too big for him and looked as tired as Jessica felt.

'I forgot how close you lived,' he said, as Jessica carefully made her way across the hallway.

She thanked the woman for her help and then walked with her supervisor to the end of the driveway. As they talked, she tried to keep a distance, hoping the gum was covering the smell of her breath.

'Did you go upstairs?' Cole asked.

'No, they reckon Kayleigh was killed by her front door and then taken to the bathroom where she was found. They're trying to keep it all clear.' Jessica blew into her hands and then pushed them deeply into the pockets of her coat. 'How did we know?'

For a few moments, Cole did not reply. Jessica thought he hadn't heard but when she turned to face him, she could see his eyes were fixed on the front door. He sighed and started walking backwards, then turned and headed towards the garden area where she had vomited. Luckily, he walked in the opposite direction and sat on a bench just inside the gate.

Jessica sat next to him, watching her breath evaporate into the air as Cole turned to face her. 'I think my marriage is over, Jess,' he said.

It was perhaps the last thing Jessica expected him to say. While most of the members of the team had relation-ship problems in one way or another, Jack Cole had made sure his relationship with his wife and children was strong above anything else. Even though he rarely talked about them, and certainly didn't bring them to any official events, everyone knew he used his free time to be the father and husband his family deserved.

Jessica did not know how to reply. All she could think was that if a relationship such as his could fall apart, then what hope did anyone else have? She answered with a pitiful-sounding, 'Sir . . . ?'

Cole shrugged. 'It's been on the cards for a while, probably since I took this job. It was easier to manage the shifts in the past but you never get away.' He held his hands up as if to indicate the time of day. 'I've been in the spare room for around four months. Obviously the kids know there's something wrong . . .'

Jessica had never had anything even approaching such an intimate conversation with the man before.

'I'm sure it will be all right,' she said, thinking it sounded like the type of thing she should say and wondering quite what had happened in the previous few days that made children and adults alike think she was a sensible person to bring their problems to. Sarcastic remarks: fine. Useful advice: there were definitely better people.

'I know you've just got married,' he continued, making Jessica feel even more uncomfortable. 'Don't listen to me, it really is great. I think I lost focus on what was important. One day you're off at the zoo with the kids, the next you're making phone calls to say you're stuck at work because of too much paperwork. It hasn't helped since Jason left.'

It wasn't strictly true that Reynolds had 'left' but Jessica knew what he meant; it had put an extra strain on everyone.

'We all think you're doing a good job.'

Jessica had not seen eye-to-eye with the man in a while but that wasn't because she lacked respect for him, more that she didn't agree with certain things he had to do.

'It's so easy to slip into a routine,' he replied. 'At first it's just staying for an extra half-hour to get through things, then it's coming in half an hour early. Then you realise thirty minutes isn't long enough. Before you know it, you're taking work home.'

Jessica knew she couldn't talk as she did all of those things when circumstances required. It was part of the job.

'It was one of her co-workers who called us,' Cole said. Jessica was momentarily confused before she realised he was finally answering her question about how they had found the body. 'Kayleigh had returned to the supermarket she works at yesterday but didn't turn up for today's shift. A lot of her colleagues were worried, so they tried her phone but no one answered. One of them lived locally, so tried knocking on her door but there wasn't a reply. I think she may have looked through the letterbox and then called us.'

'What time was that?'

The chief inspector checked his watch. 'Late, I suppose. Either way, one of our entry teams went in because the address matched the previous crime scene. I've not been to bed yet. I got the call late last night and was waiting to hear what happened.'

He rolled his sleeve back down and put his hands into his pockets.

'I probably shouldn't have called you, especially as we're going to be waiting for results anyway.'

'I'm glad you did.'

Cole offered a thin smile. 'You should be at home with your new husband, Jess. Go get some sleep, you look worse than me.'

'Thanks.'

He smiled. 'You know what I mean. You head out and we'll catch up again tomorrow.' After a second, he corrected himself. 'Not tomorrow, later.'

'Are you going to be okay?'

The chief inspector stood, then began walking back to Kayleigh's front door with Jessica a few steps behind. 'I'm going to go back to Longsight anyway. There's going to be all sorts to pull together – and that's before we get any results back.' Jessica was about to return to her car when he added, 'How did your car reg thing go, by the way?'

Although Jessica did not want to involve her supervisor too much, she had asked him for permission to trace the details of the two cars. She had access to do it herself but there had been a recent tightening of rules in regards to who could check what because a colleague in a neighbouring district had used their access to find out details of a former partner. Cole had not asked for anything other than the most basic of details.

'All fine,' Jessica said. 'Exactly what I expected.'

Circumventing various agencies was an awkward thing to do at the best of times but Jessica knew someone who worked as a family liaison officer for Greater Manchester Police. She had passed on the details of Corey and his mother and mentioned that the woman could be worth a closer look. There was nothing on her record in terms of child abuse but there were convictions for assaults and threatening behaviour which did not bode well. Jessica was at least pleased with herself for leaving it in the hands of people who could deal with it if there were a problem.

As for the mystery man, his number plate matched that of someone who most definitely was not married to Corey's mother and, from everything she had found, was still supposed to be in a relationship with someone else. Although she had toyed with a bit of playful meddling, Jessica had held off, thinking there were perhaps things she might not want to know about her own life if the situation was reversed.

Jessica returned to her flat but knew she wasn't going to get any sleep. Instead of trying, she sat in the living room, flicking through the television channels in the hope that something would take her mind away from Kayleigh, Adam and everything else that was going on. Instead, it made it worse. She had long since given up following anything other than her own cases on the rolling news channels and her secret pleasure of watching late-night reruns of early-morning talk shows was diminished by the topic of 'Your boyfriend's sleeping with me, now deal with it'.

She switched off the set and entered the bedroom quietly, looking for a warmer pair of shoes to wear out onto the balcony. Adam stirred but did not wake as she crept around to her side but Jessica's attention was drawn to the blinking light of his phone on the bedside table. She stood silently staring at the LED as it flickered on and off, wanting to summon the courage to pick it up but knowing once that line was crossed that there was no going back.

Jessica's eyes were feeling too heavy to keep awake but her mind was strangely alert as she sat in the incident room in the basement of the Longsight station. She knew exactly what she was going to be spending part of the afternoon doing, even if she wasn't going to tell the chief inspector. Before that, she did want to find out what had happened since the early hours.

Because they were now in what looked like a double murder investigation, officers had been brought in to help and press officers were having private briefings with the DCI and superintendent about 'strategy', making it feel more like a website relaunch than the end of someone's life.

The briefing did reveal plenty of details but nothing Jessica couldn't have figured out by herself. Despite extensive door-to-door inquiries that morning, none of Kayleigh's neighbours had apparently seen or heard anything untoward. Given they had also failed to hear anything to do with the break-in, Jessica wasn't really surprised – it didn't seem like a particularly caring, sharing district, somewhere the estate agent would describe as 'socially unique'.

Although they were waiting for the first set of forensic

tests to come back, someone had been on the ball enough to check the recent obituary listings in all of the local papers, where nothing had appeared about Kayleigh. They had not been able to figure out what the motive might have been for placing Oliver's notice but, if it was simply for attention or to show off, the killer could have something more sinister in store for them with Kayleigh.

Jessica left the briefing with Izzy, whom she hadn't seen in anything other than passing since the smaller meeting in Cole's office the previous week.

'You look like you're the one who was up until two in the morning with a sick child,' the constable said as Jessica held the door open for her. They walked side by side towards the stairs.

Reminded of how tired she felt, Jessica couldn't stop herself from yawning. 'You're not the first to point that out.'

'If you're up in the early hours anyway, feel free to pop around and you can look after Amber while I get some kip.'

'You're very kind but I think I'll be all right.' They started to climb the stairs as Jessica added: 'Did you find anything else about Nicholas Long?'

'Not really. I've been so busy.'

As they reached the crossroads from where the corridor branched towards Jessica's office one way and the area where the constable worked the other, they stopped and moved to the side. 'Me neither.'

'What are you going to do?'

'If at first you don't succeed, try, try and try again.'

'I thought your motto was to give up if you didn't get it first time?'

Jessica smiled weakly. 'It is but when someone pisses me off, I take extra care to go back for seconds.'

15

Jessica had no idea how much time Nicholas Long spent at his club – or even which days he was there – but a quick phone call to his house while posing as the secretary of an industrial cleaning company had easily snared her the information. Whoever it was that told her Nicholas was already at the club 'where he always is' hadn't seemed concerned about giving out private information to a stranger.

Jessica caught the bus into the city centre and walked to the club, which looked different in daylight. In the evening, the pink and black combination, along with the neon, had made it seem marginally more upmarket. In the fading sunlight, it just looked grubby, with grit and dirt on the bottom parts of the glass and smeared handprints along the top half. It didn't appear as if it had been cleaned any time recently.

She tried the front door but it was locked, so she pressed the buzzer next to it. She could hear the whirring sound from inside but there was no answer, so she tried again before resorting to holding the button in until finally Nicholas's voice crackled through.

He didn't even bother trying to hide his annoyance. 'Who is it?' he growled.

'Chinese takeaway.'

'Wrong place.' The device fizzled quiet, so Jessica held the button in again. 'I told you, you've got the wrong place,' the voice thundered.

Jessica read him the address above the door, adding: 'Shall I put it through the letterbox?'

Perhaps fearing more cleaning up, Nicholas quickly interjected: 'Just wait there, I'll come down.'

Jessica leant on the glass in the smuggest way she could. She knew she was playing a dangerous game, both because she had been told to stay out of the Serious Crime Division's business and also because of the type of person Nicholas clearly was. But she wanted to push him, to see if he would reveal something he'd prefer to have kept to himself. She sensed his connection to Kayleigh and Eleanor would be crucial somewhere, despite everything happening such a long time ago.

As the door opened, Nicholas poked his head out, peering in the opposite direction before noticing her.

'You?' His face was redder than it had been the previous time they had met, his skin wobbling in anger and confusion.

'Did you miss me?'

He looked the other way, perhaps wondering if there was anyone else with her. 'What are you doing here?'

'I thought I'd drop in for a chat.'

Nicholas stepped outside the club, still holding the door open. 'I told you to make an appointment. I've had enough of you lot harassing me.'

Jessica stood up straighter and smiled. 'I'm not harassing, I'm haranguing, there's a difference.'

'I can complain, you know, I've got rights.'

Jessica walked towards him, sliding under his arm and through the door. She had moved with such confidence that Nicholas hadn't reacted. By the time he let go of the door, she was already halfway along the corridor towards reception.

'Where are you going, hey, stop . . .'

Jessica didn't turn but she could hear Nicholas spluttering behind her as he closed the door and followed. Despite her bravado, she was relieved not to hear the clicking sound of the lock.

She continued through to the bar area and hopped onto a stool, spinning to face the out-of-breath and very red-faced man as he caught up, looking every inch like someone in a government health warning advert that involved dramatic music and words like 'cholesterol' and 'chronic heart problems'.

By the time Nicholas had reached her, his eyes were wide with fury and he barely managed to gasp: 'This is trespassing.'

'You held the door open for me.'

'I did not.'

Jessica raised her eyebrows in mock bewilderment. 'That's what it looked like. I thought you were inviting me in.'

Nicholas stared at her for a few seconds before finally recovering his composure. 'I told you I like them feisty.'

He licked his lips and reached out to touch Jessica's arm but she slapped him away. 'Are you going to offer me a drink?'

Nicholas was still breathing heavily as she took a moment to fully observe how large he was. Some people held their weight well but the club's owner certainly didn't. She could see the dark material of his suit straining around his thighs and belly. His top shirt buttons were undone most likely because he couldn't have fastened them even if he'd wanted to. The remaining hair he did have was greasily spread across his head, his teeth were yellow and crooked. He really was one of the most repulsive men Jessica had ever been close to and she struggled to hide her disgust.

As he regarded her, she could see the interest in his eyes that went beyond anything professional. If she was a man, she would have been kicked out by now. It was why she hadn't brought Rowlands or anyone else with her. Sometimes being a woman was her biggest advantage.

Seemingly making his mind up to play the game she had started, Nicholas walked around the bar and picked up a small glass, flipping it over and reaching under the counter before pulling out a bottle of whisky. A golden ribbon was wrapped around the centre with a row of stars underneath proclaiming the number of years it had spent distilling. 'I don't leave this on display,' he said, pouring himself a drink. 'Same for you?'

Jessica knew she had to be careful but also wanted him to talk. With a smile, she raised herself up from the stool, leaning across to pick up the man's glass and taking a large sip before putting it on the counter in front of her.

She tried not to grimace as it burned her throat on the way down. Christ, it was horrible, like drinking paraffin, she assumed – though she'd never tried it. Why did anyone drink this stuff?

She gasped a 'Cheers.'

Nicholas stared on incredulously before reaching under the counter to take a second glass and fill it. 'Feisty,' he purred, making Jessica's stomach churn in a way that wasn't simply down to the alcohol.

'Do you know how much this costs a bottle?' he added. When it was clear that Jessica wasn't going to respond, he answered his own question. 'Four hundred quid. I get it brought down especially from Scotland. They have only made three dozen bottles each year for the past forty years. There's a waiting list.'

Jessica didn't know if he was genuinely trying to impress her, or if he couldn't stop himself from boasting. Four hundred quid? She could have boiled some vinegar and it would have tasted the same. She was definitely in the wrong business. 'It tastes the same as any other whisky I've ever had.'

Nicholas downed his drink in one and refilled it. 'There's no accounting for taste.' He pointed towards her glass and, against her better judgement, Jessica nodded, watching as he poured another triple into it.

'So why are you here, Ms Daniel?'

Jessica felt unnerved that he had remembered her name, although not entirely surprised. 'I want to have the same chat as before.'

Nicholas put down the bottle and pulled a stool

towards him, flopping onto it and wriggling uncomfortably, like an overweight frog. Even over the bar, Jessica could see he was far too big for it.

'I thought I'd told you that I didn't know anything about the two women you mentioned. I've employed a lot of people.'

Jessica picked up her glass and took another sip. 'But you remember the women, don't you?'

Nicholas grinned, almost seeming pleased that she thought that. 'Who says that?'

'I do.'

He nodded, still shifting on the stool. 'I don't think you're as clever as you think you are.'

Jessica had another drink. Each time the liquid dribbled down her throat, it felt a little less harsh, to the point that she didn't even have to stifle pulling a face. Maybe it wasn't so bad after all? 'Why don't you tell me about Kayleigh and Ellie?'

Nicholas raised himself, finally giving up on balancing his enormous backside on the stool and instead leaning on the bar. 'How about you tell me about yourself first?'

Jessica shook her head but he pointed towards her ring finger. 'Who's the lucky man?'

Suddenly feeling vulnerable, she downed the rest of the drink, swilling the liquid around in her mouth and using the glass to mask her face. She returned it to the counter with a bang and nodded towards the bottle. 'No one you'd know.'

Nicholas poured her another generous measure, before refilling his own glass. 'Aah, but I know all men.'

'Really?'

He put down the bottle and used both hands to point around the room. 'Who do you think pays for all of this – and everything else? You should never trust a man.'

Jessica thought of what had been happening with Adam recently, wondering why she hadn't been able to pick up his phone and have a look when she had the chance. She stayed calm, enjoying the gentle burning at the back of her throat.

'Is that right . . . ?'

'While you're working late doing whatever it is you do, he's probably in here drinking my drink and touching up my women.'

'Your women?'

Nicholas grinned and nodded. '*My* women.'

Jessica could hear the menace in his voice and knew that was exactly how he thought of the females who worked for him. 'Were Ellie and Kayleigh your women?'

For a moment, she thought she saw his eyebrow twitch, as it had done the previous time they had met, but he reached forward and picked up his glass, taking another large mouthful. Jessica copied him, holding the dark liquid in her mouth and feeling the fumes drifting through her.

She was already light-headed.

Nicholas met her eyes. 'They were good-looking when they were young.'

'What else?'

Nicholas still refused to look away. 'Nothing, that's all I remember.' He lifted the bottle again, daring her to accept.

Jessica picked up her glass and downed what was left,

putting it back on the bar and nodding. Nicholas poured until the bottle was almost empty, tipping the rest into his own glass, before turning and throwing it into a large plastic container at the end of the bar. Four hundred quid gone, just like that.

'I want to see your employment records,' Jessica said.

Nicholas laughed. 'Do you now?'

'Yes.'

He nodded, as if weighing up the request, although she knew he would refuse. Jessica was fighting to keep her eyes level, knowing the alcohol was hitting her hard. She rarely drank spirits, let alone so quickly. Her eyelids had felt tired before she had come and now they were even heavier.

'You're not going anywhere near my files.'

'What if I already have a warrant?'

For the first time since he had begun drinking, Nicholas faltered. A small amount of whisky sloshed onto the counter as he wobbled, clumsily putting down his glass. 'Why would you have one of those?'

'How about if I told you one of those women had died?'

Jessica couldn't tell if she was giving him new information as there was a grey haze around her eyes that stopped her from completely taking in his reaction. He didn't seem particularly surprised.

Before he could reply, Jessica noticed a dribble of blood run from his nostril across his bottom lip. Nicholas quickly reached up to touch his face, recoiling as he saw the blood on his hands. 'Oh for fuck's sake, not again,' he slurred, turning and picking up a napkin from the back counter of the bar.

He dabbed at his face before balling up the tissue and tossing it in a nearby bin. He touched his nostril a few times to ensure it had stopped and then turned back to Jessica.

'What was that?' she asked.

'Nothing. I get them, it's fine.' He licked the tip of his finger, where a small amount of blood had dried, then wiped it on his trousers.

Jessica wanted to stand to assert some degree of authority as Nicholas was faltering but her head didn't feel clear enough to attempt to get up. Instead she tried to focus on the label of a bottle hanging behind the bar. She forced her eyes to concentrate but was struggling to figure out what was wrong, before realising it was hanging upside down in the optics. The fact she hadn't noticed that in the first place was worrying in itself but Jessica couldn't stop herself giggling slightly.

Nicholas stared at her, clearly thinking she was laughing at him. 'I don't believe you've got a warrant or anything else,' he said.

'What would you bet on that? Imagine what else they might find. Or you could just tell me what I want to know.'

Jessica couldn't tell if she was slurring her words. To her they sounded fine, but she had enough sense to know she was already more drunk than she had been in a very long time. She picked up the half-full glass and could see

Nicholas staring at it, daring her to finish what was left, probably thirty quid's worth.

'*Feisty*,' he said with a smile, although Jessica could tell the alcohol had hit him too as his eyes were flickering off to one side and lacking focus.

Jessica drank half of what was in the glass and then stared into the remaining brown liquid, her head spinning. She hadn't expected this.

'They both quit at the same time,' Nicholas said suddenly. He was trying to force himself back onto the stool he had previously given up on and looked as if he could collapse to the floor at any moment. Eventually he abandoned the idea, leaning against a sink at the back of the bar. 'I checked my files and they both left together.'

'On the same day?'

Nicholas shrugged. 'I suppose.'

Jessica knew they had left at roughly the same time but this was the first she'd heard about them going together as neither Eleanor nor Kayleigh had volunteered that. She wondered if they had been deliberately evasive and, if so, whether that had somehow cost Kayleigh her life.

'Do you remember them?'

'I always remember the pretty ones.'

Nicholas was slurring his words further. Instead of sounding sinister, it was pathetic. Jessica felt a rush of confidence. 'What do you know about them now?'

He shook his head dismissively. 'Nothing, the minute they walk, they're dead to me.'

An unfortunate choice of words, Jessica thought. 'Why did they leave at the same time?'

'I don't know.'

'Was it something to do with you?'

Nicholas tried to meet Jessica's gaze but she could see his eyelids drooping. 'I always look after my own.'

'What sort of job would they have been doing in your casino?'

'All they had to do was keep the punters inside.'

'How did they manage to do that?'

Jessica wasn't sure if she wanted to know the answer but it came anyway. 'They just had to look pretty. You'd be amazed by how long you can keep someone interested and spending money if there's a short skirt involved.' He paused, giggling: 'Maybe you can ask your fella about that? Is he a leg man? Breast?'

She picked up her drink and finished the rest in one, not wanting to think about Adam. 'If that was the case, how come you closed the place a few years later?'

Jessica could tell Nicholas was angry because he tried to speak quickly but his words skewed into each other, becoming a rant about regulations, the council and 'you lot'.

'Did you pay them well?' Jessica asked, trying to bring the conversation back to the women.

She was now feeling so self-assured that she shifted from her stool into a standing position but instantly realised it was a mistake, having to put both hands on the bar to stop herself stumbling. Nicholas noticed and she could see him smiling, although he wasn't moving very much either. Jessica tightly gripped the rail that ran around the bar and steadied herself but it was too late and the room was spinning. She tried to focus on the same bottle as before, telling herself it was upside down and that her head would clear if she could only distinguish the letters. Instead, she could barely figure out which bottle was which among the row of optics.

She glanced across to see if Nicholas had noticed but he seemed to be swaying too, although Jessica couldn't tell for sure if that was him or her. She knew it was time to leave and took one step towards the ramp that led back to the reception area but her feet felt sluggish and unresponsive. The bright green fire exit sign above the door in the distance gave her something to head for, even though the grey mist was swirling around her vision.

'Where are you going?'

Jessica could hear Nicholas calling behind her but didn't look back as there was a crash of something, or someone, falling to the floor. Instead, she focused on the sign, walking as quickly as her head would allow.

Jessica tapped her pocket to ensure her phone was still there, fumbling as she tried to remove it. She allowed herself to bump shoulder-first into the wall of the corridor that led outside. She couldn't figure out a way to make her fingers fit into the pocket of her jacket and gave up, instead using them to feel her way towards the door.

It was silent behind her as Jessica's hands closed around the door handle and pulled it towards her. As she opened the door, she thought the outside air might help clear her head but it had the opposite effect, the chill hitting her hard and making everything whirl again.

Jessica staggered away from the club, unable to recall if

she closed the door, but remembering the sensation of the cool glass on her fingers. She used her hands to trace the brickwork and windows of the nearby buildings until eventually she found herself in the public square. The cobbles were rough under her feet and the hum of shoppers hurrying through the streets made her feel even dizzier. As she tried to sit on one of the benches, Jessica felt as if she was falling, hanging onto the wooden back for support, before finally managing to settle. She could see the outlines of people: grey bustling dreamlike shapes, but nothing was in focus.

Trying again, Jessica finally managed to pull her phone out of her pocket. The screen was painfully bright and her fingers wouldn't do what her brain was telling them to. It took what seemed like an age of pressing the wrong buttons before she finally managed to call Izzy.

By the time she had lifted the phone to her ear, the other woman was already talking to her. 'Jess?'

'Izzzzzzzz . . .'

Even through her smog of thoughts, Jessica could tell the constable was frantic. 'Are you okay? I've been waiting for your call to say you were out and was about to tell Jack.'

Jessica took a few moments to take in the string of words. She knew things were bad when she could hear herself slurring a reply. 'I'm at Albert Square, come get me.'

16

The beeping of the alarm on Jessica's phone made her jump awake as she instinctively reached towards the bedside table to turn it off. The moment she moved a stinging sensation thundered through her head. She scrambled around the surface of the table but couldn't locate the source of the sound, before reluctantly – and painfully – opening her eyes. The screen of her phone was flashing brightly on the floor and she stretched to pick it up, stabbing at the front until the noise stopped, and then dropping it on the bed next to her. Where was a sodding blunt object when she needed one?

Jessica closed her eyes again and rolled onto her back, reaching for the duvet cover and pulling it tight around her, trying to suppress a shiver.

She could remember flashes from the previous afternoon: the club, Nicholas . . . whisky. As the thought popped into her mind, she could taste the liquid again, suppressing a gag as it hit the back of her throat. Jessica screwed her eyes tighter but the memories were swirling vividly. She remembered the cold breeze and sitting on a bench and then Izzy arriving and helping her into a car. After that, she didn't know.

Wondering what time it was, Jessica reached out a hand

to feel for Adam on his side of the bed. It was empty, so she assumed he must have left for work, although she didn't want to open her eyes to see the actual time. She realised she was going to be late and hoped she had either cleared it already, or that Izzy would have done something for her.

Thank God for Izzy.

Jessica felt her body shivering and realised it wasn't the cold – instead it was the fear from the previous day finally catching up with her. She remembered the way Nicholas looked at her and how he had licked his lips as if she was something he had ordered. She had been full of bravado because that was the only way to deal with men like that; beat them at their own game. Jessica pulled the duvet over her head. She could rarely remember being so scared: Nicholas was a dangerous man and she had used the fact she was a woman to try to toy with him.

She could remember her dreams from the night before more clearly than she could recall what had actually happened at the club. In her mind, Adam had been there too sitting at the bar with Nicholas, laughing and leering at half-naked girls.

Jessica tried to tell herself it was only a dream but her head was throbbing, her mind a mess of reality and night-mares. She tried to forget how terrified she had been but, before she knew what she was doing, she had thrown off the covers and was running towards the bathroom with a hand over her mouth.

*

When her eyes finally felt as if they were working, Jessica was relieved to find two text messages from Izzy on her phone. The first told her not to bother hurrying in and that Cole didn't mind, the second simply had three words: 'They quit together'.

The message was enough for Jessica to remember everything Nicholas had told her about Kayleigh and Eleanor.

There was also one from Adam, saying he hadn't wanted to wake her but that he would see her later. Jessica deleted it, bashing the screen in fury at the fact his name had the gall to appear. She didn't know if she was angry at him because of the dream she'd had, or because of everything else.

Aspirin, water and a morning moping on the balcony were enough for Jessica to finally start feeling like herself. As she sat with her feet on the railing outside watching the people underneath, Jessica phoned Izzy just after midday.

The constable answered straight away. 'Jess, are you okay?'

'I've been better.'

'Did you get my messages? You don't have to come in today, I told Jack you were feeling ill.'

'Did you tell him about Nicholas?'

'No.'

'Good.'

Izzy stumbled over her reply. 'What happened? Obviously you'd been drinking . . .'

'I don't remember.'

'You told me to remind you that Eleanor and Kayleigh

162

left at the same time but that was all. I couldn't understand a word you were saying.'

'I knew it would only be a matter of time before I
picked the Mancunian accent up.' Jessica laughed but the
other end of the line was silent.

'Why didn't you ask someone else to talk to him with
you?'

'He wouldn't have spoken to anyone else.'

'But you could have been hurt.'

Jessica could feel a lump at the back of her throat and
swallowed hard. 'I told you where I was. You knew what to
do if I hadn't called by a certain time.'

The constable's voice was quieter as she replied. 'Yes,
but anything could have happened in that time.'

Jessica didn't want to dwell on it, taking a mouthful of
water. 'I'm going to visit Ellie. Can you send me her phone
number?'

'Can't you take a day off?'

Jessica couldn't tell from her friend's tone if she was
joking or serious. 'Iz, I'm fine, send me the details and I'll
see you later or tomorrow.'

'You're forgetting though . . .'

Jessica interrupted, trying to speak with an authority
she wasn't feeling. 'Can you please just do it?'

There was a pause before the constable replied with a
terse 'fine' and then hung up.

Jessica felt bad for snapping and as soon as the line
went silent, she knew what her friend was trying to
remind her of. Although she was in the flat in Salford,
her car was still parked on the other side of the city at

Longsight. She finished her glass of water and returned indoors hoping there was still a set of bus timetables in the drawer underneath the sink.

As she walked from the bus stop to Eleanor Sexton's house, Jessica couldn't help but think that public transport was without doubt one of the worst things possible for a hangover. Everything from the whining babies to the teenagers with music pouring out of their headphones to the vague aroma suggesting that someone had mistaken the top deck for a public toilet made things feel worse. By the time she had taken the three separate buses necessary, Jessica was beginning to wish she had heeded Izzy's advice about having a day off – or at least not been stingy and called a taxi instead.

'Lara's asleep upstairs,' Eleanor said, welcoming Jessica inside with a whisper.

The woman looked weary but had clearly been very attractive in her younger days. Her hair was still just about blonde and Jessica could tell her body was trim and toned, despite it being covered by ill-fitting clothes.

'. . . I always remember the pretty ones . . .'

It hadn't been that long ago that Jessica had visited Cameron at the house. Things seemed exactly the same, with neat rows of shoes and coats inside the door and a fresh smell as if the hallway had been recently cleaned.

Eleanor led her through to the living room and went off to the kitchen to make tea. Jessica had a wander around, taking in the family photos she had glanced at on her previous visit. It was the first time she had spoken to Eleanor directly. Other officers had been to see her before but the woman hadn't had much to offer.

When she returned, Eleanor sat in an armchair, curling her feet under herself. 'How can I help you?' she asked, sipping from a mug with a pink cartoon character on the front. As if sensing Jessica's question, she added: 'It's from Lara's favourite show. I gave you an adult's mug.'

Jessica looked at the plain whiteness of her own and half-wished she had the child's one. 'I know someone has been to see you already but I'd like to ask you about Nicholas Long.'

She saw the recognition in Eleanor's eyes, before the woman glanced away towards the window. 'He used to be my boss. I told your people that. I'm not sure what else you want me to add.'

Jessica persisted. 'Was that when you worked with Kayleigh?' Eleanor nodded but didn't reply, so Jessica continued to push. 'I know someone visited to tell you what happened to her.'

Eleanor cradled the mug. 'I didn't know what to say to your people. I hadn't seen her in ages but obviously there's this strange link between us now because of what happened with poor Oliver.'

Jessica took a moment to let her dwell on the words. She didn't think Eleanor was being evasive, but perhaps there was something hidden away she had tried to forget.

'How close did you used to be?' Jessica asked.

Eleanor answered with a shrug. 'It was such a long time ago. We were good mates but a lot of that was because we saw each other every day and worked together. We were young women and I guess we moved on over time.' As if realising what could be happening, she glanced up from her mug to catch Jessica's eye. 'Should I be worried?'

'I don't know. There's nothing to say you or your family are in any danger.'

'But did whoever killed Oliver also kill Kayleigh?'

'I don't know. We're looking into it.'

Eleanor nodded. 'But why would . . . ? I don't see the connection.'

'Neither do we – I'm hoping that's where you can help.'

Jessica made sure she kept eye contact with the other woman until Eleanor looked away. She cuddled her free arm across herself, still holding the mug in the other. 'I already talked to your people about Kayleigh,' she said defensively.

Leaning forward in her chair, Jessica waited for the other woman to look at her before speaking. 'I went to see Nicholas Long yesterday . . .'

Eleanor's eyebrows flickered upwards.

'It doesn't sound as if either of you worked in the greatest of environments,' Jessica added. Eleanor nodded but didn't reply. 'He told me that you both left at the same time; the same day.'

Her eyes suddenly widened. 'He remembers us?' There was a definite tone of apprehension.

'He doesn't know anything about you now, but yes.'

'He's not a nice man.'

Eleanor's statement didn't sound fearful, she was stating a fact.

'I know.'

Both women locked eyes again and Jessica knew Eleanor had experienced exactly what she had from Nicholas – probably worse.

'Why didn't you tell us before that you had left that casino together at the same time?'

'I didn't think it was that important.'

Eleanor's voice faltered and it was clear she wasn't fooling herself, let alone anyone else.

'What happened?'

Eleanor turned to look out of the window as Jessica tried to make eye contact. A clock on the mantelpiece tick-tocked through the silence, drawing Jessica's attention. It looked like the top part of a grandfather clock, similar to one her parents had at their house. A needle metronomed from side to side, clicking as it reached the furthest points.

'That used to belong to Cameron's grandparents,' Eleanor said softly. Jessica turned to face her, wondering how long her own attention had been distracted for. 'It was made in 1899 and has been in the family ever since. It's beautiful, isn't it?'

Jessica squinted to see the detail more closely. Each number was in a perfect spidery script and there was an intricately painted background depicting a particular time of day behind each one.

'It's really nice.'

'We've never done anything to it, no batteries or anything like that. I have no idea how it works but it is amazing.'

Jessica could hear her father in her head, telling her 'they don't make things like they used to'.

'It was a different age,' Eleanor said and, for a moment, Jessica thought she was talking about the clock. 'Now, it's all about equality for men and women, gay and straight, white, black, Asian and so on, but it wasn't like that then – or at least it didn't feel like it.'

Eleanor waved her hands, trying to illustrate a point she didn't seem comfortable remembering. 'It's so different, even going to pubs where there's no smoking. Back in the casino, I remember this blue haze of smoke. You would stink of it when you got home and it was every-where; in your hair, on your clothes, even your shoes.'

'What was your actual job?'

The woman reached forward to put down her empty mug and then stared up towards the ceiling. 'We didn't do anything really. There were the trained guys who ran the tables, then the barmen. After that, there were around a half-dozen of us. We carried drinks to the tables but other-wise we welcomed guests and took their coats.'

'And you were all women?'

Eleanor nodded. 'Exactly. All young, all thin: either blonde or black hair because Nicholas didn't go for brunettes. He never hired black or Asian girls either because he had his types.'

'And you simply had to walk around looking good to keep the customers happy?'

'Pretty much, it wasn't hard.'

'So what happened?'

Eleanor again went silent and Jessica watched the

woman staring at the clock. Eventually she took a deep breath. 'One of the reasons I don't like being called "Ellie" now is because that's what I was then. It's like two different people – Eleanor the adult, Ellie the child.'

'I've heard your husband calling you Ellie.'

'He knows I don't like it. I don't know how to describe it – he says it differently.' Jessica knew exactly what she meant – Adam said 'Jess' in the way no one else could. She bit her bottom lip, trying not to think of him.

'What happened to "*Ellie*"?'

Jessica's use of the name made the woman look away from the clock towards her. 'Nothing particularly, it was just different. Back then, Nicholas had this big rivalry going with this other guy, Leviticus. They each ran various pubs and clubs and things like that – and they hated each other. There were always rumours swirling around the staff that one was going to kill the other and they were basically at war. This one night, we closed early and everyone got kicked out at the same time. We didn't know what was happening, but then it turned out there had been a firebomb attack on one of Leviticus's pubs just out of the centre. I don't know if it was anything to do with Nicholas and there never seemed to be any retribution at our end. We all went back to work the next day.'

Jessica must have appeared confused because Eleanor clarified the point. 'I'm not saying that was anything to do with what's happened now, I'm just telling you what it was like. We were always scared, especially us women. As well as all of that, Nicholas would shout and swear. He'd throw things and call you names – it wasn't a good place to be.'

'Is that why you left?'

Eleanor gulped and Jessica knew it wasn't. 'On the side, he used to lend money to people. It all used to tie in together; someone would lose a lot of money at one of the tables and they would be invited into one of the rooms at the back where Nicholas or someone else would offer them terms on a loan. We all knew it went on but it was one of those things you never talked about. Of course, it was never that straightforward, there would be some sort of small print the person had missed – or no contract at all – and the interest rates would go up so people ended up paying ten times what they owed.'

Jessica was unable to stop herself interrupting. 'Once he had you, he had you.'

Eleanor nodded. 'Exactly. You used to dread walking past the room. Once I was getting changed after shift and heard this crack, we all did, then it was just some guy screaming. If you couldn't pay, then someone would hurt you – but then you could never pay anyway because the minute you did, there would be some other penalty clause or something you had missed.'

The woman was clearly becoming distressed telling the story. She was fidgeting in the chair, putting her feet on the floor and then curling them underneath her, twiddling a strand of her hair around her finger, then letting it fall, before starting again. Jessica knew she was getting somewhere. She had waited to visit Eleanor precisely because she needed to figure out Nicholas first.

'Did you ever tell anyone?'

'None of us did, it was just one of those things. If he

was doing that to grown men, imagine what he would do to women like us.'

'What made you and Kayleigh get out?'

'With Nicholas it was all about control; he liked owning things, whether it was buildings, businesses or people. I'm not sure he ever distinguished one thing from the other. He never liked staff leaving and so he started the same with us. He would buy you something you thought was a gift and then, a few weeks later, your wages would be next to nothing. When you asked what was going on, he'd say that you owed him money for the jewellery, or the designer clothes. Of course, because you had no money to pay your rent, he'd force you to take out a loan . . .'

'. . . And then he had you.' Jessica felt a chill go down her back. She had seen Nicholas close up and the way he talked about women. Her behaviour the previous day seemed even more reckless.

Eleanor gulped, nodding in agreement. 'Right. You couldn't leave the job because you had the loan to pay back, so he had you in two ways. You would be tied to him through owing him money, then tied to him through the job too.'

'. . . *My women* . . .'

'How did you get away?' Jessica asked.

Eleanor started to scratch around her eyes, although Jessica could not see tears. 'I think even back then I knew what was going on. While the other girls took their jewellery, I always said no. Somehow I knew it was going to end the way it did.'

'So you didn't owe him anything?'

171

'No.'

'What about Kayleigh?'

Eleanor sighed deeply, taking a tissue from the table and blowing her nose before replying. 'She was more trusting.'

Jessica let the woman compose herself, allowing the silence to boom uncomfortably through the room.

'It wasn't just that,' Eleanor added. 'With the customers and men, he'd break your bones – or get one of his men to. He'd hurt you, or threaten to hurt you to make you pay. With us women . . .'

Jessica swore under her breath.

'Kayleigh owed him for a few things. The only reason any of us started working there was because it was easy and the money wasn't too bad. All you had to do was turn up for work looking half-decent and you were done. That's where the problem came – girls would keep their money and then leave after a while. Kayleigh had saved pretty well but that all ended up going back to Nicholas because of the loan.'

'But you helped her?'

Eleanor nodded. 'We were mates. You know what it's like when you're young and you look out for each other. You get more cynical as you get older. I'd kept my money too and, because I didn't owe him anything, I gave Kayleigh my savings. Between us, we bought him off and there was no way he could come back with charges, fines, or whatever.'

'Had he . . . *touched* . . . her before that?'

Eleanor shrugged, not elaborating on Jessica's choice of word. 'Probably.'

'What about you?'

'I would have *fucking* killed him if he'd touched me.'

The swear word came from nowhere. Previously Eleanor had been speaking quickly but clearly and eloquently. Although she had something of a local twang, it wasn't overbearing but, as she cursed, she looked directly at Jessica, her eyes making it clear she meant it, her accent strengthening.

'So you gave the job up together?'

'It was never one of those "hand your notice in" things, we just never went back. We moved to a different flat as well. If he had wanted to find us, he would have done – but neither of us owed him money and we hadn't done anything other than not go to work. Although he had all the loan stuff going on, he was still a proper businessman on the surface. Neither of us thought he'd come after us and he didn't.'

'Did you ever hear from him at all?'

'Not once. I saw his name every now and then in the paper or on the news but it was never for what you wanted.'

'Who's the Leviticus guy you talked about?'

Eleanor shook her head, shrugging, and it was clear she had said all she had to. The name was distinctive enough to track him down anyway.

Jessica asked if she wanted to add anything else, then made sure the woman was all right.

'Cameron doesn't know,' Eleanor whispered.

Nodding a silent guarantee, Jessica left her contact details, closing the front door gently and thundering down the steps onto the pavement. She walked so quickly that she was practically running, fury raging through her that she couldn't remember experiencing before. She had managed to contain herself in front of Eleanor but the story of the way Nicholas treated other people, women in particular, was almost too much to take. He'd had things his own way for his entire life, bullying and blackmailing people to do what he wanted them to. She didn't want to think about the things Kayleigh might have gone through all those years ago and it was no surprise the two women had been too scared previously to tell the police about the monster from their past. Now Kayleigh was dead and even though there was nothing to link Nicholas to the killing itself, he was still the person who connected the two women.

It wasn't until Jessica reached an area with no street lights that she realised she had been heading in the wrong direction away from her bus stop.

Her hands were aching and she looked at them in the light of the moon to see thin lines of blood across her palm from where she had balled her fists tightly, digging her nails in, so angry that she hadn't noticed. As she turned to go back in the correct direction, Jessica resolved that one way or the other, she was going to take Nicholas Long down once and for all.

17

Jessica was finding the weight of her silent promise to Eleanor hard to live with. Already her sleeping patterns were a mess, thanks to a mixture of mistrust towards the man next to her and a legacy that stretched back a lot further than when she had woken up in a house that was on fire. She could barely bring herself to think of what might have happened to Kayleigh and the other women who owed Nicholas Long money but that only made it harder to push out of her mind. She thought of the man's alcohol breath and his temper, plus the way she had put herself in harm's way.

Again.

After another mainly sleepless night, Jessica spent large parts of the following morning scowling at colleagues to dissuade them from asking if she was all right.

Typically, it was Izzy who saw through the act first as Jessica picked at a sausage sandwich in the canteen.

The constable slid in across the table from Jessica and stole one of the sausages off the plate. 'You look like you should be in bed.'

'I was eating that.'

'No you weren't.'

Jessica looked up at her friend, her eyes widening in surprise. 'What on earth is that?'

Izzy laughed. 'What does it look like?'

'It looks like your hair is now purple.'

'Yep.'

'Actual purple.'

'That type of observation is why you should be up for Jason's old job.' The constable was grinning while she ate the remainder of the sausage.

'When did you have that done?'

'Well, you saw me two days ago . . .'

Jessica couldn't stop herself from yawning. 'Sorry, I'm not quite with it.'

'Dave says you've been locked in your office all morning.'

Jessica put down her fork and picked up a sausage with her finger. 'I wasn't locked in there.'

'Do you need a hand?'

Jessica shook her head, not wanting to say that she had spent the morning looking into Leviticus Bryan. Because she did not want to take Eleanor's secret to anyone else unless she had to, she was determined to find something, or someone, who would give her another angle on Nicholas.

'I'm fine,' Jessica said, a little too sharply.

'Did you read the autopsy report on Kayleigh?'

Although Jessica wasn't particularly hungry, she was eating for the sake of it and finished chewing before replying. 'Exactly what we thought – killer taller than the victim, possible knee mark in her back, pretty much identical circumstance to Oliver.'

'No sexual assault.'

Jessica nodded. 'Can you cover for me this afternoon if Jack or anyone else asks where I am? I don't think he'd mind anyway but I don't want to go through him.'

'You're not going back to . . .'

'No.'

'Promise?'

Jessica looked up to catch Izzy's eye and laughed. 'How old are we?'

Izzy smiled too but her eyes didn't. 'He's dangerous.'

'I know.'

'Some things we should leave to Serious Crime . . .'

'I know!' Jessica spoke far more loudly than she intended, instantly silencing her friend. 'Sorry, I didn't mean it like that,' she added.

'I don't want you doing anything stupid.'

'That's what I specialise in.' Jessica meant it as a joke but Izzy didn't laugh. 'Anyway, it's a bit rich to be told off about doing silly things by the woman with long purple hair.'

The constable did at least smile second time around. 'I fancied a change.'

'Then why not have your nails done, or go away for a weekend? There's change and there's *change*.'

'Do you like it, though?'

Jessica smiled. 'I wish I had either the time, patience or guts to do something like it myself. What did Jack say?'

'Not much, if it was going to be an issue then it would have been when I had bright red hair.'

'True. What about Mal?'

The constable's face lit up as she grinned widely. 'Oh, he *really* likes it . . .'

Jessica rolled her eyes. 'All right, let's leave it there.'

Izzy smirked. 'How's married life?'

Jessica picked up the final sausage and bit the top off, chewing slowly and deliberately.

'You didn't do it, did you?' Izzy added.

Jessica held up her ring finger, waggling it to show her wedding band before taking another bite as the constable squinted at her, trying to work out what was going on. 'You can tell me.'

Jessica took a moment to swallow her food before replying. 'Tell me what's going on with Dave and I'll tell you what's going on with me.'

Izzy met Jessica's gaze but didn't waver. 'So how's Adam?'

'He's being a man.'

Izzy nodded knowingly. 'That's the problem with blokes, they're all so . . . male.'

Jessica put the rest of the sausage in her mouth and wiped her fingers on a napkin, before dropping it on the plate. The constable reached forwards and touched her hand. 'Seriously, you're not off to do something stupid, are you?'

'No.'

'Promise?'

'On Adam's life.'

*

Sat nav or no sat nav, Jessica didn't have a clue where she was. After she'd been directed into a cul de sac and then instructed to take a right turn into a field, Jessica told it exactly what she thought of it, before turning it off. Its final words had been 'after three hundred yards, take the second exit', even though she was facing a wide metal gate with half-a-dozen cows on the other side.

She decided to do things the old-fashioned way and reached into the pocket behind her seat, pulling out a map and opening it on the passenger's seat, trying to figure out where she needed to go.

Leviticus Bryan lived just outside Southport, north of Liverpool on the coast where there was all the drizzle and grey of Manchester, along with the added bonus of a bitter sea breeze. Getting to the approximate area had been easy enough but that was when the navigation device decided it fancied a day out at the seaside and stopped cooperating.

It took Jessica another half an hour to eventually find the right house. Each property was set back from the road with large, winding driveways. Most had large, imposing walls or hedges along the front, with huge gates to put off any potential trespassers. Or coppers.

Despite numbers being hard to spot, Jessica saw Leviticus's straight away because of the large 'LB' letters which were part of the metalwork of the gate. His property was perhaps the most imposing on the street. Although each had a large plot of land, his seemed to be wider than anyone's and the thick brick walls were certainly taller.

Jessica parked on the road and got out, staring up at the height of the wall, thinking that even if someone gave her a piggyback she would struggle to reach the top. Security lights were placed intermittently along it and it was clear you would have to really want to get in if you were going to go over the wall.

As she peered through the gate, Jessica could barely see the house itself. The driveway arched up, then looped around to the right out of sight. The metal of the gate was painted black, with nothing to place your feet on horizontally if you were to attempt climbing it. There was a wide lush green lawn on either side of the drive and a red car was just about visible far off towards the house.

Jessica walked to the speaker box to the side of the gates and pressed the buzzer, shuddering as the sound instantly made her flash back to standing outside Nicholas's club trying to get in. After a few further attempts with no one answering, she returned to her car, reversing until she was parked directly in front of the gates before turning the engine off.

She had spent the morning reading up on Leviticus and knew a ridiculous amount about him. On paper, it seemed as if the man she was waiting for had an awful lot in common with Nicholas. They had both been brought up in poverty and then made something of themselves through less than legitimate methods. While Nicholas had gone out of his way to offer a genuine front for his enterprise, Leviticus had been less careful. He had a conviction for possession of a dangerous weapon and another for grievous bodily harm. He'd spent time in prison for both offences but had apparently been out of trouble since being released four years ago.

Whether that meant he was crime-free was a completely different matter.

Nicholas's business had been exclusively based around the Manchester area, while Leviticus operated out of Liverpool. If the two setups running out of roughly the same area hadn't caused enough tension between the two powerful, wealthy and egotistical men, Leviticus then took things one step further by starting to open places in Manchester as well. On the surface, the launching of a rival pub wouldn't necessarily cause such an escalation of hostilities but Jessica figured most of the businesses were a front in one way or another for laundering money and selling drugs. That is what would have undoubtedly caused the 'war' Eleanor had described.

It probably didn't help that Leviticus was black and surrounded himself with other people of the same race. Having seen Nicholas at close quarters, Jessica doubted he was the type to openly welcome most people he didn't know, let alone someone who looked different to him.

Jessica had still been at school herself at that time but knew from the officers senior to her that policing had changed immeasurably since those days. Although most stories about corruption were apocryphal, there had undoubtedly been certain officers who'd turned a blind eye to such behaviour, hoping one side would wipe the other out and make life a lot easier for everyone.

Whether or not he was a changed man, Leviticus had shut down his businesses in Manchester after going to prison. There was little sign of him doing much in Liverpool either. Certainly from the official records, Leviticus had retired from obvious criminality.

In theory, Jessica should have approached the local police if she was crossing borders to interview someone but that would have meant escalating things through Cole and probably the superintendent. Because she wanted to keep as much of Eleanor's story to herself as she could, Jessica figured she would take the disciplinary if it came. It wouldn't have been the first time she was in trouble.

Jessica sat in her car, waiting. She played with her phone, skimming through the names and thinking of the people she had lost contact with over the years. Although she had few very close friends, there was a wealth of people she had met through her job, or through others who simply drifted in and out of her life. She thought about Eleanor and Kayleigh and the way they had once been so close, experiencing all sorts of adversity together, and yet, somehow, they still grew apart.

As she was lost in her thoughts, a car horn blared loudly, making Jessica jump. She turned to her right where there was a large silver car angled across the road with Leviticus Bryan in the driver's seat gesticulating angrily at her.

Jessica gave him a cheery wave as she stepped out of her vehicle and walked towards his door. His window was humming down as she approached and he rolled his eyes as he leant out towards her. His voice was deep and powerful as he uttered a single word: 'Bizzies'.

'How did you guess?' Jessica asked.

'You walk like one.'

The man's accent was broad Scouse, although there was an element that sounded as if he had tried to teach himself to sound more posh at some point.

Jessica crouched by his window so they were at the same eye level. 'My mum would be so pissed off at hearing that. She used to make me walk in a straight line because I was pigeon-toed as a kid.'

She was surprised when Leviticus broke into a grin. 'You're funny,' he said.

'That's not what they said when I got bottled off at the Comedy Store.'

He smiled wider, eyes twinkling in the dwindling sunlight. 'What do you want, Bizzie girl?'

'Just a quick chinwag, I'll probably have a brew if there's one on offer too.'

'What makes you think I'll invite you in?'

Jessica only needed two words to make the smile leave his face: 'Nicholas Long.'

18

'Nice place you've got here,' Jessica said, climbing out of her car and walking along the driveway towards the front of Leviticus's house. The top of the drive had a tarmac circle for cars to turn around and there were already three different vehicles parked along the edge, each large and expensive-looking.

Leviticus was waiting by the door as Jessica approached and she turned to point at the other cars. 'Are these all yours?'

'I paid for them.'

'Still got a few quid then?'

He ignored the insinuation as he unlocked the front door. Jessica stepped into a vast circular hallway, with a cold marble-like white floor and huge stone pillars on either side of a wide spiral staircase. Jessica could not stop herself from looking impressed, something which Leviticus noted with a grin.

As she glanced away from the interior towards him, Jessica noticed how grand Leviticus looked. He was well-built but it was muscle, not fat, his broad chest and strong shoulders padding out a perfectly fitted black pinstripe suit. His shoes gleamed in the artificial light, matched by the chunky gold rings on his fingers. Jessica didn't feel the same sense of trepidation she had experienced when meeting Nicholas. There was a sinister aura of aggression and danger that surrounded the club owner but Leviticus's cropped, slightly curly, silver hair made him seem grand-fatherly.

Jessica had to keep reminding herself of everything she had read on his record as he led her through to an equally impressive living room that was dominated by an enormous fireplace, with white pillars running floor to ceiling and a firepit built into the wall. 'I can get this started up if you're cold,' Leviticus said, noticing Jessica's interest.

'I'll have a tea if there's one going.'

'Are you going to have a poke around while I go to the kitchen?'

For a moment, Jessica said nothing – she had never been called on her trick in the past. 'Why? Have you got something to hide?'

Leviticus smiled. 'Milk? Sugar?'

'Just milk.'

As the man left the room, Jessica had a walk around. The living room on its own took up roughly the same floor space as the entire flat she was living in, while she doubted she would make enough in a lifetime to pay for something as extravagant as this property.

She ran her hands along the pillars, wondering if they only looked expensive, but they were solid stone and had probably been crafted solely for this house. Although there wasn't a lot of furniture in the room, it didn't feel empty. There were three large brown leather sofas and two more armchairs made of the same material. Jessica sat in one, bouncing up and down, wondering if that was a good gauge of how expensive it might be. Her feet echoed on the wooden floor, which Jessica noticed seemed cleaner than any kitchen table she had ever owned.

There were strong oak bookcases in the corner but no books; instead each shelf was filled with framed photographs.

'Do you like what you see?'

Leviticus's voice echoed as he strode into the room, carrying a tray with two cups, saucers, a milk jug and a small teapot. He placed them on a table in the middle of the room, before walking across to where Jessica was standing.

'Cute kids,' Jessica said, pointing towards a photograph of Leviticus with a woman and three boys of varying heights.

Leviticus was beaming and genuinely seemed proud. 'Whatever you may think of me, they're why you don't hear from me any longer. I thought my days of you lot popping over to pay me visits were long gone.'

'What are their names?'

'Saul, Josiah and Zechariah.'

'Biblical kings,' Jessica replied without thinking.

As she turned to walk towards the table, she saw Leviticus eyeing her, nodding. 'You know your stuff.'

'I used to go to Sunday School when I was a kid. We had to learn all the books of the Bible in order and then we moved on to the various kings.'

'Do you still go?' he laughed.

Jessica shook her head as Leviticus hunched forward,

pouring milk from the jug into one of the cups and then using the teapot to fill each of them. He stood and passed Jessica a cup and saucer. The china was dainty, the exact opposite of what Jessica might have thought someone like Leviticus would have owned.

'That's a shame,' he said, sitting on the sofa opposite her.

Jessica felt uncomfortable, so nodded towards a stuffed head hanging above one of the doors. 'Is that from a real bear?' she asked.

'Indeed, a memento from long ago.'

'I've got a mate who would absolutely love that.'

Leviticus allowed her words to hang, sipping delicately from his cup, the handle of which he held gently between his thumb and forefinger. It was almost laughable but Jessica followed his lead, thinking the cups wouldn't last five minutes in her possession as they would end up either broken or chipped.

'Nicholas Long,' Leviticus said firmly, fixing Jessica with a stare to remind her that he hadn't always been the kind, cuddly father he now appeared to be.

Jessica took another sip of her tea, refusing to allow him to dictate terms, then reached forward and placed the china on the table. 'What do you know about him?'

Leviticus eyed her suspiciously. 'Why are you asking after all this time?'

'Something's happened.'

He nodded an acceptance, putting his own cup and saucer on the table. 'I bet you think we're just the same?'

'Your records are similar.'

Still nodding, Leviticus interlocked his fingers and met Jessica's stare. 'What's on paper can be deceptive.'

'So tell me what he was like.'

Leviticus suddenly seemed uncomfortable, pulling at the lapels of his suit, flicking away specks of dust which Jessica couldn't see. 'We both ran similar businesses. Clubs, pubs . . . other things. We might have seemed like natural rivals but we actually worked together for a few years, me from this side of the border, him from Manchester.'

'How do you mean, "worked together"?'

Leviticus shrugged. 'Use your imagination. I would help him out with certain aspects of his accounting and he'd do the same for me.'

'What changed?'

'I did. Whatever you may think, Nicholas Long is a very different man to me.'

Jessica didn't disagree but she wasn't about to say that. 'You seem pretty alike to me.' She opened her palms to indicate the rest of the room. 'Vast displays of wealth, living off money made from the misery of others, violence, drugs and everything in between.'

Leviticus paused, scratching his chin thoughtfully before replying. 'Just because I welcome you into my home and extend my hospitality to you, don't think you know me, Ms . . . ?'

'It's Jessica but I didn't hear you denying any of that.'

He said nothing but reached forward, refilling both of their cups. He sat back in his chair, again holding the cup daintily in one hand, cradling the saucer with the other. As odd as it appeared, it also seemed natural.

'In the type of business I used to be in, there was always an unwritten rule about female family members. As much as you might hate each other, as much as you might compete, you always left people's mothers and wives out of it.'

Jessica shuddered as a chill went down her spine. 'What did he do?'

Leviticus sipped his tea, staring towards the ceiling. Jessica could hear the rattle of the cup on saucer before the man steadied himself. 'My mother.'

He spoke the words in the same tone as Eleanor had told her about Kayleigh the previous day. Before Jessica could respond, Leviticus continued. 'He's a ruthless, brutal man.'

'What did you do about it?'

The delicate clatter of cup on saucer began again as Jessica saw his hand shaking. 'I was arrested on the night I was going to do something about it.' Jessica thought of the possession of a dangerous weapon conviction she had read next to the man's name. 'I came out a different person,' Leviticus added. 'By then, things were different anyway. Most of my businesses had fallen through.'

'Where does all of this come from?' Jessica asked, indicating around the room.

'I'm not a stupid man, I planned for all eventualities.'

Jessica nodded, not wanting to know anything further but Leviticus didn't give her a moment to interrupt in any case.

'When you hear of the way he treated his ex-wife, you

understand he's not the kind of man to forgive anything lightly.'

Jessica knew from their files that Nicholas had a former wife, Ruby, but assumed she had simply been traded in for a newer, younger version.

'What happened?' she asked.

Leviticus shook his head. 'Any man who raises his hand to a woman is a coward.'

As she looked around, Jessica realised the room was a tribute of sorts to Leviticus's family. There were photographs of his wife and children everywhere, not just the bookcases in the corner.

'How does your wife feel about all of this?' she asked.

Leviticus peered at Jessica and then turned away, taking in the vast room. 'She accepts me for who I am – and who I was.'

'That's easy to say when you have vast wealth.'

Jessica wasn't trying to wind the man up but he didn't seem offended anyway.

'What would you have me do?'

It seemed a fair question. Jessica thought of the way Nicholas had been using his money to create an illusion of respectability. The authorities had presumably investigated Leviticus at some point and not found anything to indicate they should seize his money or possessions. As if reading her mind, Leviticus added: 'Not everything I did would have interested you lot.'

He stood quickly, placing his cup and saucer on the tray and pointing towards Jessica's still-full cup. 'Do you want that?'

Jessica shook her head.

'I can get you something else if you want?'

'I'm fine.'

'Come with me,' he said.

Jessica followed as he walked past the staircase along a hallway and through a door that was wedged open at the bottom. She blinked as she entered, the brightness of the room a complete contrast to the artificial light from the rest of the house. The kitchen had a row of white work-tops along each side, with a huge window that stretched almost from the floor to the ceiling at the far end. Sunlight beamed through, bouncing off the surfaces, making Jessica rub her eyes.

As Leviticus made his way to the sink, which was around half the size of the bath in Jessica's flat, she rested a hand on the solid worktop, trying to picture just how heavy it would have been to install. Everything she had seen of the house had a similar expensive style.

Jessica glanced up to see Leviticus watching her, drying his hands on a tea towel. Everything about his movements oozed authority – but it was a natural charisma he exuded, as opposed to the forced aura that Nicholas had.

'Come look,' he said, nodding towards the window. Jessica walked across the room, running a hand along the full length of the worktop as she did. 'What do you see?' Leviticus asked.

Jessica peered through, looking from side to side. There was an enormous lush green garden, stretching in every direction. On one side was a large tree, with a swing tied to one of the branches. A football goal was in the other direction.

'How old are your children?' Jessica asked, ignoring his question.

'Between eight and fourteen. This is all they've ever known.'

'Football pitches in their back garden?'

Leviticus stepped away from the window and leant against the counter top. 'You're not seeing it.'

Jessica looked out of the window again, taking in everything she had spotted previously, before finally noticing what he meant.

'It's like our own private prison,' he told her. 'I'm not complaining, we have an amazing house, cars, a garden I could only have dreamed of when I was young, we go on holidays all around the world – and yet we're surrounded by massive walls, security lights and cameras.'

'Is this all because of Nicholas Long?'

'Among other people. It's not an easy thing to retire from.'

Jessica didn't know if he was trying to get her sympathy, or simply defending himself against her assumptions that he had it easy because of his wealth. She didn't know why he cared about her opinion.

'Why did you start to operate in Manchester in the first place?' she asked.

Leviticus drummed his fingers gently on the counter, probably realising she knew more than he had given her credit for. 'Greed. I wasn't happy with everything that I had and wanted more.'

Jessica was impressed at his honesty. 'What made you leave?'

'There was only one way it was going to end up: with one or both of us dead. I didn't want that. Ultimately, he was better than me at that side of things. He keeps impeccable records of everything; staff, accounts, who owes him money, the lot. I was never that good at all that. He always had other people to do his dirty work for him. They were always completely loyal for whatever reason. You'd hear about networks of people he had through the city: journalists, police officers, people in the council who dealt with planning and so on. He knew what he was doing in Manc, I didn't. He may have been everything you've read about him but he's a businessman too and knew how to play the game.'

'Had you already left Manchester by the time . . . it happened?'

Leviticus nodded. 'He had already won but that wasn't enough. It was all about sending a message to me personally. My mother was in her seventies and lived in a bungalow I bought for her. I wanted to get her a nice big house, somewhere to live comfortably, but that was all she wanted. It was on the outskirts of the city in a quiet cul de sac. She was no threat to anyone – she spent most of her day baking for the local kids and then she'd cook chicken once a week when I went around. Cooking was what she lived for as she got older. But one day, they came for her.'

He shuffled awkwardly, taking off his suit jacket and

placing it carefully on the worktop. Through his shirt, Jessica could see just how well-built Leviticus was. His chest stretched the material, his biceps were bigger than her thighs. As he turned, Jessica could see vast sweat patches on his back and under his arms and wondered if his confidence in talking to her was more bravado than she first thought.

If anyone should know the signs, then she should.

'Are you sure I can't get you something else?' Leviticus asked.

Jessica knew he was trying to change the subject. She wondered how many other people he had spoken to about his mother over the years.

'Why are you telling me all of this?'

Leviticus sighed, running his hand through his hair. 'I assumed that's why you were here – because you'd heard things too?'

'What things?'

He tilted his head, squinting towards her, as if trying to work out if she was playing him. 'I thought you were here to talk about Nicky, his son?'

Jessica knew Nicholas had a son with the same name as him but no one had spent much time looking into the teenager. She tried to shield the surprise. 'What have you heard?'

Leviticus spoke slowly, clearly wondering if he was making a mistake. 'That he's just turned eighteen and is ready to step into his father's shoes.'

Jessica nodded but he wouldn't say anything else until

she was looking into his eyes. 'Nicky's an animal,' Leviticus warned solemnly. 'And I've heard he's not too keen on waiting his turn.'

19

There had been no reason for anyone to look into Nicky Long's background but that didn't stop Jessica ploughing through every piece of information they had on the teenager. His age was the key thing; as a youth with no criminal record, there had been little cause for any of them to investigate beyond his father. Even with Izzy's help, all Jessica had been able to establish was that Nicky had finished at a private boarding school a few months earlier, had turned eighteen, and was now apparently living in Manchester with his father and stepmother. Jessica noted that Nicholas's current wife, Tia, wasn't that much older than Nicky. His actual mother was Nicholas's former wife, Ruby, who had been a teenager when she had Nicky.

The more Jessica found out about Nicholas, the more she marvelled at the fact he had kept himself out of prison for as long as he had. Perhaps even more remarkable was that, despite the long line of people he had apparently crossed, he was still going strong. She thought of her own anger at him for the way he'd behaved towards her, not to mention the fury she felt having heard about the things he had done. She almost admired the restraint someone like Leviticus had shown after being released from prison, although wondered how different things might have been if he hadn't been picked up for weapon possession all those years ago.

Jessica knew there was going to come a time where she'd have to share everything she knew with Cole but he was so distracted because of the lack of a DI and everything else that needed doing, for now she was getting away with pretty much what she wanted. Before that point came, Jessica wanted to put as many of the pieces together as possible.

'Are you ready?' Jessica asked Rowlands, who was in the passenger seat of her car.

The constable had been silent for the entire journey, something that was beginning to annoy Jessica. He blinked rapidly, as if just waking up, and then put a hand on the door handle. 'I'm fine.'

Before he could open the door, Jessica touched him on the arm. 'I need you to be on form today. You're here for a reason – and it's not your sad but partially impressive knowledge of "Star Wars".'

She was hoping for a laugh which didn't come. Instead he opened the door and got out, waiting for Jessica as she rounded the vehicle and checked the address on her phone. 'I bet this isn't what she expected when she married one of the richest businessmen in Manchester,' she said, looking each way before crossing the road.

Ruby Long lived in the middle of a row of terraced houses in the Wythenshawe area. The house next to hers had a skip outside and there was a smell of burning as Jessica noticed a bonfire in the field at the end of the road. The houses were all red-bricked with sloping brown-tiled roofs and small front yards barely wider than the adjoining pavement. Ruby's property was filthy on the outside, with black soot-like dust splattered across one of the downstairs windows. Jessica could hear a cross between a giant bumble bee and a jumbo jet zipping along the road parallel to where they were. Before approaching Ruby's door, she waited as a boy who couldn't be older than eleven or twelve turned the corner at the end of the road, dropping one leg to the ground and spinning a moped around before speeding towards them.

Against her better judgement, Jessica stepped off the pavement, standing in the centre of the road and holding an arm out to make it clear she wanted the biker to stop. The groaning of the engine was almost deafening as the youngster skidded to a halt next to her.

'Where's your helmet?' Jessica asked him, wondering which of the various offences being committed in front of her eyes she should mention first.

Up close, the boy looked even younger, although his voice had broken and he had an angry inflection in his voice. 'Who the fook are you?'

Jessica pulled the keys out of the bike's ignition and told him she was from the police, rolling her eyes as the expected mouthful of abuse arrived. After establishing that he was apparently 'eighteen' and that his licence was 'at home' – although he couldn't remember where he lived well enough to tell her – Jessica spent fifteen minutes waiting for a local patrol car to come.

When the uniformed officers arrived, it was clear they were already very familiar with the boy who had spent the time in between calling Jessica a lot of words she was pretty sure she hadn't known when she was his age – even if he did turn out to be eighteen.

As one officer placed the boy in the back of the patrol vehicle to return him home, the other tried to figure out what they were going to do with the bike. He offered Jessica a 'thanks' that didn't seem overly genuine, pointing out the biker was 'twelve, maybe thirteen'. Jessica's joke about the lad having two kids by two different mothers was met by a stony-faced agreement that she probably wasn't far wrong.

'Welcome to Wythenshawe,' Rowlands said as Jessica finally got around to knocking on Ruby's front door.

The inside of Ruby's house wasn't as dirty as the outside but there was something unerringly familiar about it. The carpet was the same shade of red as that in Nicholas's club and the decor of bright, glittery tat felt similarly forced and fake. Rowlands noticed it straight away, pointing out the wooden border that ran along the walls.

Ruby herself wasn't exactly happy to see them. Although Jessica had called to arrange a time when they could talk, she opened the door with a 'I wondered where you lot were' and then turned, walking through the house, shouting 'and take yer fooking shoes off' over her shoulder. Nice to see you too.

Jessica slipped hers off easily but Rowlands hopped from one foot to the other, nearly overbalancing as he tried to untie the laces on his boots. Six months previously, she would have playfully nudged him with her shoulder but she wasn't sure if they had the same relationship nowadays.

'Over, under, in and out, that's what tying shoes is all about,' she said. 'Just do that backwards.' After what seemed like an inordinately long time, the constable finally dropped his boots to the floor, revealing socks with cartoon characters on.

'You're worse than Adam,' Jessica said, walking in the direction Ruby had headed in.

She found the woman sitting in an armchair in a living room that was as garish as the hallway. The walls were painted red up to the border and then a slightly off-white above it. There were at least half-a-dozen mirrors and a haze of smoke hanging around the ceiling. Jessica remembered the way Eleanor had described the casino and couldn't help but wonder if Ruby was somehow creating her own low-rent version.

Ruby scowled at the officers, cradling a cigarette in her hand. Her expression only told part of the story as her face was brown bordering on orange, her skin wrinkled and leathery, making her look far older than the mid-thirties that she was. Jessica could only assume that was what a lifetime of cigarettes left you with.

She took another drag, before stubbing it out on an ashtray balancing on the windowsill. Jessica sat on the sofa, with Rowlands next to her. 'I was hoping for a bit of background on your former husband,' Jessica said.

Ruby shrugged, reaching into a handbag by her feet, pulling out a packet of cigarettes and taking one out. She offered the pack towards them in a gesture Jessica hadn't expected, although she did seem pleased when they both turned her down.

'I've not seen him in years,' Ruby said, hunting around the floor before realising she had left the lighter on the windowsill next to the ashtray.

'What about your son?'

Ruby didn't look up as she lit the cigarette. 'Him either.'

'How long ago did you split up?'

She breathed in deeply, holding the smoke in her mouth before finally exhaling as her eyes closed in pleasure. 'Ten years ago when he hooked up with that tart he's married to.'

Nicholas certainly liked his women young. Jessica knew that Ruby had been eighteen when she'd had Nicky – and they were already married by then. Meanwhile, if Tia was now in her late twenties, that meant she was also a teenager when she had got together with Ruby's then-husband.

Jessica was roughly the same age as Ruby and it seemed creepy that the woman in front of her had a son who had just turned eighteen. She barely felt old enough to have a child now, let alone having one who was already an adult.

'How often have you seen Nicholas since?' Jessica asked.

Ruby shook her head dismissively. 'Not much, maybe once a year?'

'Do you have any contact with your son at all?'

The woman held the cigarette close to her mouth but didn't touch it to her lips. 'What's it to you?'

'We're looking into a few things surrounding your former husband.'

Ruby smiled, exposing yellow teeth that somehow fitted with her skin tone, like a womble with a crack habit. 'Anything that could get him sent down?'

Neither officer replied but Ruby got the message that it would be a good time to tell them anything she knew.

'How did Nicholas get custody of your son?' Jessica asked, being careful to use the word 'your' instead of 'his'.

The smile disappeared from Ruby's face as she puffed heavily on the cigarette. 'You've not got a clue, have you, love? Have you ever met him?'

Jessica nodded.

'Well then, you'd know that if he wants something, he gets it. The minute he said he wanted custody, he was always going to get it. If I'd gone up against him in court, he would have found a way to get to the judge. If he couldn't do that, he'd go through Nicky, promising him all sorts to tell people I'd done things I hadn't. If all of that failed, he would simply make me disappear. There was no point me even opposing him – at best I'd lose, at worst, I wouldn't be here now.'

The matter-of-fact way she spoke was horrifying and Jessica didn't doubt for a second that what Ruby had told her was true.

Ruby must have seen the realisation on Jessica's face because she smiled again. 'Don't worry, love, he's like that with everyone. He didn't even want Nicky – he sent him off to some boarding school to get rid of him – it was only ever about making sure I couldn't have him.'

As if sensing what she was thinking, Ruby glanced from Jessica to Dave, then back again. 'Up until about a year ago, I was living with this guy. We'd been together for eighteen months or so and things were going okay. We were talking about getting married – but then he didn't come home one day. Then he wasn't here the next day either, or the day after that. I called you lot but nothing ever came of it, he just disappeared.'

Jessica felt Rowlands glance towards her, which Ruby clearly saw. 'It's not what you think,' she said, nodding towards him. 'I got a call at three in the morning about a month later. You never know what it is when the phone rings at that time, do you? But it was that fat fuck, he was pissed as always, giggling. He asked how my relationship was going and kept laughing. I was going to hang up but then he said I shouldn't worry. I asked what he meant and he said I should take heart that it took a six-figure sum to make him go away.'

'Nicholas paid your fiancé to leave?' Jessica couldn't believe she was asking the question but Ruby finished off her cigarette before stubbing it out.

'That's what he does. It doesn't matter that he doesn't want me any more, he doesn't want anyone else to either. He thought it was hilarious that I'm living here on benefits while he paid someone else that amount to leave me. It's the way he works.'

'We're looking into a few things,' Jessica said, wanting to offer the woman some hope.

Ruby shook her head. 'You'll never get him for anything, you must know that? He'd rather go down shooting and take a couple of you lot with him. That's the type of vindictive bastard he is.'

Jessica tried not to take the image literally. 'What was it like living with him?' she asked, although she could guess the answer.

Ruby reached forward and took another cigarette out of her bag, lighting it and sucking the smoke deep into her lungs before holding it in and eventually breathing out. 'Everything you can imagine and worse.' She twisted her body around and lifted her shirt, showing them an area at the bottom of her back around her kidneys. Even from the other side of the room, Jessica could see a patch of skin far whiter than the tanned brown of the rest of Ruby's body.

'That's where he held an iron on me because I wasn't ready to go out on time.'

She allowed her shirt to fall and then bent her ear forward, pulling her hair out of the way to reveal a zigzag-shaped mark. 'I'd gone shopping one Saturday and missed the bus. I got home forty-five minutes later than I said I was going to. This was before the days of mobile phones, so I had no way of letting him know because the only money I had was for the bus, not for a payphone. He would only ever give me an exact amount for things. When I got home, he refused to open the front door at first.' Anticipating Jessica's question, she added: 'He never let me have a front-door key.'

Ruby paused for another puff of the cigarette. 'He eventually opened the door but when he was halfway through, he smashed it back into me. I fell backwards and this side of my face got caught in the door. At first, because

I was in the way, he couldn't shut it but, as I was lying there, he looked down at me and slammed it as hard as he could. My ear was caught in the door and was torn off.'

Jessica couldn't prevent herself from wincing but Ruby seemed unperturbed, pointing to the inside of her thumb. 'When I was pregnant with Nicky, we were hosting this dinner party for some people he knew. I wasn't feeling very well and kept being sick but he barricaded me in the kitchen and told me to get on with it. I didn't know what happened but I guess I fell asleep for a moment because I was woken up by the fire alarm going off. It was nothing serious but something under the grill had burned. He came storming in, saying I was trying to kill him by burning the house down. I was so tired, I didn't even know what was going on – but he grabbed my hand and forced it onto this red-hot ring on top of the cooker. I was screaming and could smell my own hand burning but he was shouting in my face, telling me I'd regret trying to burn his house down.'

Ruby paused to have another smoke, although Jessica had the feeling she could have catalogued many more injuries.

'Surely there were questions from the hospital?' Jessica asked, knowing how naive she sounded. It was a human reaction, not a police officer's.

Ruby exhaled and smiled thinly. 'Let's just say I fell down the stairs a lot. If you went to a different casualty unit each time, no one even noticed.'

It was far from the first story of domestic abuse Jessica had heard but, coupled with everything else she knew about Nicholas Long, a genuinely terrifying picture was emerging.

'Aren't things better now?' Rowlands asked. Jessica heard his voice falter and realised he was taking it worse than she was.

Ruby smiled another toothy grin and held her arms into the air. 'Look around, honey, this ain't much fun either.'

Jessica had been wondering why Ruby was letting them into all of her secrets but realised the woman was past caring. As she finished stubbing out the cigarette, Jessica knew the saddest thing was that Ruby would run back to her former husband in a heartbeat if the option was there.

She wanted to comfort the woman, to tell her it couldn't be that bad, but she knew anything she said would sound patronising.

'There's not much else I can tell you, sorry,' Ruby added, straightening her clothes.

'What was Nicky like as a child?' Jessica asked, doubting the woman would be able to give her any information to back up what Leviticus had told her.

'Nicholas found everything funny, as long as it didn't affect him. Nicky would pinch and punch me and his dad would laugh along so he thought it was okay.'

'But you still wanted custody?'

Ruby shrugged. 'Boys will be boys. They're always up to something. He was still my son.' She quickly corrected herself: 'Is my son.'

Jessica couldn't think of anything else to ask. She had hoped for some insight into Nicky but instead ended up hearing one more awful chapter in the life of the boy's father.

'You can show yourselves out,' Ruby concluded as Jessica and Rowlands stood.

As she waited in the hallway with the constable struggling to put his boots on, Jessica couldn't help but swear under her breath.

'Sounds like a lovely chap, doesn't he?' Rowlands said quietly.

'You don't know the half of it.'

'I do have one idea you might be interested in.'

'There's a first time for everything.'

'No, seriously. Your newspaper ad thing, it was something Ruby said.'

Jessica could tell from the way he was speaking to her normally that he thought he was onto something.

20

Jessica peered across the table at the two individuals and pointed to the newspaper in front of her. 'If either or both of you were responsible for this, now would be a pretty good time to speak up.'

When neither of them answered, she looked sideways at Rowlands. He spoke with the exact tone she wanted him to, like a big brother to a younger sibling. 'Look,' he said chummily, 'if it was you and you tell us now, we're prepared to let things go. If you keep this going and we later find out it was either of you, then you will be in serious shite.'

Jessica could tell it had worked.

Terry shifted uncomfortably in his chair, rubbing the back of his neck. Richard had sensed his friend's nervousness and slumped in his seat.

'It was supposed to be a joke,' Richard said quietly, refusing to look up from the table. 'We thought Ollie would find it funny when he saw his name in the paper but didn't think he'd actually . . . y'know . . . a few days later.'

Jessica said nothing, allowing Rowlands to speak. 'You do realise that in the history of school pranks, this is not only one of the shittest but also one of the most poorly timed?'

His words echoed around the empty classroom as neither student dared look up from the table.

'What's going to happen to us?' Terry asked, his voice cracking halfway through the sentence, partly through emotion, partly fear.

Jessica exchanged a look with Rowlands, holding his eye to allow the tension to build. 'Nothing for now,' Jessica said firmly. 'But we both know who you are and what you did. If either of us ever hear you're in trouble again, then we will rain some serious shite down upon you.'

She allowed her words to hang, before adding, 'Now get out of here.'

Richard and Terry jumped to their feet in unison, muttering a 'thank you' before racing towards the classroom door and the relative safety of the corridor. The truth was that neither of the young men had committed any sort of offence, other than one of stupidity – and if they started convicting people for that, they'd need some pretty large new prisons. Jessica didn't think a few idle threats could do them any harm.

When the room was empty, Jessica caught her colleague's eye. 'I quite like our bad cop, bad cop routine.'

Rowlands smiled, then stood and walked across to stand by the window. 'We should take it on tour.'

'You'll have to start speaking to me properly first.'

The constable didn't reply for a few moments, before eventually saying: 'Different world here, isn't it. At my school, the toilets barely worked. Here, they've got their own operatic society.'

Jessica went to join him by the window. 'Let's hear it then.'

'What?'

'How you guessed all of this. We could've come in here and had them tell us they didn't know anything about it.'

Rowlands turned to face Jessica, leaning against the glass. '"Guess" is the right word. I think it had been floating around the back of my mind anyway after Iz told me you'd been here to talk to Oliver's friends. I thought about my own mates and how we'd arse around. It was never anything like this, mind, we'd hide each other's clothes after swimming, or give each other dead legs.'

'Sounds mature.'

'Well, exactly, but when Ruby was going on about boys being boys, I thought that Oliver was a bit different to us.' He pointed towards the door Terry and Richard had just left through. 'Those two don't seem the type to go around pissing in a Lucozade bottle, then leaving it around the changing rooms after rugby practice.'

'You did that?'

The constable shrugged but offered a half-grin. 'Maybe. The taste is about the same. Anyway, the point is I thought they'd be doing something a bit more high-brow. Placing an ad predicting their friend's death seemed the type of unfunny thing they'd come up with. The fact he ended up being killed days later was just . . . unfortunate.'

The way he said the final word sounded a little callous but Jessica knew what he meant. 'Something always seemed a little off,' she said. 'There was never anything predicting Kayleigh's death and it never really fitted. The two killings were brutal, not something whimsical that someone would choose to predict beforehand.'

Rowlands crossed the room and sat opposite Jessica. 'I guess our killer isn't as clever as we thought.'

Jessica made sure her friend was looking at her as she replied. 'We could have figured this out ages ago if you were talking to me properly.'

She expected the constable to brush off the remark and pretend nothing was wrong but instead he squirmed as awkwardly as Terry and Richard had done minutes before.

'Can I tell you something?' Jessica asked quietly. Rowlands nodded but she couldn't read his face. 'I went back to see Nicholas a second time.'

'On your own?'

Jessica nodded. 'Iz knew. I wanted to see what he was like on his own with a woman.'

The constable loosened his tie. 'I can guess.'

'You wouldn't even know the half of it.'

For as long as Jessica had known Rowlands, he'd kept up a front of bravado. Although some of his boasting about women in his younger days had no doubt been true, at least in part, it had taken Jessica a long time to realise that he was very similar to her. As she told him Eleanor and Leviticus's stories, she could see in his face that he was as horrified as she was.

'. . . And you put yourself in a room alone with him?' he replied.

'I didn't know all of that at the time,' was the only justification Jessica could think of.

'Have you told Jack or anyone else yet?'

Jessica shook her head. 'What good can it do? All it proves is the type of person he is, which we partly knew already. There's nothing to link him directly to Oliver or what happened to Kayleigh.'

Dave loosened his tie further and undid his top button, breathing out deeply. 'Do you reckon Serious Crime would be interested?'

'Do you think Eleanor, Leviticus or Ruby might want to give evidence against him? Even if they did, much of it is dated, circumstantial or one person's word against another. And what would they do him for anyway, other than what they're already looking into him for?'

Jessica could see the constable shared the same feelings of injustice she did. While they had officers out checking the speeds of motorists, someone like Nicholas Long was seemingly free to continue going about his business.

Although there was silence in the room, there was a hum of activity from elsewhere around the school. Students were hurrying to and from lessons, others whooping on the various sporting pitches.

'Shall we go and tell everyone what conquering heroes we are?' Dave asked, sliding his chair backwards with a screech.

Jessica didn't move. 'I miss you,' she said quietly.

The constable stopped, hands fixed to the back of the chair as he was half-standing. 'Sorry?'

'I miss you mucking around and taking the piss. You're such a dick but you made it fun coming to work. Me, you and Iz are a good team.'

Jessica had been wanting to tell him that for weeks but

everything fell out in one unrehearsed sentence. As soon as she had spoken, she half-wished she could take it back but the emotion of hearing the endless stream of degradation Nicholas had poured over those around him had worn her down.

Rowlands seemed frozen, half-bent over the chair. Jessica could feel him staring at her but she didn't acknowledge him. Finally, he stood and walked back to the window.

'Are you going to at least tell me what's up?' Jessica demanded, raising her voice.

'Things have been complicated.'

'That's it?'

Jessica scraped her chair back and walked to the window to stand next to him. They both stared towards the sports fields where a group of children were playing lacrosse.

'What type of a game is that?' Dave asked with a forced laugh.

'Is it to do with you breaking up with Chloe?' Jessica asked, refusing to let him change the subject.

'I've been out with plenty of girls since then.'

'That's bollocks. If you had, we'd have all heard about it.'

Out of the window, play stopped as one lad was tackled roughly by another. The teacher and the other students crowded around as the two started pushing and shoving. Almost simultaneously, the familiar pitter-patter began as rain descended, bouncing off the tarmac of the car park that separated the school from the field.

'I guess some things don't change regardless of what school you go to,' Dave said, as one of the boys shoulder-charged the other to the floor. The teacher dived in to try to separate them.

Jessica didn't reply, watching in silence as the adult pointed and shouted at both of the students before sending them towards a building on the far side of the pitch.

'It wasn't Chloe,' the constable finally said.

'So what was it? You've been weird ever since the fire.'

Even though she wasn't facing him, Jessica could hear Rowlands gulping. 'Exactly. I saw it all, Jess. I was at your house when they put you in the ambulance. Your face was covered in black stuff and you weren't moving. Everyone had gone to focus on Adam and I thought you were dead. I thought they'd given up on you.'

Jessica waited for a moment, the broken memories of that night running through her mind. When she replied, her voice cracked and didn't sound like hers. 'I know you told me Jack, Jason and everyone were there but I guess I didn't know that meant you.'

Outside, the game was descending into farce, with players sliding in the mud as the teacher stood in the middle of the field, blowing his whistle and bellowing.

Dave didn't take his eyes from the game as he replied. 'There was this paramedic who asked if I was all right and it was only then I realised you were off to the hospital. Jack told me to go, so I raced away. I was driving like such an idiot that I caught the ambulance up.'

'You stayed with me the whole day.'

'Yes.'

'You held my hand.'

'You gobbed on my shoe.'

Jessica laughed. 'I don't remember that.'

Dave snorted too, although his voice was faltering. 'I didn't know if you'd wake up, Jess. All this back and forth we've had over the years, all the arsing around and taking the piss out of each other . . . I was sitting in the room wondering what might happen if you didn't wake up.'

'But I did.'

The constable didn't reply as they watched the match come to an end. The rain was falling so hard that it looked like a wall of water instead of individual drops. Over the top, they heard the teacher's whistle blaring as everyone, including him, turned and ran towards the building on the far side.

'My old PE teacher would have left us out in that,' Dave said. 'He used to wear the same tracksuit every day, this horrible blue and white shiny thing. He was called Mr Haythorn, but we called him Mr Gaythorn when he wasn't around.'

As childish as it sounded, Jessica couldn't stop herself giggling.

'He was a right bastard. If you ever turned up late, he'd make you run a full lap of the field. If you didn't do it quickly enough, he'd make you do another one. He made us play rugby on an icy pitch once. Everyone was getting injured but he didn't care.'

Jessica waited until all of the players had reached their building.

'That doesn't explain why you've been weird with me ever since,' Jessica said, just loudly enough to be heard over the noise of the torrent hitting the roof.

At first, she thought the constable hadn't heard her. 'I'm glad things are working out for you, Jess,' he finally said. 'Adam's a good guy.'

Jessica felt the lump returning to her throat that had never been far away in the past week. She tried to swallow but instead it made her feel worse. 'It's not as rosy as you might think,' she eventually managed to say. 'Something's going on with him but I don't know what.'

Rowlands didn't move, staring out at the now-empty field. 'Some of my friends got married and said the first few months were awkward as they got used to each other.'

Jessica bit her lip. 'Just tell me what's wrong.'

Dave finally turned away from the window. They were barely a foot apart, staring at each other. His eyes were a mixture of sadness and determination and she realised that she rarely looked at him directly. With suspects or witnesses, she would draw eye contact, sometimes waiting in silence until they gave it to her. With her friends, she rarely did that, assuming she knew what they were feeling.

His voice croaked awkwardly. 'It's you, Jess.'

'What's me?'

The rain continued to hammer on the top of the building as Jessica raised her eyebrows to query what he was saying.

'As I sat next to you in the hospital, holding your hand, not knowing if you were going to wake up, I knew it was you.'

Jessica saw his throat begin to bob and realised he was moments away from tears. Placing a hand on his shoulder, she struggled to know what to say, feeling drawn into the emotion of the moment. 'I woke up . . . I'm here. I don't know what you're trying to tell me.'

Dave placed a hand on her chin, stroking it gently, and she finally figured out what he was trying to say. By the time the words came, she had already taken a half-step back in shock.

'I love you, Jess.'

21

Nicholas Long surveyed the piles of cash in the club's safe with a grin. It was one of his biggest pleasures, something he always did himself. The increase in people paying with cards annoyed him, although, because of the type of club he ran, there were still plenty happy to pay in cash in case the name of his establishment appeared on their credit card statement.

He had spent the past forty-five minutes bundling the notes into neat even piles to count the day's takings, slowly drinking his way through a bottle of gin. Some of the people in the circles he kept preferred to stick to one type of drink but he liked the variation.

When he was happy that everything added up from the bar, Nicholas walked through to the reception area to take the entrance money. Before doing so, he went along the corridor to the front door to check that Liam had locked up properly. It was no surprise that he found the door secured as it should be; his bar manager had never failed him before in anything that had been asked of him, let alone with menial things such as shutting the club up. When he was done, Nicholas would leave via the fire exit in the way he always did.

After emptying the final till, he pushed everything into a money bag and then, suddenly feeling out of breath, turned and sat on the sofa. Nicholas could feel sweat on his head and wondered if he had eaten something dodgy. If it was Tia who had been at fault, he would make sure she knew about it the following day. He grinned at the thought of yanking her out of bed by the hair when he got home, demanding to know what she'd done to him.

Grunting as he stood, Nicholas felt a sharp pain in his chest. His eyes were drawn to the blinking light underneath the security camera in the top corner of the room, angry at his awkwardness being documented. Staggering as quickly as he could manage, he went back through the doorway into the main part of the club, using the edge of the bar to keep himself upright.

Nicholas's mind wandered to the detective who had visited him a few days beforehand. He stared at the stool she had been sitting on, wondering what exactly it was that she wanted. There was the obvious thing, that the police had been trying to take him down for years, but she had something about her. At first, his plan had been to see how far he could push her, although he had been surprised at how she stood up to him. Still, that wasn't anything that couldn't be put right if it ever came to it. He always took much more pleasure from quieting those who thought they could go toe-to-toe with him.

The pains in his chest began to fade as Nicholas tried to remember what she looked like. He let go of the bar and walked as steadily as he could towards his back office. As he passed through the first door, he flicked the latch, locking it to ensure the main part of the club was sealed. The hallway felt colder than usual, although it had an almost sobering effect as Nicholas blinked away the confusion.

As he entered his office, he suddenly felt a weight of apprehension. Constantly having to look over his shoulder, having to anticipate what might be coming, was something he had become used to over the years but the recent spate of panic attacks was beginning to worry him. The biggest concern was making sure no one else got to see him in that state but Nicholas could feel something building from his stomach as he collapsed into the chair behind his desk. He was panting for breath, and grabbed at the bottle of gin on his desk, leaning back and swigging until he began to cough. He could feel the effects of the alcohol going to his head, his heart continuing to race.

Nicholas had been telling himself that he should visit a doctor but he wasn't the type to bother talking about anything. The useless bastard would probably instruct him to lose weight and stop drinking anyway, as if that was the magic cure to everything. He'd take a pill over that any day, although he knew what he really needed was someone new and exciting to keep him interested. There were a few girls in the club who were potential candidates but it wasn't as if there was a shortage of others who would be happy with the initial money on offer to come and work for him. That had always been the way.

Finally, Nicholas began to feel his body returning to normal, the gin apparently doing the trick in settling his nerves. He opened his eyes to take in the room and, as the small voice in his head told him he shouldn't be paranoid, he realised there was no one there.

He had been grasping the money bag tightly in his free hand and emptied it onto the table, concentrating as he stacked the notes into piles.

As he reached the end, Nicholas heard a banging from somewhere nearby. Holding his breath, he slowly opened the top drawer of his desk, sliding out the pistol he kept there. Although he had a licence for it as part of his constant efforts to keep everything above board, he was supposed to keep it somewhere secure. Still, if he were ever raided, that would be something that could be argued in court; he was more concerned about his immediate safety.

The noise had made Nicholas's head clear completely, his vision as sharp and in focus as it had been forty years ago. He bounced the metal in his hand, feeling the weight of the gun as he quietly slid his chair backwards and edged across the room towards the hallway. He put one hand on the doorframe and poked his head out, quickly glancing each way at the empty stretch of concrete, before withdrawing back into the office.

His office was almost opposite the door which led into the club. On the left was a small cupboard where the cleaners kept their things, while on the right was one door which led into the girls' changing room and a second where the toilet was. At the far end of the corridor was the fire exit.

Nicholas peered around the corner again, noticing a crack between the fire door and the frame. He once more withdrew to his office, trying to think of any legitimate reason why it might be open. He exited through it every night but, as far as he could remember, had closed it fully the night before.

As another bang sounded, Nicholas peeped around the frame to see the fire door clattering into place, seemingly blown by the wind. He stepped into the hall, holding the gun, flicking his eyes from side to side looking for movement but reaching the end without noticing anything. Nicholas rested one hand on the fire exit and realised it had popped back into place. He pressed down on the bar across the centre and pushed it open, instantly feeling the wind rushing across his face. Stepping out onto the path that ran along the back of his club, Nicholas checked both ways, but it felt like a gale whipping through his clothes, making him shiver.

Realising he was holding a weapon outside the club and that he should be sensible, Nicholas stepped back inside, closing the door behind him, waiting and listening. At first he couldn't hear anything except for the wind, but then he realised his heart was pounding and the hairs were standing up on his arms. He straightened himself, and it dawned on him that the burst of adrenaline had been refreshing – he hadn't felt that edge of excitement since the old days.

Nicholas flipped the gun's safety device back into place and pushed it into the waistband of his trousers before nudging the toilet door open with his shoulder.

He washed his hands first, something he had done since he was young, and then unzipped his trousers as he stood over the bowl, thinking about which of his girls would make a good Mrs Long the third.

Lost in his thoughts, Nicholas didn't hear the steps of the intruder rushing behind him. Before he knew what was happening, there was something wrapped tightly around his face as he gasped for breath. He swung his elbows back, but the person shoved him sideways, smashing his skull against the side of the sink.

Nicholas felt his head spinning as he hit the ground but the impact had at least given him a moment when whatever was around his face came loose, allowing him to take a breath. He was still facing down, desperately trying to turn around, but could feel the person's knee hard in his back, the material tightening around his mouth.

He tried to kick his way free but Nicholas knew he was beaten. Pink stars formed around the edges of his eyes, leaving him with the sole thought that someone was going to have a good laugh when they found him dead in a puddle of his own piss.

22

Jessica stared at Rowlands not knowing what to say. She took another step backwards, nearly tripping over the outstretched leg of a chair.

'I'm sorry,' Dave mumbled, staring at his own feet.

Jessica tried to reply but her thoughts weren't clearing quickly enough for her to process any words. Before she could compose herself, the silence was broken by her phone ringing. She collapsed backwards into the chair she had almost fallen over and pulled it out of her jacket pocket.

'Hello.'

At first, she couldn't register who was trying to talk, the person's words a cluttered mismatch of stops and starts. Jessica stood and stepped back towards the window to get a better reception, physically pushing Rowlands away from her.

'Can you repeat that?' she asked.

After hearing Cole tell her the news that had just come through, Jessica dashed across the room, grabbing her coat and shouting over her shoulder as she fumbled for her keys.

'Nicholas Long is dead, let's go.'

*

Jessica couldn't remember the last time she had driven so recklessly. She broke every speed limit and eased through every traffic light, green or not, as she sped from Worsley towards the centre of the city. The rain wasn't helping but she was as focused on the road as she possibly could be, looking for gaps in the traffic and opportunities to gain a few seconds, using the concentration to block out the double hit of information.

Dave Rowlands loved her.

It was no wonder he'd been so awkward over the past few months. Those knowing looks from Izzy suddenly made sense. Jessica didn't know how she had missed it.

If that wasn't enough, Nicholas Long was dead; the man she had spent the past few days hearing horrific stories about, the person she had vowed would be taken down one way or the other. Someone else apparently agreed with her.

Aside from swearing under her breath, the journey to Nicholas's club was completed in silence. If Rowlands had dared say a word, she would have stopped the vehicle and made him get out, rain or no rain.

By the time they arrived, half of Albert Square was cordoned off, along with the streets around the club. Jessica parked behind one of the marked police cars and got out, not waiting for Rowlands to follow. She took out her identification and was waved towards the scene by an officer in uniform she didn't recognise. There were four officers standing outside the front of the club, but they let her through. Jessica knew the inside layout all too well, walking along the dark corridor towards reception and then cutting through into the main area. A few officers were milling around and one pointed her towards the back offices.

Cole was standing in the hallway as Jessica entered, panting for breath. 'Are you all right?' he asked, but Jessica didn't know if he was referring to her breathlessness or if he somehow knew what else had been happening.

'Is he really dead?' she asked.

'Definitely.'

'You saw the body?'

'He's still there if you want to.'

Jessica wouldn't usually go out of her way to see something so morbid but after everything she had heard recently, she felt an irresistible urge. The chief inspector stayed where he was as Jessica edged forward. At the far end of the corridor, there were people working in white paper suits and hair nets. One of them noticed Jessica but the look in her eyes must have told them that she was coming to look at the body regardless of what they thought.

The Scene of Crime officer nodded towards her and turned. Jessica stepped carefully along the hallway, being careful not to touch anything, as she was led to the entrance of a toilet at the end. From the doorway, she could see the unmistakeable shape of Nicholas Long's body on the floor, a pistol lying next to his hand.

'He was on his front when we arrived,' the officer said.

'Was he suffocated?'

'Probably.'

Jessica treaded forward gently, glancing from side to

side. She saw a chip had been taken out of the sink, a piece of the white ceramic on the floor next to Nicholas's hand. Jessica crouched and leant forward to see the contorted look on his face as the officer said 'steady' over her shoulder. She looked down at a pool of liquid on the floor she had somehow missed. All of a sudden the smell hit her and she didn't need to ask what it was. Jessica stood again, stepping backwards carefully, having seen everything she wanted to. She took no particular pleasure from viewing the corpse but couldn't deny there was a definite feeling of satisfaction he couldn't hurt anyone again. Facedown in a puddle of his own making seemed just about right too.

Rowlands was hovering uncomfortably next to Cole but Jessica ignored him as she spoke to the DCI. 'It seems like it's the same person who killed Oliver and Kayleigh.'

'Yep.'

'Can we have a quiet word?' Jessica glanced sideways at Rowlands to indicate that meant without him. Cole nodded and pushed the door open to the main part of the club, walking across to the long sofa where Jessica had seen the girls lounging on her first visit to the place.

The red velvet material felt cheap and uncomfortable as Jessica slid in next to the chief constable, before telling him everything she had found out over the past few days from Eleanor, Leviticus and Ruby. If he was angry, he didn't show it, instead replying with a simple: 'So what you're saying is that we have a few suspects?'

He smiled thinly at her.

'I'm sorry for going around you.'

Cole scratched his head and laughed slightly. 'I'm not as out of the loop as you might think.'

'Oh.'

Jessica waited for him to elaborate but he said nothing, the knowing smile fixed on his face. Jessica broke the silence. 'Who found him?'

'The bar manager – Liam someone or other. He's off being spoken to now. He says he came to open the place up and found his boss where we did, then called us straight away.'

'Did you talk to him?'

'No, we'll get a statement today, then you can read it through and go back to him tomorrow to see if anything has changed.'

Jessica narrowed her eyes. 'Are you suspicious of him?'

'Maybe – he seemed a little too cooperative. Plus we've started going through the CCTV and it shows him arriving half an hour before he told us he did.'

'Perhaps he got the times wrong?'

'We'll see. We've been talking to this other guy too, the bloke from the front desk.'

Jessica could still remember the way she had confused him by reading the name from his tag as if it were magic. 'Scott?'

'Yes, him. He was here when we arrived as well.'

'Have you seen the CCTV yourself?'

'I was about to have a look when you arrived.'

The chief inspector turned, beckoning Jessica towards the door that led to Nicholas's office. Inside, a man was sat behind the large desk, pressing buttons on the computer as the images on the screen skipped forwards and back-wards. Cole introduced Jessica to one of the members from their computer team and told her he was heading back to the station to deal with the media fall-out. He didn't even blink when she suggested Rowlands would be better utilised back at the station. Jessica wondered if his comment about 'not being out of the loop' extended to more than what she had been up to in the course of the job.

Before he left, he nodded towards the filing cabinets lining the room. 'These are all locked,' he said firmly.

'Okay . . .'

'They have to stay that way.'

Jessica hadn't thought about looking for a key to get into them and wondered why he was telling her before it dawned on her that the Serious Crime Division would be desperate to get to the contents. Finding a legal way to do that was by no means a certainty and simply helping themselves would likely create more problems than it solved if any of Nicholas's associates were ever brought to court.

Jessica didn't bother asking how he knew they were locked before nodding an acceptance. The other officer stood to offer her his seat and, although she wasn't usually concerned if men opened doors and gave up their chairs for her, she didn't complain.

'Have you found anything?' she asked when they were alone.

'Not really. Obviously the body was found along the hallway but there are no cameras around there.'

'Life's not that easy.'

'Exactly. Anyway, there are four cameras.' He pointed towards a button on the keyboard which Jessica pressed to flick from one view to the next. Once she had the hang of it, he talked her through them, although she could see for herself. 'There's one outside of the front door pointing at the pavement outside, another in the lobby facing the sofas, a third above the bar directed at the row of stools, then a final one next door.'

'In the changing rooms?'

'Charming, hey?'

Jessica was only half-surprised. Nicholas Long didn't seem the type to be that bothered about employment laws. She doubted 'his' women would report him considering everything she had heard about the type of person he was.

'What have you found?' Jessica asked.

The man directed her through a few screens until she reached a list of file names. 'These are what I've already clipped up, although there isn't a lot to look at.'

Jessica started the first one from the previous evening, which showed Liam and Scott leaving together, the bar manager securing and checking the door before they headed out towards Albert Square.

The next showed Nicholas staggering into the reception area, taking money from the till and then falling onto the nearby sofa. He seemed to be struggling for breath, before eventually composing himself and slowly making his way towards his office after leaning on the bar for support.

'He doesn't seem very well there,' Jessica said, stating the obvious.

'That was about an hour after the other two left. Watch this bit again.'

He reached across Jessica to scroll the footage back and she watched the door next to the bar snap firmly into place. She knew that you needed to know the code to get through from the bar side.

'Did anyone else go through that door afterwards?'

'No, I've checked through the whole night of footage, and the next person to come in was your guy who called it in earlier this afternoon.'

'So whoever killed him was either hiding in this back area or came in through the fire exit?'

'I guess so.'

'They must have really wanted to kill him.'

'Well, there is one other option . . .' The officer turned and nodded towards an empty space on the floor. 'There was a safe there. Your team have already been through it but the money had gone apparently. It could have been a robbery that went too far.'

It sounded unlikely considering the man had been killed in a similar way to Oliver and Kayleigh, but they could never discount anything.

'Are there any cameras out back?' she asked.

'Not that are linked up to here – you'll have to get your teams on it. There'll be some around the square and probably the other streets nearby but whether you'll get anything is a different matter.'

Jessica already knew that was true. Many of the cameras struggled to catch anything that wasn't directly underneath a streetlight, making it easy enough to make your way around undetected if you really wanted to.

'Will you feed all of these back to us?' Jessica asked.

'Of course but we'll take everything back to the labs first. Who knows what else we might find?'

Jessica realised that this was exactly the type of opportunity the Serious Crime Division had been waiting for. Now that Nicholas was dead, they would finally be able to poke through a few things they would not previously have had access to. If they got really lucky, they might be able to implicate one or two other local 'businessmen'.

As she exited into the hallway, Jessica stopped to watch the officers carefully removing Nicholas's body through the fire exit. She followed them into the alleyway that ran along the back, looking up towards the tops of the buildings around to see if there were any CCTV cameras. There weren't, leaving them with the question of how the killer got in. The obvious answer was that someone who worked there had left the fire door open, ready to either return themselves later, or for someone else to do the deed.

Jessica peered at the door, concluding it was pretty much like any other fire exit she had ever seen. It had a metal bar that ran horizontally across the centre, with another connecting vertically.

'I've not touched it,' Jessica said defensively as she saw one of the officers returning.

The man grinned an acceptance. 'I never said you had but you're thinking it must have been left open, aren't you?'

Jessica stared quizzically at him. 'Yes . . .'

'That's not strictly true, look.' The officer pulled on a pair of blue latex gloves and pushed the door shut. 'You think we're locked out now, don't you?'

Jessica accepted a pair of gloves from the man and put them on, stepping closer to the door. There was no handle on the outside; instead she ran her hands around the grooves between the door and the frame, wondering if they were wide enough to push her fingers into. She checked the hinges but the screws were on the inside, then stepped back, shaking her head. 'Go on.'

The man began moving along the alley away from her, before stopping to pick up something from the floor. He walked back towards Jessica and showed her the object. 'This is some sort of roof slate. I promise you I didn't plant this. Hopefully it works now.'

He crouched and pushed the slate in between the bottom of the door and floor. He wiggled it gently at first then, after seemingly finding a spot he was happy with, stepped back and kicked it hard. To Jessica's amazement, the door popped open. The man bent back down and picked up the slate, tossing it behind him.

'How did you do that?' Jessica asked.

'It only works on old-fashioned fire exits. It would never work nowadays.' He pointed at the vertical metal pole connected to the door. 'What happens usually is that when you press down on the horizontal bar, it lifts this vertical one out of the ground so the door springs open. If you know what you're doing, you can make the same thing happen by popping something hard but flat into the groove at the bottom of this pole.'

Jessica stared at him, open-mouthed. 'All this time and I never knew that.'

'No reason you should.' The man shrugged. 'I guess it depends where you grew up. Some kid at school showed me it years ago. We used to go into the locked classroom at lunchtimes and move our teacher's things around. She could never figure out what was going on.' The man suddenly seemed embarrassed. 'I was only a kid.'

Jessica grinned. 'Fair enough, who would have thought you'd now be putting that knowledge to good use?'

As she walked towards Albert Square, she thought that what she had just been shown put a new slant on things. Previously she had assumed someone who worked there must have been responsible, directly or not. This meant it really could be anyone.

As she left the alley to head for her car, Jessica could hear a commotion. To her right, towards the front entrance to the club, there were half-a-dozen police officers standing side by side in front of a line of police tape, their arms stretched out wide. Next to them was someone holding a video camera but it was the group of young men standing on the other side of the road who were the obvious concern.

A riot van skidded to a halt not far from where she was standing, officers pouring out of the back and dashing towards the scene. The young men were all wearing black, some with bandanas tied across their faces. Jessica came as close as she dared and could feel the tension in the air, with threats and abuse being shouted across the street.

As the riot squad lined up with their shields and

helmets, the person with the video camera started running towards her, their gear making it clear they were from a television news channel. Jessica started edging towards her car as the stand-off continued: the police on one side of the road, the youths on the other.

As the cameraman slowed close to Jessica, a woman she recognised as a local news presenter came from somewhere behind her and stopped next to the man.

'Did you get it?' Jessica heard her ask.

Before the cameraman could reply, Jessica interrupted. 'What's going on?'

The presenter replied, 'You police?'

'Yeah.'

'Have you been inside?'

'What's it to you?'

The woman smiled and nudged her colleague, who was looking into the viewfinder with the camera pointed at the floor. 'How about we tell you what we've got and you tell us what you saw.'

'I'm not talking on camera.'

The presenter exchanged a look with her colleague. 'Fine, as long as we can still quote an unnamed source.'

The two women stared at each other, waiting for the other to go first. Jessica could hear the noise of the confrontation growing louder. 'All right, fine,' she replied, giving the briefest of details about what she had seen inside the club, omitting everything about suffocation, guns, stolen money, or fire exits that weren't as secure as they first seemed.

The presenter seemed happy to have confirmation

of the death. 'So Nicholas Long is definitely dead?' she asked.

'Yes.'

She looked at the cameraman. 'All right, fine, show her.' As the man turned the camera around so Jessica could see the digital screen, the woman continued, 'There's been all sorts of stuff on the Internet this morning that he was dead. One of our producers grew up on Moss Side and he said he'd heard chatter this morning.'

'What about?'

'You know Nicholas Long was idolised there?'

'Yes.'

'Watch.'

The footage had been taken around the corner where the police were now lining up. The person being interviewed on camera appeared to be a teenager, although the hood and bandana covered all but his young eyes.

'Why are you here?' a man's voice asked off camera.

The youth's eyes darted nervously away from the camera before staring defiantly into it. 'It's the feds, innit? They've gone and fucking killed him and now we're gonna smash the place up.'

23

Jessica sat alone thinking the timing of Nicholas's death and Dave's revelation could not have been worse. She had already planned how her evening was going to go from the moment Adam told her he was going to be working late at the university. Usually, Jessica would have taken him at face value but something hadn't sounded right, not to mention the way he had been behaving recently.

She was trying to block out what Dave had told her but using the job as a way to escape, as she so often would, was hard because he was a part of that. Izzy had allowed Jessica to swap cars with her for the evening without asking any questions other than 'You're not going to do something stupid, are you?'

Jessica tuned in the radio to the local stations, waiting to hear if anything was going to spiral out of the incident in the city centre. Although the news had mentioned a police presence, there was nothing more.

She realised she could be in for a long night sitting in a car if Adam genuinely was working late but she parked in between street lights on the road that ran adjacent to the university's staff car park. With the lamps placed handily around the area, Jessica could see exactly where Adam had parked and there was little chance of him spotting her, even if he did somehow know to look for Izzy's car.

A steady stream of students began to pass Jessica's vehicle as the clock on her phone eased around to the time she knew Adam usually finished. She watched the groups passing, thinking they seemed to be getting ever younger, before realising she was one step away from complaining about 'kids today'.

Jessica turned her attention to the door at the side of the building, wanting to believe Adam really was staying late and wouldn't emerge. At five minutes past the time he was due to finish, she was feeling a little ashamed of herself for doubting him. By fifteen minutes past, she had put the key back in the ignition and was ready to pull away, before the voice at the back of her head told her to wait five more minutes.

As Adam emerged from the building with his bag over his shoulder a couple of minutes later, Jessica felt a sinking feeling in her stomach, a sense that something was about to go horribly wrong but that she was simply a bystander, unable or unwilling to step in. Jessica noticed he had on different clothes than he had been in that morning. He always wore similar things to work, dark trousers with a shirt, over which he would wear a lab coat. He was now wearing a pair of smart jeans with a casual shirt he usually only wore on a night out, along with his best jacket.

After he got into the car, Jessica watched him talking into his mobile phone, smiling and laughing. She tried to think of an innocent explanation of who it might be. Although he didn't have any family, that didn't mean he might not be meeting up with someone he used to know from school, or someone he went to university with, or perhaps even a work colleague.

None of that would explain why he had told her he was working late though.

He hung up and switched on the headlights. Jessica turned the key of Izzy's car, feeling the power roar through it. She slid down into her seat as Adam drove past, waiting a few moments before slipping into the traffic behind him.

Although rush hour was over, there were still plenty of people trying to get home or to whatever theatre or concert was on that night. Or just driving around in circles specifically to annoy her. Jessica had never really done much in the way of vehicle surveillance, and now relied instead on what she had seen on television shows by staying two car lengths behind. She followed Adam along Oxford Road onto Deansgate, with no idea where he was heading as he kept driving north. The traffic was stop–start until they reached the outskirts, with all the signs pointing towards either Prestwich or the motorway ring road.

Just as she thought he was going to join the M60, Adam indicated, turning left off the main road. Jessica was so surprised, she almost missed the turn herself, swerving late as the person in the car behind beeped their horn.

It took her a few moments to realise where she had turned into. The road branched off into two, the left lane leading to a Tesco, the right twisting around on itself before ending up in a car park for a restaurant and hotel. She hoped Adam would turn left into the supermarket, as if he had somehow come this far out of his way to pick up some groceries. Instead, he stayed on the road that led to the hotel.

Jessica eased off the accelerator and stopped, checking her rear-view mirror to see with a small amount of relief that no one was behind her. She crept the vehicle forward, watching as Adam drove his car front-first into a space opposite the entrance of the restaurant. It was an American-style one with a black-and-red awning hanging over the door and branding everywhere, just in case you walked in the front door and forgot where you were. Jessica waited as Adam switched off the headlights. In the moment of darkness, she pressed the accelerator, powering around the corner past where Adam had stopped into the middle part of the car park, where she reversed into a space.

As she peered up, Jessica saw Adam hurrying across the tarmac into the restaurant. There were around a dozen seats at the front of the diner and perhaps half-a-dozen slightly further back. She picked up her phone, wondering whether she should call him, when a blonde woman stepped out of the car she had parked next to. As she had reversed, Jessica hadn't even noticed her but the woman was holding her phone in one hand and a bag in the other. Her hair was bright and bleached, curled into a short bob, and she was wearing tight-fitting jeans with a matching jacket.

The woman tottered into the restaurant wearing heels Jessica wouldn't have even attempted to try on and, for a minute or two, everything seemed to slow down. Jessica wondered if she would have to get out of the car and go in herself to see what was happening, or if there was a completely innocent explanation and that Adam had popped out for a bite to eat, with the woman nothing to do with him.

The car was beginning to steam up and Jessica balled her sleeve to wipe the window. She was halfway through clearing the windscreen when she felt her heart jump. A waiter was strolling along the front window with Adam and the blonde behind him. When they reached the table at the end, Adam and the female slid onto opposite sides, the server handing them menus and writing down what she presumed were drinks orders.

They were smiling and laughing. All of them.

Jessica swore at the condensation, before giving up and getting out of the car, leaning against the driver's side door in the darkness and shivering as the breeze zipped across her. She folded her arms but it wasn't the wind that was making her tremble. The blonde with the stupid curly bob reached across with her stupid tanned hand and touched Adam on his stupid arm.

Jessica could feel her throat tightening, the sickness that had been crippling her stomach so often recently ripping through the rest of her body. She pressed herself against the vehicle, using it to hold herself up. Somehow, she forced herself not to cry, fighting every instinct she had, trying to think of an innocent explanation for why he could be in a restaurant miles from their house with an attractive blonde after telling her he was working late.

Could it be because she was always working herself?

Early mornings, late nights and everything in between? Perhaps it was because he was annoyed at her for not helping with the decision about where they should live? Maybe he was simply bored?

Perhaps it was because of what had happened in America?

Jessica bit her lip, remembering what he was like when they first met; always apologising, stammering over his words, clumsy, awkward, socially inexperienced. She watched him through the window laughing as the waiter passed them drinks and they raised their glasses in an unknown toast. Suddenly she was angry, furious that she had helped him become the person he now was and that he was using it against her, taking the confidence to chat up curly-haired blonde tarts.

She stared through the darkness as the lights from inside the restaurant illuminated the area in front of her. Even from a distance, when Jessica looked properly, she could see the woman was a bit older than her, which only made things worse. If Adam was going to dump her for some slutty student with a push-up bra, that was one thing, but it would be a humiliation too far if it was for someone born before her. Someone who spent half her life getting her hair dyed and curled instead of doing a proper job.

Jessica could feel the edges of her phone digging into her palm as she squeezed it tightly. She looked at the screen, unlocking it and scrolling through to Adam's name on her contact list. Pressing the button to call him, Jessica watched as he broke off mid-conversation and reached into his pocket. He took out his mobile phone and glanced at the screen, presumably seeing her name and then pressed a button. Jessica was ready to start speaking, thinking he had accepted the call, but instead her phone beeped and went silent. The words 'call failed' appeared as Adam put his phone back into his pocket.

Jessica stared at the now-blank screen wondering what she should do next. In the moment it took her to breathe in, the rain started as suddenly as it had done when she had been watching the schoolchildren play lacrosse earlier in the day. She found it hard to believe that so much had happened in such a short period of time. That morning, she had been a different person, wondering how she could play a part in bringing down Nicholas Long. Now he was dead, one of her best friends was in love with her, Adam was copping off with some other woman, and Moss Side was seemingly on the brink of a riot.

And she was getting wet.

Jessica pocketed her phone and stood still, watching Adam and the blonde from across the car park, the rain dribbling down her face. She closed her eyes and breathed in the cool air, allowing her body to shiver as the freezing rain ran down her back.

By the time she looked up, the waiter was back at the table with two plates of food. The one he placed in front of Adam seemed to consist mainly of meat and chips; the woman's was a big bowl of salad which made Jessica hate her even more. At least if someone was going to steal him away from her, they should have the good grace to get fat in the process.

Jessica ran her hands through her hair, pulling it away from her face and apologising silently to Izzy for getting the interior of her car wet as she opened the door and climbed back inside. She watched as Adam and the woman ate their meals, chatting, smiling and laughing the whole way through. Jessica continued staring, not knowing why she didn't march into the restaurant and demand to know what was going on. The rain continued to rattle off the metal of the car, deafening her until, finally, they finished eating and stood.

There was a tiny inkling of solace as Jessica realised neither the woman nor Adam had brought a proper coat but even that was ruined as she watched him handing the blonde his jacket. The final straw came as they dashed side by side to the hotel next door, clattering through the front door to get out of the rain.

Jessica couldn't describe how she felt, any anger she expected to have cancelled out by a feeling in her stomach of wanting to be sick. She continued to stare at the hotel but there was no movement.

Her throat was so swollen that it was hard to breathe but Jessica composed herself to turn the key just as the rain began to ease off.

The radio jumped into life halfway through the newsreader's sentence but his message was as clear as it could be – the threats of the teenage protestors that morning that they would 'smash the place up' were in the process of coming true.

24

Moss Side was separated from Longsight by the Royal Manchester Children's Hospital. With the high number of battles between youths from estates belonging to the two communities, that meant the medical facility was in the perfect location a few years back. When Jessica worked in uniform, every officer knew Whitworth Park at the back of the hospital was the place where the gangs of Moss Side would square up against their rivals from Longsight every few weeks.

Since then, much of the gang warfare had died down, or at the least the lower-scale trouble. But while stabbings, drug charges and public disorder figures had decreased, firearms offences were up.

There were specialist teams in Greater Manchester's Police service trained to deal with gang-related crime but neither they, uniform, or anyone else had been prepared for what happened on the night of Nicholas Long's death.

After arriving back at the flat, Jessica watched the news on the television in the bedroom, before turning it off, rolling over and pretending to be asleep the moment she heard Adam's key in the lock. He whispered an apology for being late and she struggled not to tense as he kissed the back of her head.

The following morning, Jessica headed straight to Moss

Side, where smoke was still rising. Police had cordoned off the roads heading in and were checking each car attempting to enter and exit, leading to long queues in the surrounding district. Jessica parked Izzy's car a short distance away and walked. She struggled not to shiver, her decision to stand in the rain the previous evening returning to haunt her. Her hair was still matted and knotty, despite the fact she'd had a shower.

The morning itself was dry and bright, although the air smelled of burning as one of the uniformed officers waved her through and told her where the rest of the team were.

Jessica saw the initial burned-out car at the end of the road – the first of half-a-dozen. There was a host of officers crowded around, with a fire engine parked on either side blocking the roads. Stones and broken glass littered the tarmac as Jessica tried to step around the debris.

She realised quickly that the only reason Cole had asked her to attend was to keep up appearances. The chief superintendent was strolling around the scene with two news cameras in tow and there were officers massed throughout. She could guess the way things had happened that morning, with the high-ups requesting every district from across the city send an officer or two to at least make it appear as if they were reacting to what had gone on the previous evening.

A man in a suit Jessica recognised as a detective sergeant from their neighbouring North division caught her eye and she weaved her way around one of the vehicles, making sure she stayed out of the camera's view.

'You got the short straw too then?' he asked. He was at

least fifteen years older than Jessica with curly grey hair and a slouch that made it look like he'd long since given up.

'I'm thinking of changing my middle name to "shat upon",' she replied with a weak smile.

The man laughed. 'If nothing else, it will get you funny looks at the airport.'

'What are we even doing here?' Jessica asked.

'Just follow me and look busy.' He turned and walked away from the cars. 'I'm Geoff,' he said, offering his hand.

'Jessica,' she replied, shaking it.

Geoff began pointing at rocks as they walked. 'If we stay together and walk around pointing at rocks and bottles like this, anyone watching from a distance might think we're gathering vital evidence, rather than simply making up the numbers in a show of force.'

Jessica copied him, pointing at a broken piece of glass. 'Haven't we got specialist teams to go through scenes like this?'

He crouched, picking up a rock and showing it to Jessica, then holding it up to the light as if he had noticed something important. 'They've already got most of them in custody, it's just kids, teenagers and young blokes who fancied a tear-up. We're only around because the cameras are here – people will want to see lots of officers on the news this evening and in the papers tomorrow.'

Geoff stood again, walking back towards the cars with Jessica by his side.

'How long do you think we'll have to hang around?' she asked.

He nodded towards the chief superintendent. 'As soon as the cameras go, he'll be off within five minutes, then we'll get back to some proper work five minutes after that. Then the local lot can get on with things without us trampling around in the way.'

'What happened? I saw some of it on the news yesterday but it wasn't a good night for me.'

'Did you hear about Nicholas Long being killed?'

Jessica didn't want to say how involved she was in the case, replying with a simple 'yes'.

'He came from around this area,' Geoff continued as they walked. Every now and then, he would point at a random half-brick, just in case the cameras were focusing on them. 'He paid for some social club around here and apparently lots of kids looked up to him and so on. As soon as word got around that he had been killed, the rumour mill went into overdrive and, before you know it, every little scroat and thieving shitbag was on the street moaning about "feds" and "cops", plus every other Americanism you can think of.'

Jessica tried to give most people the benefit of the doubt, especially when they had grown up in an area of poverty, telling herself it was easy to look down on others when she had parents who loved and cared for her. That didn't mean she didn't sympathise with and largely understand Geoff's cynicism.

'I saw some of them in town yesterday,' Jessica replied.

'Aye, someone sent all of the riot squad into the centre. As soon as this lot realised they wouldn't be able to cause any trouble there, they all came home and smashed their own area up instead. I doubt many of them had even met Nicholas Long, let alone knew he came from here. He was just an excuse to go out and cause trouble.'

'Anyone hurt?'

'Not really. Lots of scared locals but I think they mainly damaged objects rather than people. I heard a few of ours got carried away. Still, you never know if someone's going to pull a gun on you when you're out this way, do you?'

Jessica didn't reply as she wasn't entirely sure what she thought about that. They arrived back at the burned cars just as the chief superintendent was leading the cameras away to talk to some nearby locals. She wondered if they had already been screened by a press officer to prevent them saying anything unexpected on camera. A few of the other members of CID began to make eye contact with each other, wondering if they could return to their real jobs yet, as uniformed officers waited around, wanting to get to work properly.

'Do you think there'll be anything else tonight?' Jessica asked.

'Have you been to your station yet?' Geoff asked with a smile.

'I came straight here.'

He turned so he was facing away from where the cameras might be and broke into a laugh. 'Where are you based?'

'Longsight.'

He laughed even harder. 'Just down the road then. Wait

until you get in, then you won't need to ask that question.'

As Jessica walked through the station's front door, she knew instantly what Geoff had been trying to tell her. A queue of people was winding out of the door as she pushed her way through to reception. She offered the desk sergeant a sympathetic grin, heading towards the main floor where the constables worked. She had a quick look from side to side to make sure Rowlands was nowhere to be seen, then moved quickly across to Izzy's desk and swapped car keys.

'Are we full downstairs?' Jessica asked.

Izzy smiled. 'Everyone's full. They arrested everyone out on the street last night but there wasn't anywhere to fit them all. The cells are jammed at all the local stations and we can't get people in and out quickly enough. There aren't enough duty solicitors to go around and we've had angry parents storming in and out all morning. Some of them have already been processed and shipped off to the magistrates but their parents are still turning up here. Some of the ones involved in the more serious stuff are being kept downstairs too.'

'I got sent out to the estate this morning to make up the numbers.'

'Is it as bad as it looked on the news?'

'Not really, most of it happened at the end of one road.'

Izzy didn't appear too relieved. 'Still, one riot a year is one too many, we're not going to hear the end of this for months. Next thing you know, we'll have a five-step plan about how to spot a riot and what to do about it. Step one: is anyone throwing stones? Step two: where are the stones coming from?'

'So young, cynical and purple,' Jessica smiled back, before straightening when she saw Rowlands entering the room. 'I've got to head back to Nicholas's club to talk to the staff. Are you coming?'

Izzy seemed confused. 'Aren't you taking Dave?'

'No.'

Jessica's reply was deliberately firm, meant to end the enquiry, rather than to invite more.

Izzy took the hint. 'Whenever you're ready then.' She paused before adding: 'My car is in one piece, isn't it?'

'Why wouldn't it be?'

'It's just . . . your reputation . . .'

Jessica rolled her eyes. 'Let's go. I'm driving.'

On the surface, Nicholas Long's club looked the same as it had on every other occasion Jessica had visited it but by the time she reached the back set of offices and rooms, it had changed dramatically. A thick piece of chipboard had been bolted in place of the old fire door. Jessica led Izzy through the hallway, showing her how everything had been. The toilet was unrecognisable, the sink ripped out and exposed water pipes sealed off with a plastic stopper.

After checking how everything had been left, Jessica and the constable went back through to the main part of the club. Half-a-dozen women were sitting on the sofas in the same spot as the first evening Jessica had come by. Their attire was very different on this occasion, tight jeans and combinations of jumpers and tops, rather than skimpy underwear.

Jessica and Izzy stood next to the security door as the assembled workers eyed them suspiciously.

'Do you fancy talking to them?' Jessica asked quietly, not wanting them to hear. 'I don't think I give off the right vibes.'

'Why would you think I would?'

'You just look . . . trendier.' Jessica indicated Izzy's tied-back purple hair.

The constable narrowed her eyes before responding. '"Trendier"? Is that a nice way of saying I look a bit like a stripper?'

'If that's how you want to think of it.'

'I'm not sure if I should take it as a compliment.'

'Either way, I think they'll talk to you more than they will me. I've had a bunch of dirty looks already.'

Izzy nodded. 'Who are you going to talk to?'

'The bar manager, Liam, and the guy who works on the front desk – Scott. I've already taken a look at their statements and I want to go over a couple of things. The times are all over the shop.'

Izzy nodded at the women. 'We've already got statements from this lot too, haven't we?'

'That's not really why we're here. This is supposed to be a less formal thing to discuss wider issues of what it was like working for Nicholas.'

'Is there anything you want me to ask specifically?'

'Skirt around it and do your girly thing but see if you can find out if any of them were sleeping with him. Just bear in mind it might not have been entirely a two-way thing.'

'Is it going to matter now if they were?'

Jessica shook her head. 'Probably not but there are so many people that may have had it in for him, it wouldn't do any harm to know if he was having an affair.'

Izzy took a deep breath, readying herself. 'Is this why you brought me instead of Dave?'

'Well, that and the fact Dave's a dick.'

Izzy laughed, thinking Jessica was joking. 'What's new about that?'

Liam and Scott were both sitting on stools at the far end of the bar talking quietly. As they saw Jessica approaching, they stopped, standing as if she had commanded them to.

The dim light glinted off Scott's styled spiky hair. Instead of the smart clothes he had been wearing at their last meeting, he was dressed in jeans and a T-shirt. In his suit he had looked like an usher at a wedding, thrust into the job at short notice with a suit one size too big, bought by his parents so he could grow into it. If anything, the casual clothes made him appear even younger.

On the other hand, there was little Liam could do about his brutish appearance. He too was wearing jeans with a T-shirt but his arms were practically bursting out of it. While Leviticus was well-defined, he had a charm about

253

him that Liam certainly didn't. With a voice that was squeaky and held no authority, Jessica could see why Nicholas had been happy to bring Liam in on work experience. He was someone who could be moulded into something far more useable.

'How can we help?' Liam asked in a tone higher than usual.

'I'm going to talk to you one at a time in the reception area,' Jessica said. 'You first,' she added, pointing at Scott.

She led him through to the porch, sitting on one end of the sofa and nodding for the man to sit at the other.

'Am I in trouble?' he asked nervously. 'I did speak to you yesterday.'

'I wanted to run through your statement and to clarify a few things about your relationship with Nicholas Long.'

'Okay . . .'

'How did you come to work here?'

Scott answered instantly without thinking. 'Word gets around when Nicholas is looking for someone to hire. He had a bunch of us in on work experience, not here, at one of the pubs he owns out Rusholme way. I helped out with the barrels.'

'How long ago was that?'

Scott ummed for a few moments, his slight frame shrinking into itself as he glanced at the ceiling, counting on his fingers. 'Three years or so?'

'How did you end up working here?'

Scott looked away nervously. 'I'd been here a few times just for, y'know . . .' He peeked up to catch Jessica's nod. 'Anyway, through that I'd started chatting to Liam. A few months back he told me they'd be looking to take someone extra on and that he'd put in a word with the boss.'

'Is Liam your best friend?'

'I suppose . . .'

'What's he like?'

Jessica saw a minor look of panic shoot across Scott's face but she recognised it as the expression most males gave when they were asked to talk about other men, as if admitting they liked someone as a mate meant they were secretly attracted to them too. She stared at him, eyebrows raised, letting him know she wasn't in the mood for immature blokes on this particular day.

'I guess . . . he's a good guy . . . ?' Scott's inflection made it sound like a question.

'Is he or isn't he?'

Scott squirmed awkwardly and Jessica wanted to shout *'it doesn't make you gay'* in frustration.

'He looks out for you,' Scott finally replied in what Jessica guessed was about as ringing an endorsement as she was likely to get from him.

'Talk me through what happened the night before last.'

Jessica already knew from the CCTV that the club had been serving drinks after their licence said they were supposed to have closed for the night. Because it was something Liam should have been on top of – and because it didn't matter in the bigger picture – she didn't say anything as Scott told her a white lie about everything being 'normal' and them closing 'on time'.

Aside from those issues, he said they had gone to his

own flat after locking up to play computer games until the early hours, something they did regularly. As he pointed out, they worked odd hours.

Liam's version of events on the night Nicholas had died matched Scott's. He had been hired in a similar way to Scott, but had moved up quickly in Nicholas's organisation to the point that he was now some sort of right-hand man. As well as being the bar manager for the club, he worked one day a week as a regional manager, visiting the other pubs and clubs Nicholas owned to ensure everything was running as it should be. Jessica didn't push what exactly that might mean, although she thought the Serious Crime Division might be paying him a visit sometime soon to ask more probing questions.

The more she spoke to Liam, the more Jessica could see what Nicholas clearly had. He was happy to make eye contact but there was a vulnerability there. He refused to say anything negative about Nicholas, proving his loyalty, but the fact he was comfortable talking about accounting showed he had an intelligence too. Coupled with his physique, it was quite a combination. She wondered quite how deeply entrenched in Nicholas's other pursuits he might be.

Jessica's final question was as much for her own gratification as the investigation. 'Who's going to be the new boss with Nicholas gone?'

Through their talk, Liam had been leaning forward and using his hands as he spoke, even though it didn't seem particularly natural for him. As Jessica asked the question, he crossed his arms defensively. 'I had a phone call yesterday.'

'Who from?'

'The other Nicholas, his son.'

Jessica had been wondering how long it would be before the younger Long came up. 'What did he say?'

'He wants to meet. I think it would have already happened if you hadn't have been coming down today.' Liam had spoken affectionately about his old boss but clearly didn't have the same feeling towards the man's son.

'Have you met him before?'

Liam nodded. 'Once. His dad brought him in to give him the tour around a year ago. I knew he had a son but he was off at school somewhere and would only come home for a few weeks each summer.'

'What was he like?'

At first Jessica thought Liam was going to say something derogatory but he stopped himself mid-sentence, perhaps wary of the fact that the eighteen-year-old was possibly going to be his new boss. 'He's . . . different.'

Jessica knew Nicky was someone she should try to meet sooner rather than later. And Leviticus Bryan's earlier assertion that the young man wasn't too keen on 'waiting his turn' was a particularly interesting choice of phrase, given what had happened to his father.

25

Jessica had been wary of spending time alone with Adam recently, even before watching him in the restaurant with the mystery woman. Since then, she had done everything she could to avoid him, although she saw the irony of text messaging him to say she was working late when she instead went and moped in the nearby pub. Far from seeking an explanation, she didn't want to hear what he might have to say, worried about the effect it might have on her professional life if she let her relationship fall apart while she was still in the middle of a case. She felt she owed it to Kayleigh, Eleanor, Oliver's parents and everyone else to find out what was going on, then she would figure out the best way to deal with what was happening at home.

The other problem was that the Longsight station was becoming less and less of a respite too. Avoiding Rowlands was hard to do, meaning she either spent all of her time in her office, or made sure she travelled in a pair, walking around with DS Cornish or someone nearby if she needed to go anywhere.

They were still dealing with the fall-out of the Moss Side disturbance too, with half of the cells still full three days after it had happened. The enormous police presence on the morning after had worked in one way, with the media backing rather than criticising them, although even that had an edge to it, the insinuation being they should shoot anyone under the age of eighteen who happened to be on the streets after dark. Jessica knew one or two people within the station who probably shared that view but that wasn't helping either.

With at least two area taskforces being set up, as well as the shifting of resources to the gang crime unit, few officers seemed to know what they were supposed to be doing. It wasn't helping that DI Reynolds hadn't yet been replaced.

What also wasn't helping was that ever since she had been drawn into the whisky-drinking with Nicholas, Jessica could feel something wasn't right with her body. For the first few days, she had put it down to her own stupidity but it had gone past that now. The constant tiredness was something she had experienced in the past but her limbs were beginning to ache and she frequently felt hungry, even after just eating. She woke each morning knowing she should visit the doctor but not wanting to hear what he might have to say. At the same time, she feared she would burst into tears and be signed off work with stress.

Instead, Jessica kept acting as if nothing was wrong.

She was somewhat surprised to be called into an early morning briefing by Cole, and even more concerned when he told her to come to the media room rather than his office. Although it was technically called the Press Pad, most officers went out of their way to call it anything but. The reasons for his choice of location became clear when Jessica saw the number of people there, including

Izzy, three other detective constables and a handful of uniformed officers.

Not to mention Rowlands.

Rather than talking at them, the chairs had been arranged into a near-circle. Jessica deliberately sat a quarter of the way around from Rowlands, next to the chief inspector. It was far enough away not to have to speak to him but not opposite, meaning she didn't have to look at him either. Small briefings she could deal with, but this was the type of corporate shite she hated: 'blue-sky thinking', 'pushing the envelope', 'moving forward', 'thinking outside the box' and any number of other made-up phrases that people came up with. Basically, let's all sit in a circle and talk at each other until someone pulls out a weapon and puts everyone out of their misery.

Cole offered her a weak smile and she wondered how things had been going with his wife. They hadn't had any time alone since they had talked in the gardens outside Kayleigh's house and they had never had a close enough relationship for her to assume she could ask. She knew she wasn't one to talk but the areas under his eyes were dark and the wrinkles on his forehead seemed to have doubled over the past month or so. He looked as if he could do with an entire weekend in bed.

After everyone had settled, Cole explained that things were awkward with officers being pulled in all directions, often with no notice. Through careful negotiating, he had managed to ensure that everyone in the room, with the exception of himself, would be free to continue investigating the deaths of Oliver, Kayleigh and, almost by default, Nicholas Long. He did point out that the Serious Crime Division were also investigating Nicholas's activities, although they hadn't yet taken on the man's death because they weren't too keen on looking into the elements relating to Oliver and Kayleigh. It was typical that the deaths of real people were being thought of as an impediment, rather than a spur into action.

After a few introductions, he told them time for briefings such as this would be at a premium in the coming weeks, so they should get as much out into the open as possible and share any ideas.

'I do have some early results from Nicholas's body,' he added. 'It's as we expected. He died from asphyxiation in much the same way as Oliver and Kayleigh. There's an additional gash in his head from where it looks like he hit his head and a significant amount of pressure was placed on the bottom of his spine.'

'Was anything found at the scene?' one of the keener constables asked.

'You should all have diagrams and photos of the area. The sink is covered in fingerprints, so identifying any that don't belong to staff members, or Nicholas himself, is going to take some time, if not prove impossible. A handgun was recovered from the scene but the numbers match what we have on file for a weapon legally registered to Nicholas himself. It shouldn't have been out of his house but that's a different issue. Taking anything from that is proving difficult given the fact it was found in a puddle of urine. They've taken the whole of the fire exit door to check as well.'

Cole tried to explain how someone could open a fire exit from the outside but wasn't doing a good job, so Rowlands talked everyone through it. Jessica stared off into the distance but was unsurprised he knew the trick. The chief inspector emphasised that it only worked on old-style doors and that most buildings weren't so easy to get into. He also pointed out that none of this ignored the possibility that someone who worked in the club had deliberately left it open.

Jessica talked the officers through Scott and Liam's statements, as well as her additional chats with them both.

Izzy had not had the most productive of times speaking to the female workers. None of them seemed to share the disdain for Nicholas that Eleanor did but the constable described it as a consistent mix of fear and awe, something Jessica could understand from her dealings with the man. None of them would open up further than describing their own movements on the night Nicholas had been killed. It also seemed apparent a few of them were working without the knowledge of their family, something which complicated things further.

Jessica talked about the impression Leviticus and Ruby had given her of the man and they all knew about the suspicions around his business dealings and the position he held within the community. Finding someone with a motive was never going to be difficult, which left them trying to connect possible suspects back to Kayleigh and Oliver's killings.

Two officers were tasked with tracing back everything they had in their files that could link the three people, with another small group working with the local CCTV footage. The initial examinations had found nothing from the cameras around the streets and Jessica doubted they'd get anything. It was still worth looking into, despite how time-consuming it would be.

When one of the officers asked who was likely to be taking on the business, Jessica said she had heard Long's son Nicky seemed probable.

'We've tried to make contact with both Nicky and his stepmother, Tia, but neither have so far been that cooperative,' Cole added. 'We took a statement with a few of the basics in, such as the fact that Nicholas often doesn't arrive home from the club until five or six in the morning, but not much more.'

Another officer was given the task of finding out anything about Nicky, although Jessica knew it would be a struggle because of his age.

As they were getting ready to split up, Cole did reveal one interesting fact, insisting it couldn't leave the room. 'Serious Crime are going big on getting access to the filing cabinets at Nicholas's club,' he said. 'They're off to court later this week to try to argue they have the right to search them. Basically, if you're at the premises, stay away. If you're not, forget I ever said this.'

Jessica hung around, waiting until it was just her and Cole, noting that Rowlands hadn't stopped to chat. Although the chief inspector had stood to send everyone on their way, he then sank back into his seat, as Jessica dragged hers around so she could see him face to face.

'Is everything all right?' she asked.

Cole offered a short 'fine' without looking at her, letting her know that any conversation unrelated to work was off limits.

She knew the feeling.

'Do SCD think they'll win in court?' she asked.

His demeanour brightened as he laughed at the suggestion. 'They've got no chance, they're just trying it on. If they had enough evidence before, they would already have the files. They're hoping they'll get a lenient judge because of everything that happened in Moss Side this week. Nicholas's wife has a lawyer on the case to stop anything we do.'

Jessica remembered Leviticus telling her how meticulous Nicholas was with his record-keeping, although one thing had always bothered her about the statement. 'What I don't get is why someone like Nicholas would keep records of everything if it might come back to bite him at some point. He must have known the agencies were desperate to get hold of them?'

Cole smiled, but the wrinkles around his eyes folded into one, making him look even more tired. 'Why would Richard Nixon record everything that went on in the Oval Office? It's not to do with knowing it could implicate you, it's the arrogance of assuming it won't matter.'

Jessica couldn't argue, having seen the man's ego close up.

'I need to visit Nicky,' she said.

'I know.'

'Are Serious Crime going to mind?'

'Probably, but what they don't know and all that . . .'

Jessica couldn't be sure but she thought he had winked at her. 'We're going to have to be careful,' he added.

He was already on his feet before Jessica realised that meant he was coming too.

26

Despite the length of time they had worked together, Jessica had never been in Cole's vehicle. He had a 4x4 that was under a year old and drove like Jessica's mum, which was the worst insult she could think of. Actually, sod that, he drove like her grandmother, who'd been dead for years.

When she was younger, Jessica had always liked going in a car alone with her father but every journey would be prefaced with the words 'don't tell your mother'. While her dad would zip around the local country roads and speed up over the humpback bridges, her mum would stick rigidly to the speed limit and obey every road sign. She often wondered if it was this which led to her driving having a bad reputation around the station.

Their journey south into Didsbury was conducted mainly in silence, the tick-tocking of the indicator and the dull poshness of the person on the radio providing a backdrop to a life Jessica knew she had to avoid.

Jessica used to live in the area herself, although Nicholas's house was in a far more affluent spot. Her flat had been part of a newly built development of townhouses just off the main road but the property they were heading to was a mile past that at the back of a housing estate with a cul de sac to itself. If you hadn't known it was there, you wouldn't have found it, with signs sending you off to the nearby rugby and golf clubs and no indication there were any additional houses.

Cole drove steadily, with the air of someone who knew the area well, skipping along a selection of side streets and avoiding the major commuter routes.

There were no huge gates or enormous walls shielding Nicholas Long's property from the rest of the road as Cole pulled onto the driveway, which itself was an intricate pattern of yellow and red brickwork. Jessica stepped out of the car, peering behind to find the yellow bricks under her feet spelling out an enormous upside-down 'NL' when set against the red. She walked along the length of the letters, which curled into each other, showing an intricacy of design which would have been impressive had it been in calligraphy, let alone created with bricks in a driveway.

The house was in a mock-Tudor style similar to the school she had visited, with vast thick black beams offset against bright white walls. Jessica couldn't see how far the property went back, but there were three wings, as well as a central block that had a huge wooden door, styled to look like a drawbridge. A separate building off to their left had huge garage doors in the same style at the front, big enough to fit at least three cars side by side.

'We're in the wrong business,' Cole muttered as a joke, but he was only half-wrong. For all these years, Nicholas had somehow found a way to stay out of trouble and this was the house he had built with the proceeds. That came on the back of everything Leviticus had, which, despite his protests of feeling trapped in a prison, she knew full well had also been funded partially through the misery of others.

Wrong business indeed.

How to announce their arrival baffled them both for a few moments before Jessica realised the handle hanging next to the door which she thought was decorative was actually a doorbell. It reminded her of flushing the old-fashioned toilets in her primary school but she pulled the chain and they heard a tinkling tune from inside.

Jessica's stomach was rumbling uncomfortably in the way she had become used to ignoring but after a minute or so, they heard a heavy bolt being withdrawn before the door swung open. A small woman with dark curly hair and a purple uniform stood looking at them quizzically. Her accent sounded Eastern European, although Jessica couldn't deny she had a better grasp of English than many of the local youngsters they picked up.

She told them to sit on a sofa just across the threshold, carefully bolting the door back into place and disappearing into an adjacent room.

Leviticus's property had been impressive but it wasn't a patch on Nicholas's. The insides kept the same style as the exterior, large dark beams running along the walls, inter-spersed with fake candles. Everything they could see, from the sofa they were sitting on, to a large table opposite, to the frames around the doors, was made of the same thick heavy-looking wood. Jessica could see why Nicholas employed a maid; keeping everything tidy would be a full-time job in itself.

'How much do you reckon this place cost?' Cole asked as they both took in the hallway.

'Seven figures? Eight?'

They were interrupted by the clicking of heels as someone Jessica assumed was Tia Long entered the room. She was wearing a short dark skirt with a matching jacket over a tight white blouse. Her black hair was tied tightly away from her face, which was tanned and made up to perfection. Her legs were a similar colour, which certainly hadn't been gained from the overcast Manchester skies.

She walked with the confidence of someone who couldn't believe their luck. 'I'm on the way to visit my solicitor,' Tia offered as a way of greeting. She insisted there was nothing she could add that wasn't in her statement, pointing out that, although she had said it was fine for them to visit, 'I didn't actually think you'd turn up'.

Before she could leave, Cole added: 'Is Nicky still around?'

Tia's snort of 'yeah but good luck' did not bode well as she told them he was somewhere in the house and then unbolted the door, letting herself out.

Alone in the hallway, Jessica didn't get the opportunity to speak before Cole. 'Let it go.'

'Let what go?'

'You know. Just think what you might be like if you were in a situation living with a man like him. You'd be skipping out of here cock-a-hoop too if you found out he'd died.'

Jessica couldn't deny that but he then answered her follow-up question before she could ask it.

'We'll still look into her, don't worry.'

With the echo of the door closing still sounding around the house, Cole led the way through the door the maid had entered a few minutes earlier. It led into a long corridor with doorways on either side. Jessica could see daylight, following the chief inspector as he walked to the end, which opened into a kitchen.

The maid from before was nowhere to be seen but there was an older woman wearing the same uniform chopping up potatoes on a large worktop in the centre of the room. Her eyes widened in a panic at the sight of people she didn't know but Cole held up his identification and asked where Nicky was. Her grasp of English wasn't as strong as the first maid's. Instead, she shrieked an accented 'Mister Nicky' so loud it made Jessica wince.

The reason for the woman's call soon became obvious as a man with a baseball cap on backwards sauntered out of an adjoining room with a tube of crisps in his hand.

'Pipe down, would you?' he said aggressively before noticing Cole and Jessica in the doorway. 'Who are you?'

Cole introduced himself and Jessica, adding: 'I thought your stepmother told you we were coming?'

Nicky chewed a crisp with his mouth open, laughing. 'Yeah right, mate, I don't have a mum.'

Jessica was trying to place his accent but it was a mixture of everything, part local but with an over-pronunciation she guessed came from his private education. He was exactly how she would have pictured him: short hair gelled forward, expensive clothes and the inbuilt aggression of a pitbull being held on a leash while being poked by a stick.

Everything he said sounded like a threat and his body language might as well have been backed by a tattoo across his forehead reading 'bring it on'.

'We were hoping to talk to you,' Cole said politely.

Nicky nodded, chewing another crisp. Without speaking, he strolled past, leading them through the house, past the entrance into the far wing and then opening the doors into a room that was so big it contained a full-size snooker table with a row of sofas on either side. The decor unsurprisingly matched the rest of the house but a large window at the far end filled the room with daylight.

The teenager had the swagger of someone beyond his years and marched up to a rack of cues, picking one out and offering it to the DCI.

'Fancy a game?'

The chief inspector was clearly flustered in a way Jessica doubted he usually would be by an eighteen-year-old. He stumbled over a reply before declining.

'Do you know who killed Dad?' Nicky asked.

'We're still bringing all of the information together at the moment.'

'So no then?'

'Not yet,' Cole replied.

Nicky was tapping the cue on the edge of the table but even the way he was holding it made it look like a weapon. He told them exactly what he was intending to do with the cue to whoever it was that had killed his dad.

The attitude to authority was something he clearly shared with his dad but Jessica could see there was something far more reckless about him. Nicholas would never have threatened anyone in front of a police officer, he would keep anything like that behind the scenes, while maintaining his public persona.

'If you were doing your jobs properly, you would already know who did it,' Nicky replied after his ticking off, as he picked the balls out of the various pockets and began arranging them on the table.

'This is why we are talking to as many people as we possibly can,' Cole said.

Nicky hammered the white ball into the reds he had just arranged, sending them hurtling across the table. 'Do you think I had something to do with it?'

He hadn't asked as if he was outraged at the suggestion, more as a challenge.

'I didn't say that,' the chief inspector replied, his voice level in a way Jessica could never have managed herself. It was pretty clear why he had come. 'But we need to get a full picture of everything, which is why we are currently talking to as many people as possible.'

Nicky smirked at Jessica, letting her know as if she didn't already that he was trying his best to wind them up. As Jack had pointed out about Tia in the hallway, Nicky was another who most likely couldn't believe his luck. She didn't know what type of relationship he had with his father but, from what she had seen of Nicholas, he didn't seem the type to be close to anyone. Sticking his only child in a boarding school for an extended period hardly gave the impression he was concerned about him. Ruby had told her Nicholas was only interested in winning, not in their son, so it was perhaps no wonder this was how he had turned out.

Jessica initially assumed Cole had come along to stop her saying anything stupid under provocation but, after a little more back and forth, he mentioned something she hadn't expected.

'The other reason we came was to ask you for a favour,' he said, as straight-faced as he had been throughout.

Nicky put the cue on the table and looked up, half in amusement, half bemusement. 'Are you having me on?'

'Not at all.'

Nicky looked towards Jessica, making sure it wasn't a joke, but she had as little idea of what was going on as he did. 'Go on then, Grandad,' he said.

'I take it you saw everything that happened in the city centre a few nights ago?'

Nicky grinned. 'Did you have fun?'

'We were hoping that, given all the good work your father did for the area, you might be able to come to the community centre later today to talk to some of the local young people. I'm sure a lot of them would look up to you.'

Jessica couldn't believe what she was hearing, doubting Nicky had ever been near the estate his father came from. He certainly hadn't spent any time living there.

Nicky took off his cap, smoothing his hair forward. There was a grin apparently fixed to his face as he left them hanging. 'What's in it for me?' he eventually asked.

'We were hoping that with everything your father helped to create that perhaps you would want to build on his good work?'

273

Jessica knew Jack must be annoyed at the sycophantic way he was being forced to grovel and realised orders must have come from the chief superintendent or higher. It was no wonder he hadn't left it to her as she would have stomped in and told Nicky he was going to do it, or she would find a way to make life difficult for him.

He would have laughed in her face.

'I'm a bit busy tonight,' Nicky said. 'There are a few things on TV, or I might take one of the cars out for a drive. They are mine now, after all.'

He winked at Jessica, as if expecting her to laugh along.

'We can't force you to, all I can say is that it would be very much appreciated. We'll make all the arrangements to pick you up if you want, we don't need you to talk for long, it will just be to a lot of people roughly your age. I suspect they're looking for someone new to lead them.'

Jessica sensed Cole had chosen the word 'lead' carefully enough to insinuate there was status to be gained, knowing full well Nicky would never have the gravitas his father had managed to buy for himself.

Nicky's stance didn't change but Jessica could tell he was going to agree moments before he did. The DCI promised someone would be in touch within an hour or two but, as they turned to leave, Nicky called them back.

'You do know I'm taking over, don't you?'

He spoke confidently, picking the cue back up.

'Regardless of what Tia thinks, or anyone else says, this is why Dad brought me back. I'm taking over the clubs, the pubs, the lot.'

Cole didn't respond and Jessica wouldn't have trusted

herself to. Instead they walked out of the house to the car and drove away.

They were barely at the end of the road when Cole pulled over to the side, leaving the engine idling. He looked at Jessica. 'Thoughts?'

'I wouldn't have been so diplomatic if it was me.'

'I know. What else?'

'Someone's going to have to keep a very close eye on him.'

'Exactly.'

27

Although it wouldn't have been her way of doing things, Jessica had to admit that bringing Nicky onto their side, at least temporarily, had somehow done the trick. His speech outside the boxing club his father paid for, along with the myriad of arrests, had calmed things far more than she could have guessed. After a week of recriminations and accusations, it also meant the police's day-to-day workload was more or less back to normal.

That didn't mean they had got anywhere.

No useable fingerprints had been recovered from the sink and the fire door had provided them with nothing either. Hours had been put into scouring the local CCTV footage and, although they had a few hooded figures hurrying around the surrounding streets during the early hours when Nicholas had been killed, there was nothing specifically to say they were anything other than people heading home after a night out.

Jessica stared at herself in the washroom mirror, thinking how everything from the past few weeks had aged her. She had even started wearing make-up to cover the paleness under her eyes, knowing she should visit a doctor soon. The nausea wasn't easing and she felt tired all of the time. Each day, she kept telling herself she would go tomorrow.

'No Adam?' Izzy asked chirpily.

Jessica hadn't heard her enter. 'I thought it was a work-only thing.'

It was a lie but that was what she had told him.

Izzy tilted her head to the side and Jessica knew she wasn't fooling anyone. 'Mal's at home with Amber anyway. This is pretty much the first night I've been out on my own since having her.'

'I wouldn't get too excited.'

The constable waved her hand dismissively. 'Aah, stop moaning. You're the only one who hasn't got dressed up.'

'I was busy at the station and only got here a few minutes ago.'

It was a half-truth; she had only just arrived but, instead of being busy at the station, she had deliberately waited around in order not to have to go home.

'You look nice,' she added quickly, changing the subject.

Izzy did a twirl and was clearly delighted. 'It took me ages to find a dress the same colour as my hair.'

'You *are* very purple,' Jessica conceded. 'But you do know the worst thing to do in a comedy club is stand out?'

'Really?'

'Everyone who comes on stage will single you out.'

'We'll have to sit near the back then. What time's your friend on?'

'Hugo? I don't know, last I think.'

Izzy stepped into a cubicle and locked the door behind her. Jessica was ready to leave when she heard her friend shouting over the top. 'Dave said he's really funny.'

'It depends on whether you mean funny-weird or funny-ha-ha.'

'Have you seen his act?' the yelled reply came.

Jessica realised her friend was happy to conduct a full conversation, regardless of where they were. It was the exact kind of thing she would have done as a teenager with Caroline. She peered closer into the mirror, rubbing her eyes.

'Hugo' was the stage name for a friend named Francis she had met through Dave. 'Not *this* act,' Jessica said. 'But pretty much everything he does is a sort of act.'

'How do you mean?'

Jessica untied her hair, letting it fall behind her, then combed it with her fingers, trying to pull out a few of the knots. 'He's a bit different. You'd really like him.'

'Do you like him?'

'In small doses.'

As she pulled out a loose hair, Jessica could hear Izzy laughing from the cubicle. 'Like Dave then?' Jessica didn't share the enjoyment. Possibly taking her lack of an answer the wrong way, the constable added: 'Cheer up, it could be worse, we could be at a different club tonight.'

After his talk at the boxing club, Nicky had launched himself into his father's business as he had promised. Jessica had no idea if he had any experience, but knew Liam was sensible enough to show him the basics. Driving to work a couple of days previously, Jessica couldn't fail to notice the huge banner hanging across the road advertising the 'grand reopening' of Nicholas's club. There were tackier versions on posters around the city with a silhouette of a half-naked girl and an unfunny play on words, which Jessica knew would attract younger men, and they were also offering buy-one-get-one-free on all dances. Business-wise, Jessica had no doubt it would be a big success but there was something monumentally distasteful in the women's services being offered as if they were a supermarket product. With the business front being relaunched, Jessica couldn't help but wonder how much of his father's other activities Nicky might also be involved in.

Just as Jessica was beginning to feel uncomfortable, she heard the toilet flushing and the cubicle door opened. Izzy breezed towards the sinks and washed her hands. 'Are you all right?' she asked. 'You're not yourself.'

There was so much Jessica could have told her but instead she shook her head, offering a conciliatory, 'I'm just a bit tired.'

Izzy put an arm around her shoulders and led her out of the bathroom, where Jessica gasped in surprise.

'What are you doing here?' she asked, as Caroline approached and hugged her.

Jessica hadn't seen her in a couple of months, with most of the text message conversations they had revolving around the flat. Jessica insisted she didn't want to keep being a burden, with Caroline saying she didn't mind.

'You invited me,' Caroline replied, as Jessica returned the hug.

Caroline was looking as dressed-up as she always did when she went out, wearing a tight bright blue dress exposing her exotic olive skin, her dark hair hanging loosely.

'Did I?'

Caroline stepped back and put her hands on her hips in mock indignation. 'It's nice to be wanted. You emailed a few weeks back, saying you were all going out. You asked if I wanted to catch up.' Jessica suddenly remembered doing just that – it was at a point when she thought Adam would be coming to see Hugo's show.

'Where is Adam?' Caroline asked.

'He couldn't make it,' Jessica blurted out, before realising she had told Izzy a different lie.

'Aw, that's a shame, I've just been catching up with Dave.'

Caroline placed a hand on Rowlands's chest in a way Jessica didn't appreciate. She then said hello to Izzy.

'Is anyone else coming?' she added.

Izzy answered: 'Jason was going to but ended up saying it wasn't his thing, my husband is looking after our baby, Jess says Adam couldn't make it, Dave's perpetually single, so, unless you're bringing anyone, I think this is us.'

Caroline nodded, grinning. 'Right, who wants a drink?'

Dave went for his usual pint and Izzy asked for a glass of wine. Caroline suggested they get a couple of bottles but Jessica said she only wanted a soft drink.

Jessica had only agreed to come because of Izzy. She certainly hadn't fancied an evening with Rowlands, but then it was just as awkward hanging around Adam. The fact Hugo had asked her to watch his new act was a draw too. He had been doing various magic shows around the city regularly since they had met but had never asked her to attend anything. Now he had a regular night at the comedy club on Deansgate Locks, she figured she owed him at least one.

The upstairs bar had largely emptied, everyone making their way down to the lower levels as the show was due to begin. Because they were running a little late, it at least brought about Izzy's wish that they could sit at the back, hopefully out of harm's way.

The place was built into the arches underneath a railway bridge and, although the bar at the top was on street level, the comedy club was underground. It was arranged with the stage at the bottom, tightly packed seats stretching up and around to form an amphitheatre. Jessica had never been before but it took some getting used to as the entire building shook every time a tram passed overhead.

Izzy's theory that sitting at the back wouldn't get them noticed hadn't worked too well as there was a row of dim spotlights above them, which only made her purple dress seem shinier. The compere had certainly noticed, first trying to chat her up from the stage, then joking about her 'grumpy friend', which Jessica didn't appreciate.

Although the early acts were funny, Jessica couldn't bring herself to laugh in anything other than a forced way. Caroline seemed to be enjoying herself – a bit too much when the host was joking about Jessica – and Izzy was definitely having fun.

A row of women at the front who Jessica assumed were part of a hen party were shrieking by the time Hugo stumbled onto the stage.

For the whole time she had known him, Jessica had

never been able to figure out how much of him was an act, and how much was simply him. His hair was long and tied back into a short ponytail and he was wearing a brown striped suit with a blue trainer on one foot and a red one on the other. It would look ridiculous on anyone else but, on Hugo, it kind of worked.

Jessica knew he was a talented magician but the first part of Hugo's act consisted of him getting tricks drastically wrong. He asked a woman a few rows back to choose a card at random from a pack he offered her. As he shuffled nonchalantly with one hand, he dropped the whole deck and then, after she had chosen, he ripped open his shirt to reveal a T-shirt with a three of diamonds on the front. The woman held her queen of spades up for everyone to see.

After that, he asked a man towards the back to think of a number between one and a thousand, then took off his shoe to reveal a number printed on the bottom of his sock which read '666', even though the man had chosen '243'.

Finally, he gave a pad and a pen to a woman in the front row, telling her to draw any animal she wanted. After a bit of back and forth, he took off his other shoe to reveal a picture of an elephant drawn in biro on the bottom of his foot.

It would have been terrific if it wasn't for the fact the woman had drawn a turtle.

At first there were huge amounts of laughter, largely because of his confused facial expressions, but it soon reached the point where the audience were becoming restless, wondering if he was genuinely that bad.

At the rear of the stage was a table that had been there

since the start, with a yellow-headed puppet that had massive eyes, wild spiky hair and a large flapping mouth sitting on top of it. Hugo crossed to the back and launched into a ventriloquist act with the puppet he told them was named Dom. Hugo soon showed how funny he could be with lightning-quick responses from Dom tamely insulting audience members and almost always making himself the butt of the joke. It drew huge laughs and Jessica couldn't stop herself from chuckling, mainly because of the ridiculous sight of the puppet talking in a broad Mancunian accent as Hugo shifted seamlessly from that into his own.

Hugo eventually returned to the front of the stage where he bowed and took the applause, although Jessica hadn't been overly impressed with the actual tricks. As he was about to leave the stage, Dom's voice shouted loudly: 'Oi, dickhead, we're not done yet.'

Even though Hugo was nowhere near it, Dom's mouth flapped open, leading to gasps and laughs in equal measure. Hugo's lips weren't moving but the voice was coming from the direction of the puppet.

Hugo played it straight and Jessica knew from experience that she shouldn't have doubted him. The pair argued back and forth, before Dom demanded someone competent be brought onto the stage. He continued to insult various people with their hands up, before finally settling on 'the purple one at the back'.

Izzy got a big cheer as she carefully made her way to the stage. Hugo asked her to tell the crowd her name and then got scolded by Dom for touching her bottom – even though he clearly hadn't.

Dom continued to insult Hugo, with Jessica trying to see if there was anyone else behind the table, or if there were strings somehow controlling his mouth. The puppet said Izzy was making him feel 'hot' and asked her to help him out. Jessica could tell the constable was nervous, but also finding the epilogue hilarious, as, on command, she removed Dom's shirt and shoes to reveal the queen of spades stitched into his chest, the number '243' on one foot, and a turtle on the other.

The grand finale coincided with a tram thundering overhead but the applause was far louder as Hugo bowed. Izzy made her way up the steps beaming and clapping, while Dom called her a 'fat cow' as soon as her back was turned. Hugo walked to the curtain and took a final bow, only for a pair of pink knickers to fly over the top of his head. He picked them up and gave a thumbs-up to the crowd, pocketing them and walking off.

The compere could barely make himself heard as he wished everyone a good night since it was clear who had stolen the show. Izzy couldn't stop laughing, telling everyone around them that she had no idea how Dom was managing to talk, let alone how Hugo could have possibly brought off the rest of the trick. Caroline kept saying it was the best thing she had ever seen.

'Do we get to meet him now?' Izzy asked Rowlands excitedly.

'Jess?' Dave said, raising his eyes, and speaking to her for the first time since they had been in the classroom together.

'Lead the way,' Jessica replied, largely because she

suspected Izzy would have bashed the door down to get to him anyway.

Rowlands had clearly been before and led them through a side door after swapping a handshake with the security officer, who knew his name. They didn't have to worry about where to find Hugo as the half-dozen women who had been in the front row were hammering on a door at the far end. Dave reopened the side door and told the security officer, who radioed for help, leading to a scene Jessica wouldn't have believed if she hadn't watched it herself – seven burly men physically having to eject six middle-aged women from the building, as they thrashed and kicked in an effort to get through the dressing-room door.

As the security officer came back and told them they were clear to see Hugo, Jessica touched his arm to get his attention. 'Were they groupies?' she asked.

The man laughed. 'They come here every week. Why do you think I have to stand here? After the show, they went all the way upstairs, then went through the staff toilets to get back down here. They'll be waiting out front when you all leave.'

'Really?'

The man laughed again. 'Whatever you do, love, don't walk out of here holding his hand, they'll tear you to pieces.'

Jessica had no intention of walking out holding Hugo's hand but the fact he had fans who were so devoted they couldn't bear to see him with another female was astounding. Caroline, who had met him at her wedding

285

and a Christmas meal, seemed star-struck. But it was Izzy in particular who could barely contain her excitement as Dave knocked on the dressing-room door and Hugo welcomed them in.

Hugo seemed oblivious to the attention and was sitting cross-legged on a table watching a cartoon on the television while playing with an abacus. Jessica's gaze was drawn towards Dom, who was sitting on top of a guitar case in the corner. He was lovely and soft as she picked him up, searching for anything that could have made his mouth move independently. As she turned it around, Dom's voice snapped: 'Oi, get yer hand out of my arse'. The puppet's mouth hadn't moved, but Jessica still jumped, looking around to see everyone, including Rowlands, grinning at her.

'Very clever,' she said, crossing the room and playfully punching Hugo on the arm.

As she knew he would, Hugo shrugged his way through Izzy and Caroline's questions, as if the entire act had been something that had just happened, continuing to focus on the abacus.

Just when it seemed as if no one was going to get any sense out of him, Hugo hopped up and took his shoes off before moving across to the sofa in the corner.

'I'm going camping next weekend,' he said with no prior indication that might be what was on his mind. 'Who fancies it?'

Dave shook his head, although said he might another time. For a moment, Jessica thought she was going to have to remind Izzy she was married, such was her apparent infatuation, but she reluctantly said she had a child and husband at home. Caroline, on the other hand, was more than up for it and was talking about what she should pack when Hugo looked across the room. 'Jess?'

'I don't do camping.'

'Why not?'

'Because I have a perfectly good roof to live under.'

'Come on, Jess, it'll be fun,' Caroline pleaded.

Jessica had been friends with her for a long time and knew she was definitely not outdoor-minded. When they had been teenagers, she wouldn't even cross the field to get to college in case she got muddy, instead making them both walk the full way around. Jessica reminded her of that but was met with a very mature raspberry noise.

'Right then, it's just me and you,' Caroline said with a smile that Hugo hadn't appeared to notice. Instead he was trying to clean the biro-drawn elephant from his skin by licking his thumb and wiping vigorously. Jessica was impressed at the level of detail given it had been drawn in pen on the bottom of his foot.

Izzy's raised eyebrows confirmed to Jessica that they were each thinking the same thing when it came to Caroline's excitement about time alone with Hugo.

Jessica excused herself and made her way upstairs. One of the barmen was sweeping the now-empty club but he didn't question her presence as she entered the toilets. She was washing her face and hands when the door went and she turned to see Izzy again.

'I'm not stalking you around the toilets of Britain, I promise,' she said, slightly slurring her words. Jessica guessed it was the first time she'd had any serious amount of alcohol in a long time.

'If I was going to go cottaging with any girl in Manchester, then rest assured it would be you.'

Izzy laughed and walked across to Jessica, pulling her into a hug. 'I've had a brilliant night,' she giggled. 'I wish I could just take him home and keep him in a cupboard, then bring him out for my own amusement.'

'I think you'll have to fight Caroline for him, not to mention his groupies outside.'

As she tried to laugh, Jessica felt her stomach lurch but she managed to stifle the heave, instead turning it into something close to a hiccup.

'I know I keep asking you but are you all right?' Izzy asked.

'Just a dodgy tea last night.'

'Come on, Jess . . .'

'What?'

'Everything's always a dodgy meal or a lack of sleep, or you've been drinking water all morning, which is why you're in the toilets so much. You can't think no one's noticed?'

'Who's been talking?' Jessica had replied more aggressively than she meant to. When Izzy didn't answer, she asked again, demanding a response.

Izzy reached out and stroked Jessica's hair away from her face. 'No one, Jess, just me. I'm worried about you.'

'Oh . . .'

'You've got to talk to someone about whatever's going on.'

Jessica blinked quickly to stop the tears and thought about telling her friend about Dave's admission, then about Adam, before deciding to mention the biggest thing on her mind.

'I'm late,' she said quietly, staring at the floor.

'What for?'

Jessica didn't have to repeat herself before Izzy gasped and pulled her in for a hug.

28

Jessica quickly regretted saying anything to Izzy. Her friend had jumped to the obvious conclusion, telling her to go to a doctor or, at the absolute least, buy a testing kit. Jessica pointed out she had been late in the past, especially when she was young, but the constable refused to listen, asking question after question, including whether Adam knew. He was the biggest reason Jessica had held off from finding out one way or the other as she didn't want anything to do with him – or his blonde woman.

By the time she arrived home, Adam was sleeping but Jessica lay awake, telling herself everything could be explained because she was run down by the long hours and stressful job.

The following morning, she made sure she got up before Adam's alarm went off and got dressed in the living room before going to the station. She had a brief chat with Cole before heading out again, making sure there was no danger of running into either of the constables she was trying to avoid.

Most of their leads had gone nowhere, with nothing to link Oliver to Kayleigh to Nicholas. They had been diligently checking alibis of people who might have it in for him, despite the length of the list, but anyone realistic, including Nicky and Tia, had been accounted for. The forensics team had struggled to salvage anything useable from the scene of the businessman's death and Jessica knew the day was approaching when she would have to revisit Owen and Gabrielle Gordon to apologise for getting precisely nowhere.

Meanwhile, the reopening of Nicholas's club had caused problems the night before – but only because there were so many people trying to get in. Someone who Jessica assumed was Liam had hired extra security for the evening, but they had called for police when a group of men turned aggressive after being told the club was full. Nothing had been damaged and no arrests made but, because it was the council's job to decide whether licences should be awarded, one of the councillors had requested a member of the police visit the newly refurbished club to give their opinion. It certainly wasn't Jessica's job but after hearing what had gone on, she volunteered anyway, if only to get out of the station for as long as she could get away with.

When she arrived, Liam was waiting at the front door, dressed smartly in a suit. 'Good to see you again,' he said, sounding genuine.

As soon as he opened the door, Jessica could see that things had changed. The wall that had created the initial corridor had been ripped out, so there was one large reception room with a new bar at the rear. Scott, who was wearing a matching suit, was restocking the fridges, and acknowledged Liam as he walked through.

'What's with the gear?' Jessica asked, nodding at Liam's suit.

'Nicky's idea.'

'Really?'

'Oh yes, he's full of ideas . . .'

Liam didn't sound completely impressed by it but Jessica conceded that the redesign was a large improvement on what had been there before. The red carpets and walls had gone, replaced by a subtler ivory colour that made everything seem less tacky. Well, less Turkish knocking shop, more IKEA beige.

Liam led her through to the main area, which was styled in the same way. The long bar had been taken out, replaced by something half the size, and the far end curtained off. Nicky certainly hadn't wasted any time making the place his own.

'What's in there?' Jessica asked, nodding towards the curtain.

'Private areas.'

Jessica wished she hadn't mentioned it. Liam sat her down and got her a glass of water, talking her through what had happened on their opening night. Aside from some over-promotion, it sounded as if they had done everything more or less as well as they could, with the extra security officers largely dealing with things. If it hadn't been for a particularly drunk group of lads, no one would have been any the wiser.

As Liam appeared happy to talk, Jessica thought she would try her luck. 'How's Nicky?' she asked.

Liam glanced towards the security door before answering. 'He's not his father.'

'How do you mean?'

'He has different ideas, dangerous ideas. His dad knew what to leave at home and what to bring here.'

The statement was cryptic but Liam seemed to realise he had said too much, quickly correcting himself before Jessica could follow it up. 'He's a kid, he doesn't know how things work. He wants everything done instantly and doesn't understand they take time. I'll give him one thing, he's full of ideas, but for every good 'un, there are half-a-dozen dreadful ones – like shrinking the bar, for instance. That's where all the money comes from.'

'Aren't you the manager?'

Liam laughed. 'Yeah, right. I'm not sure I'll be around much longer. He'll drive this place out of business. Whatever you might think about what goes on in the private areas here – and it's probably not what you think – the fact is it's very profitable. You don't need to go throwing around drinks promotions or free dances or whatever. This isn't that kind of business – he'd be better off at one of the smaller pubs figuring out how everything works.'

'Why does he focus his work here, then, if he's running the whole empire?'

The obvious answer, especially for an eighteen-year-old, was the girls, but Jessica suspected this was also where the 'real' work went on.

Liam gave nothing away. He was good at playing things down, another reason Jessica guessed Nicholas had given him the job. 'This is where his dad worked, I guess?'

'Doesn't Tia get a say?'

'Pfft. I don't know who'd be worse but it doesn't

matter anyway. When Nicky came in shouting the odds the other week, he said she was taking the house, while he got the business. For whatever reason, it was what he wanted.'

'Where is he, then?'

Liam shook his head. 'Oh, he's in the back. He'll be watching all of this.' He nodded at a camera above the security door pointing towards them. 'There are cameras everywhere now. The kid's paranoid whoever killed his dad will come back for him. He doesn't realise his dad was a somebody, but he's a nobody.'

Jessica hadn't completely understood how devoted Liam was to his former boss until the way he phrased his final sentence. He was clearly still full of admiration for Nicholas, with Nicky an inconvenience he hadn't got around to walking out on yet.

'I may as well go say hello,' Jessica said, standing up.

'He doesn't usually like visitors.'

'I couldn't care less, I'm supposed to be making sure there's not going to be any more trouble so let's go.'

Jessica marched towards the door, even though she didn't know the code. Liam hurried after her, pushing in front and shielding the numbers with his hand as he unlocked it and held it open for her.

'Don't say I didn't warn you,' he muttered.

Jessica crossed the hallway and pulled the door handle down on Nicholas's old office, shunting it open. In contrast to the rest of what she had seen, this area looked identical to before, the familiar row of filing cabinets on one wall and the framed newspapers on the other. Nicky had been facing away as she entered, not watching the monitors as Liam had suggested. As the door opened he spun around, swearing loudly at her to get out. Unlike when she had visited Nicholas, Jessica wasn't trying to be provocative but the first thing she noticed was that Nicky was wearing an identical suit to the other two men. He was covering his mouth with his hand, eyes wide and panicky.

'Are you all right?' Jessica asked.

Nicky looked angry but didn't take his hand away. 'Yes, piss off,' he shouted, although it was muffled.

Jessica was about to turn when blood began dripping from Nicky's hand onto the desk.

'Get out,' he shouted again, although that only sent more blood spitting across the desk. When it was clear Jessica wasn't leaving, he eventually reached across to pick up a tissue, revealing a mouthful of blood.

Nicky dabbed inside his lips with the tissues, eyes full of anger that she hadn't left.

'What did you eat?' she asked.

Nicky threw a blood-covered tissue towards her. 'Eat? You stupid bitch. I didn't eat anything, I've just got bleeding gums. Now get out, you're not supposed to be here.'

As he threw another tissue at her, Jessica walked backwards out of the room, closing the door and moving into the main part of the club.

Liam was sitting on a bar stool. 'I did warn you,' he said.

Jessica shook her head. 'He was bleeding.'

Liam shot up, about to rush to the door, but Jessica held out a restraining hand.

'Nothing's happened, well, I don't think so. He says his gums are bleeding.'

Liam eyed her suspiciously before sitting again. 'His dad was the same. He'd get nosebleeds all the time and sometimes there would be dried bits of blood around his mouth. At first I thought he was eating all sorts of weird stuff. It's not the kind of thing you'd ever ask about but it got to the point where you couldn't ignore it.'

'What did he say?'

'Not much, he said he had some disease.'

'What disease?'

Liam stuck out his bottom lip, puffing loudly. 'Von something or other. I couldn't tell you.'

'Did he say what it did?'

He shook his head dismissively. 'You met him, would you have wanted to ask? Do you think that was what killed him?'

Considering he'd been suffocated, Jessica didn't think that at all but she did have an idea that made Liam's question not quite as stupid as it sounded.

She said goodbye and hurried to her car, taking her mobile phone out of her pocket and wishing she could think of a better way to get things done. Adam answered on the second ring with a cheery 'Jess'.

Jessica didn't bother with niceties. 'Do you know any doctors at the university who might specialise in blood disorders?'

'Why? You're okay, aren't you?'

'I'm fine, it's not about me – I just need to speak to someone quickly.'

'We've got a couple of people who might be able to help. If you drive over to the uni, I'll see if I can get someone to talk to you.'

'Great, text me the names so I can go straight to them.'

'Don't you want to stop by for a coffee?'

'I don't have time, sorry.'

Jessica was about to hang up but Adam said, 'Jess?'

'What?'

'We've not had an evening together in ages . . .'

'I've been busy.'

'Are you going to be home later?'

'Why?'

She heard him take a deep breath before responding. 'I think we need to talk.'

Jessica knew it was the moment she had been waiting for. She swallowed hard, told him it was fine, then hung up.

The academic Adam had set Jessica up with ticked every stereotypical box you could hope for if you were trying to picture a professor. He had black velvet patches on the elbows of his brown corduroy jacket and wild grey hair which seemed to be in a constant battle to prove the laws of gravity didn't actually exist.

She didn't know what Adam had told him but by the time Jessica arrived in the reception of the university, a man was already waiting for her, springing to his feet and shaking her hand vigorously. He introduced himself as Professor Kenyon, although he assured Jessica she could call him Ken. Jessica wondered if that was a nickname relating to his surname or if he was genuinely called Kenneth Kenyon, then figured she didn't want to know the answer.

Ken led her to the cafe and insisted on buying her a coffee, despite her protests. She didn't know the technical term, especially as he was the supposed medical expert, but her layman's opinion was that he was slightly mad.

He did at least appear to know his stuff though. After finally settling at a table, Jessica sipped her coffee as he enthused about the jam roly poly and custard he had bought himself. As soon as she mentioned a blood disorder that was called 'von something', the man's eyes lit up.

'Von Willebrand disease,' he said matter-of-factly, shovelling a spoonful of custard-covered cake into his mouth.

He started to speak about a Finnish scientist but Jessica hurried him on to what concerned her. 'What actually is it?' she asked.

Ken spoke far too quickly and, before she knew it, he was talking to her about platelets. She interrupted, asking him to put it into language she could understand.

Unperturbed, he took another spoonful of custard, before having another go. 'When you get a cut, the blood clumps together and forms a scab,' he said, which Jessica nodded along with. 'When you have von Willebrand's, your blood doesn't clot in the same way, which means you continue to bleed for longer.'

'How long?'

'It depends on how serious it is.'

'How do you catch it?'

'It's usually inherited from a parent.' Ken used the spoon to slice himself another piece of cake, blowing on it, before putting it in his mouth.

'So if your dad has it, you'll get it?'

Ken shook his head, still chewing. 'Not necessarily, it's about a fifty per cent chance.'

'So if one child has it, another one won't?'

He looked at her sideways as if she was a student who had asked a stupid question, although the smear of custard around his lips didn't give him the gravitas he was perhaps trying for. 'Not at all, it's like tossing a coin. Each time you flip it, it has half a chance of coming down tails, regardless of what happened last time.'

'So two children could both end up with it?'

Ken picked up the final piece of cake. 'Exactly, but not just two. You could have ten children and all of them inherit it – or none of them. It's an equal chance every time.'

Jessica nodded, fairly sure she understood, and watched while the man finished his dessert before glancing towards the food-serving area, presumably wondering if there was any more.

'I met someone who I think had it,' Jessica said. 'He got this bad nosebleed.'

'Sounds about right.'

'Would it be right that his son's gums could bleed?'

Ken nodded emphatically. 'Probably, yes, if he had inherited it. You can have some really impressive bruises too that are all sorts of colours. It can create problems during surgery of course because it's hard to stop the bleeding, while aspirin is off limits. It's particularly bad for females, for obvious reasons.'

Jessica squirmed uncomfortably, thinking he couldn't have picked a worse time to tell her that. She took a notebook out of her jacket, ensuring she had asked everything she wanted to. She then got Ken to spell out the name of the disease so she could look it up herself.

As she stood to leave, Jessica realised there was something else. 'Can I ask you one final thing?' she asked politely.

The man was running his finger around the edge of the bowl but looked up, grinning widely. 'Of course, dear.'

'Is your first name Kenneth?'

'Oh no, of course not.' He looked at her with the same 'are you stupid look' he had before, although she had little time to query why he had asked her to call him by a nickname when he added: 'It's Kendall.'

'Kendall Kenyon?'

He licked the remaining custard from his fingers. 'That's right,' he confirmed, as if it was the most natural revelation. 'Perhaps you've read one of my theory papers?'

Jessica shook her head and said her goodbyes, thinking that, if that's what the custard did to you in this place, she had made a wise decision turning it down.

*

Kendall's information had given Jessica something to think through but without checking more details, she only had the inklings of a theory. She would much rather have continued to work but, seeing as Adam had apparently chosen tonight as the night he was going to finally come clean, Jessica figured it was as good a time as any to get the showdown out of the way.

Wanting to avoid both Dave and Izzy, she went to a restaurant around the corner from the university and treated herself to some chicken and chips, at least wanting to confront Adam on a full stomach.

She ate slowly, keeping an eye on the clock as she wanted to ensure he would get home before her. Usually she would have gone out of her way to avoid the main roads but now Jessica willingly sat in the evening traffic, crawling a few car lengths at a time.

By the time she had parked and taken the lift up to their floor, Jessica was ready for whatever Adam might have to say. She had worked out a few different speeches, some more venomous than others but ultimately she wanted to tell him that she understood. As much as she hated him for lying and going behind her back, she couldn't deny that she was hard to live with. She deliberately worked long and late; she didn't sleep well, she had a short attention span, she swore a lot and it was her who had originally broken up with him a few years ago.

Whatever he had done, she accepted she deserved at least some of it.

Jessica took a deep breath and entered the flat, ready for

anything except for the scene in front of her. Adam was sitting on the sofa grinning, as the blonde woman from the restaurant sat next to him cradling his face in her hand.

29

Although Jessica had been prepared to forgive him and go their separate ways, she wasn't ready for the outright slap in the face of him inviting the other woman around. Jessica stood, staring in furious disbelief as the pair gazed into each other's eyes.

'I think yours are darker,' the woman said, before Adam noticed Jessica in the doorway.

'Jess, you're back,' he said, jumping up from the sofa and bounding across the room.

Jessica hadn't closed the door but she was glaring daggers at him. 'Who the hell is that?' she shouted.

Adam was within touching distance of her but took a step back in surprise at the spite in her voice. 'Jess . . . ?'

Jessica didn't wait for him to say any more, turning and running out of the door and along the corridor. She hoped the lift would still be there but as she pressed the button, the annoying voice taunted: 'lift coming . . . up'. Seeing Adam racing towards her, Jessica stormed through the door next to the elevator, rushing down the stairs two at a time. She could hear him calling after her but wasn't interested in whatever he had to say.

By the time she reached the bottom, his voice had grown silent and she barged through the double doors, heading towards her car. She was practically running as she rounded the corner to find Adam, who had presumably waited for the lift, sitting on her car bonnet. Blinking back tears, she ran at him, ignoring his outstretched arms and punching him hard in the chest. He staggered backwards, his eyes telling the story of surprise.

'Jess . . . ?' he protested again, but she wasn't ready for excuses.

'Why did you bring her here?' she shouted, pushing him away as he tried to reach for her.

'Georgia?'

'I don't care what her name is – I saw you. I followed you that night you were working late when you went out with her instead. I sat and watched you chat and laugh in that restaurant.'

Adam's eyes widened as he moved a loose strand of hair away from his face. 'It's not what you think.'

'I saw you going into the hotel afterwards.'

Jessica swung an arm out towards him, catching him in the sternum before he reached out and grabbed both of her hands to restrain her.

Jessica struggled but his grip was firmer than she had ever known it. She wanted to be strong but instead she felt the tears streaming down her face.

'Jess, I was only checking the room where she was staying, honestly, that's all.'

'Why were you there at all?'

Adam continued to grip her wrists as she flailed. 'Because she's my sister. Well, half-sister . . .'

Jessica finally stopped struggling as Adam released her.

She couldn't stop the tears but shoved her hair out of her face. 'You're an only child.'

Jessica remembered standing in the kitchen of Adam's grandmother's house when he first told her the story of how his mother had died during childbirth. His father had killed himself not long afterwards because he was only interested in his wife, not his son.

It was that day she knew she was in love with him.

There were tears in Adam's eyes as he responded. 'That's why I didn't tell you before – I didn't know if it was true either.'

As she leant against her car, Jessica couldn't stop crying. She used her sleeves to try to dry her eyes but the tears kept coming. Eventually Adam pulled his jumper over his head and handed it to her. 'Just don't blow your nose,' he said with a forced laugh.

The lump in Jessica's throat was so large that she could barely breathe, let alone speak. In her head, she was trying to put the pieces together but it didn't seem real.

'I had a letter out of the blue a little while ago,' Adam said. 'You never know nowadays if it's someone trying to scam you. It was from a woman named Georgia who had an address in Bath. She said her father had recently died and she had been sorting through his things. She found a letter that had come from her mother. She was brought up all these years thinking her mum had abandoned her.'

Jessica used the jumper to wipe her eyes but the tears continued to come. 'How did she find you?'

'The letter came from someone named Janet Boyes, which was my mum's maiden name. It told Georgia's dad to stop contacting her but because her full name was there, Georgia started digging into things and found a marriage notice for my mum and dad. When my mum died, it was in the papers, so she discovered a son named Adam Compton and started trying to find me. She saw on the university's website there was someone with my name working there, so wrote to me on the off-chance.'

Jessica remembered the envelope she had found in the bin.

'The computer . . . ?'

Adam reached out an arm and although Jessica didn't allow him to embrace her, she didn't push him away either. After letting his arm drop again, he sighed and apologised.

'When I got that letter, it had an email address and phone number at the bottom. I wanted to believe it was true but Georgia didn't know all the details either. We started emailing each other, piecing together the timeline of what might have happened but I suppose it was a bit too much for me. I've spent my whole life thinking I was on my own and then this happened. I wasn't ready to talk to you because I wasn't ready to admit it to myself either.'

Jessica was also an only child and tried to think how she might react if someone turned up claiming to be related to her. Would she keep everything quiet until she was absolutely sure? She tried to tell herself she wouldn't, but the fact she hadn't yet told Adam what she had told Izzy only proved she was no different.

'So is she actually your sister?'

Adam smiled in the way that had first drawn her to

him; it changed his face from being someone she would look at and forget into *her* Adam.

'Yes, she's three years older than me and was born in Manchester. Her dad took her down south around a month before my parents got married.'

'Why?'

'We don't really know. In the letter she found, it's just from our mum telling her dad never to contact her again. It sounds like they had some sort of affair. For whatever reason, our mum didn't want her in the same way my dad . . . didn't want me.'

Adam's voice cracked as he finished his sentence and Jessica reached out towards him, pulling him towards her as he grasped at her.

'I'm so sorry,' he sobbed.

Jessica wanted to apologise herself but the lump was bulging in the back of her throat, tears streaming down her face.

It felt like hours before Adam finally released her, taking her hand. 'We should probably introduce you properly.'

Jessica snorted half a laugh, realising what a horrendous scene she had made. 'She's going to hate me already, isn't she?'

Adam shrugged. 'I've seen you make worse first impressions.'

Jessica giggled, more tears running down her face. She started to walk towards the lifts but realised Adam hadn't moved and was still holding her hand. She turned to face him but his expression had changed as he looked into her eyes.

'Do you trust me?' he asked.

His voice sounded so aggrieved that Jessica didn't know where to look.

'Yes . . . I mean . . .' She paused, trying to find the words, before admitting: 'I don't know what I mean.'

Adam nodded, knowing she was being honest. 'We've got to trust each other.'

'You didn't trust me enough to tell me about Georgia when your letter arrived.'

'I know.'

They stared at each other before Adam cracked first, his giggling soon spreading to Jessica.

'I thought I was coming home for you to break up with me,' she said as they walked slowly across the car park.

'Why would I do that?'

'I don't know, that's just what I thought. Isn't that what "we have to talk" is code for?'

Adam shrugged. 'Can we make a pact to tell each other things in future?'

Jessica hesitated as Adam pressed the button for the lift. The voice told them it was 'coming down'. 'I've got something to tell you,' Jessica said.

'Anything.'

Adam squeezed her hand to tell her he meant it.

'Can you trust me for a day or two?'

The lift doors pinged open as Adam pulled her close and kissed her on the top of the head. 'Whenever you're ready.'

Adam stepped into the lift but this time Jessica kept

hold of his hand, not moving. 'I've got something I need to do,' she said.

'For work?'

'Yes.'

'Do you have to do it tonight?'

Jessica thought of what she had found out that day and who she needed to see next. The photos of Oliver and Kayleigh's bodies flickered through her mind.

'I don't know, maybe.'

'Can you come and meet Georgia first and do everything tomorrow?'

Jessica kept hold of his hand, thinking of all the times she had run off, prioritising work ahead of Adam and Caroline, not to mention her parents. Adam's eyes were asking her to put him first, even if it was just for this one time. As he let go of her hand, Jessica stepped into the lift a moment before the doors pinged closed behind her.

Jessica set her alarm for early the next morning but it was Adam who eventually woke her with a gentle shake and whisper in her ear.

'What time is it?' Jessica mumbled, rolling towards him.

When Adam told her, Jessica kicked the covers off, dashing towards the wardrobe.

'Why didn't my alarm go off?'

'It did.'

Jessica had a blouse halfway off the hanger as she turned to face him.

'You slept through it,' he added.

'Why didn't you wake me?'

'Because you needed a rest.'

Jessica was ready to protest but knew he was right – everyone had been telling her that and for the first time in weeks, she had slept completely through the night. Even hearing the words made her feel more alert, as if the realisation she had slept well was more invigorating than the sleep itself.

'Do you want to talk tonight?' Adam asked, as Jessica reached into the wardrobe.

'Maybe.'

'Last night didn't go so bad in the end, did it?'

Jessica dressed quickly as she spoke. 'When is she coming back up north?'

'I'm not sure. We could visit her?'

Not knowing exactly what the day might entail, Jessica crouched and hunted for a sensible pair of shoes. 'I've never been to Bath.'

'Me neither but Grandma came from that area.'

'Aren't they all farmers around that way?'

Adam laughed and put on a fake accent. 'Ooh arr. I guess we'll find out.'

By the time he kissed her goodbye, Jessica was fully dressed, phone in hand, ready for the day.

As Jessica sat in Eleanor Sexton's living room, she realised she should have been prepared for the questions the woman might ask, instead of focusing on what she needed to find out. The look on the woman's face was more one of bemusement than pleasure but Jessica couldn't have held it against her if she had been pleased.

'He's really dead?' Eleanor said, cradling a mug of tea exactly as she had the last time Jessica had visited.

'Yes he is.'

'Did you see him?'

'Yes.'

Eleanor paused for a moment, thinking, then she smiled. 'I saw it in the papers and heard it on the news but he was just one of those guys you think can't die. I know it sounds mad.'

Jessica understood what she meant. 'I've got one other thing I need to ask,' she said.

'Okay.'

'When you and Kayleigh left Nicholas's casino, which of you suggested that you needed a way out?'

Eleanor scratched her head, narrowing her eyes. 'Why?'

'It might be important.'

'I don't know, maybe me?'

'Really? Think about it. Did Kayleigh come to you to ask for help getting away, or did you see she was in trouble?'

'I suppose I knew she was in trouble, so I suggested we left.'

'And it was your suggestion to give her money to pay off the debts?'

Eleanor shook her head. 'I don't remember. It might have been the type of thing where she said she still owed him money, so I offered.'

'But it was her telling you she was in trouble that made you offer?'

'I suppose . . . but it was my idea after that.'

Jessica knew the key to getting your own way was to make the other person do what you wanted, all the time thinking everything was their idea. She didn't point out that suspicion but could not stop thinking about what Eleanor had told her the last time she was there.

'. . . With the customers and men, he'd break your bones – or get one of his men to. He'd hurt you, or threaten to hurt you to make you pay. With us women . . .'

Jessica asked the only question she needed the answer to: 'Could she have been pregnant?'

Eleanor sounded shocked. Evidently the idea had never crossed her mind. 'Kayleigh?'

'It sounds as if everything happened pretty suddenly.'

'It did but . . .'

'How often did you see her in the year or so after you left the casino?'

Jessica could see the pieces falling into place as Eleanor took her time before responding. 'Not much. We stayed friends but it was usually through letters. We met a few times but not that often.'

Jessica nodded and stood to leave before Eleanor asked the obvious question. 'If she was pregnant, where's the baby now?'

30

As Garry Ashford held the lift door open for Jessica, she told him her one demand. 'Keep that Ian guy away from me because if he looks me up and down, even from a distance, I might just punch him repeatedly until his stupid face is no longer shiny.'

'I would pay to see that,' Garry replied.

Jessica didn't smile, raising her eyebrows to tell him she was serious.

'All right, fine,' he conceded. 'But he does work here and you don't.'

'I'm on official police business.'

'Really?'

'Officially unofficial. Either way, keep him away from me.'

As they emerged onto the main floor of the *Manchester Morning Herald*'s newsroom/bomb site, Garry led Jessica around the edge, telling her to wait in an office. Five minutes later, he returned to say Ian had been dispatched to an address on the far side of the city 'that may or may not exist' to interview a woman 'who also may or may not exist'.

'Either way,' he added, 'you've probably got an hour and a half before he gets back.'

Garry showed Jessica to a store room at the farthest end

of the floor. At first, she thought it was packed with junk, but her heart sank as he announced this was the paper's official archive.

The room smelled of wet shoes and the brown colour of the stacks of newspapers seemed to have somehow seeped into the dull, faded yellow walls. A fan whizzed overhead but the sound was more of an annoyance than the breeze was a help. Everywhere Jessica looked, there were either unlabelled boxes, heaps of papers, or tables piled on top of each other. It was the sort of place you ended up visiting when someone had died three months previously and no one had noticed.

'Are you going to help?' Jessica asked.

'I'm pretty busy.'

'I wouldn't ask if it wasn't important.'

'Haven't we done this before?'

Jessica grinned as she had been thinking the same. 'Not quite, I'm only after one thing, I even have a roughish date for you. I can call you my sidekick if you like?'

Garry cracked: 'It could be anywhere – and that's if we even have the correct issues. This place isn't complete, it's just what moved with us when we switched floors.'

'All the more reason for you to help . . .'

He rolled his eyes but Jessica knew he was going to give in, offering him her most girly 'thank you'.

After Garry returned from delegating work, she told him exactly what she was after and they began checking through the piles. Some were in date order, others had seemingly been stacked on whatever surface was closest. Jessica instantly discounted anything that looked too new, trying to be careful not to make too much of a mess. Within fifteen minutes, Garry had identified a heap of around two hundred papers from the relevant time period. Jessica helped him clear a space on the floor and they sat opposite each other, flicking through them one at a time.

'This is a bit like a fort I built when I was a kid,' Garry said.

Jessica was sitting cross-legged but looked up at the newspapers towering above her, the gap they had created just wide enough for one person to fit through.

'How old are you?'

Jessica took a newspaper from the stack and scanned the front page before turning inside. Although she was fairly sure the story she was looking for would be on a front page, she didn't want to take the chance and have to check everything again. Garry was flicking through another issue, skimming his hand along each page before turning.

Not looking up, Jessica spoke softly. 'Can I tell you something?'

'I guess . . .'

He didn't sound sure.

'Dave told me he loved me.'

Garry stopped, holding the paper open as Jessica felt him staring at her. She continued skimming, not looking up.

'Dave Rowlands?'

'Yeah, your mate.'

It had been a point of contention between them that Dave had been Garry's source for a series of stories a few years before. The journalist had never officially told her that they had been friends but Jessica had dug into their university records to discover the pair of them – plus Hugo – were all students together.

'I suppose it took him long enough.'

'You knew?'

Garry took another paper from the pile and opened it. 'Everyone he hung around with knew.'

Jessica thought of the looks between Dave and Izzy and the way Chloe had questioned her the previous Christmas over whether they had ever had a relationship.

'Everyone?'

'Everyone.'

It was Garry's turn to keep his eyes to the floor as Jessica stared at him. He had a large grin on his face as he continued to look through the paper. 'What's so funny?'

'Like I said: I'm surprised it took him this long.'

Jessica felt confused. To her, the constable had always been a mate, someone she would joke around with, take the mickey out of, and go out for a pint with. She had never seen him as anything more.

'What do you mean?' she asked.

Garry stopped and looked at her. 'It's always been you, Jess. Even when we'd be in the pub, he would be going on about work, but it was only ever you, not the job. At first it was "She's given me all this stuff to do", then it was "She's always off doing her own thing" and then, gradually, it became "She's the only one who bloody does anything" and so on.'

Jessica was too shocked to speak because she could

suddenly see it too. She could remember a boy at primary school whom she had spent three years tormenting – but the only reason she had done it was because she liked him. At that age, there was never anything serious in it. To an adult, she could see it was different. For her, winding Dave up was a part of friendship, for him it was clearly more.

'I never knew . . .'

Garry put the paper aside and picked up another. He sounded more serious when he spoke again. 'You shouldn't hold it against him if you don't feel the same. He's a good guy.'

Jessica said nothing, not knowing how to reply, turning her attention back to the paper in front of her before reaching for another.

'Do you remember a few years ago,' Garry went on. 'You were in trouble at work and I wrote that profile piece that ended up getting you off the hook?'

'You did all right out of that too,' Jessica pointed out. Garry's byline had been everywhere and he ultimately got a promotion from it.

'Who do you think asked me to write that?' Garry replied.

They both reached for a new paper at the same time, watching each other. Garry clearly saw what she was thinking and fell silent. Jessica didn't want to respond.

With the two of them working quickly and the papers stacked in something approaching a logical order, she was surprised by how easily they found what she was after. The enormous photograph on the front page helped, Jessica noticing it upside down as Garry took it from the pile.

'That's it,' she said, dropping what was in her hand. She shuffled around until she was sitting next to him on the floor. The date of the paper was just under seven months after Kayleigh and Eleanor had left the casino.

They read the article together before Garry turned inside. 'Is that who you're after?' he asked, reaching the end.

'I suppose so.'

'"The Casino Kid",' Garry said, reading the headline. When Jessica didn't respond, he asked the question she already knew the answer to. 'Who would leave a newborn baby outside a casino?'

Jessica thought of her own circumstances, wondering how she might act if her suspicion turned out to be true. 'Someone who didn't want to get pregnant in the first place.'

'I wonder what they called the baby,' he continued, although Jessica had a pretty good idea.

She stood gingerly, paper in hand, trying not to complain about the ache in her back.

'Have you got what you need?' he asked.

'Yes and I found out one of the things I couldn't figure out – how he knew who his father was. The place where he was left was enough for him to eventually put two and two together.'

Garry seemed confused but he knew Jessica wouldn't give him specifics. As she headed for the door, he called one final question after her: 'Are you going to let him down gently?'

For a moment, Jessica thought he was talking about their killer, but then she remembered there was more than one bloke she had to deal with.

31

Jessica took a deep breath, feeling as nervous as she ever had.

'Are you all right?' Cole asked.

Jessica tried to act calmer than she felt. 'I'm fine.'

She didn't know exactly why she was so on edge but she suspected it was because of the secret she had told DCI Diamond and what it could mean. She had tried her best to convince herself that it was simply tiredness or illness.

Maybe it was.

'We've got other people who can do this,' the chief inspector added.

Jessica thought of Adam and hesitated for a moment before responding. 'I'm fine.'

He didn't seem convinced, but Cole nodded, turning his attention to Rowlands. 'And you?'

'I'm fine,' Dave said. 'We go in, tell him "You're nicked, son", then come back out and go for a pint. Easy.'

Jessica was hoping it would be that simple, even though the voice in the back of her mind was telling her something would go wrong.

Cole stepped away from them, indicating the van parked across the street. 'We can hear everything going on. If you need help, just say the word.'

Jessica and Rowlands both nodded.

'If your guy's on the front desk, grab him and go. Don't get the others involved. We've got the back covered, we all know the floor plan.' After one final look, he added: 'Okay, let's do it.'

He walked back towards the van as Jessica and Rowlands made for the door of the gentlemen's club. Dave placed his hand over the hidden microphone under his shirt, gripping it tightly. He nodded towards Jessica, who reluctantly followed his lead by covering the one clipped to her bra.

'I'm sorry for what I said to you at the school,' the constable whispered.

'It's fine.'

'Obviously it's not. You haven't spoken to me in weeks.'

Jessica released the microphone, letting him know the conversation was over. She clenched her teeth tightly, thinking of the reason she had volunteered to make the arrest. It wasn't so she could take the credit, simply as she had explained to Cole that she thought he might come quietly if they went in softly. If he didn't, they could take the harder approach.

'Did they get what we needed from his flat?' Rowlands asked, letting go of his own microphone.

'More than we hoped for.'

'So you were right?'

Jessica didn't reply, striding to the front door and pushing it open. Rowlands followed into the club that used to belong to Nicholas Long to see the man they were looking for standing in front of them, stacking glasses behind the newly installed bar.

The constable edged towards the serving hatch to the right.

'Hello, Scott,' Jessica said softly but firmly.

He seemed confused but put down the glass. 'Liam and Nicky are out back,' he replied, barely acknowledging them.

'It's you we wanted to talk to actually.'

Scott stared at her but Jessica could see in his eyes that he knew the game was up. He glanced from one officer to the other, holding his hands out to his side, palms facing towards them.

'How did you know?' he asked quietly, eyes flicking between them.

'We've been to your flat.'

Scott spoke gently, as if mindful of alerting anyone else. Jessica wondered how Nicky might take it if he knew the man who killed his father had been working a few metres away from him.

'Do you want me to come with you?'

'Yes please.'

Scott began to lower his arms slowly as Rowlands moved closer to the hatch. In a moment that seemed to take both a millisecond and an hour, Jessica knew what was going to happen; the clues had been there all along. Cole had told her the Serious Crime Division had been looking to pin illegal weapon possession on Nicholas but had never managed it.

Liam's words from days ago raced through her mind and she realised he had been trying to warn her what was going on without deliberately betraying his boss.

'. . . *He has different ideas, dangerous ideas. His dad knew what to leave at home and what to bring here . . .*'

Scott reached under the bar quicker than Dave could move and pulled out a sawn-off shotgun, bringing it to eye level to cover the constable. Rowlands stopped moving, holding his hands up in surrender.

Everything happened in slow motion, Scott slowly turning the gun around until it was pointing at her, as Dave spoke clearly: 'He's got a gun.'

It was for the benefit of the officers listening outside but Scott's face screwed up in confusion.

With the weapon facing away from him, Rowlands took a half-step forward but Jessica knew he had misjudged the situation. Before she could say anything, it was too late. Scott swung around, pointed the gun at the constable's chest, and pulled the trigger.

32

EARLIER THAT DAY

After finding out almost everything she needed, Jessica phoned Cole to tell him what she knew, asking him to set the wheels in motion for a warrant. They only had circumstantial evidence but it would probably be enough. Before that, she had one final person to visit, although she had to be quick.

Liam was stunned as he opened his front door to see Jessica standing there. She had been surprised to find he lived a few streets away from where the disturbances had been nights earlier. A large clean-up had been in force in the days since she had last been to Moss Side and there was now no trace of the burned-out cars.

'Can I come in?' Jessica asked as Liam eyed her partly out of suspicion but largely out of confusion.

He didn't speak for a few moments, instead tilting his head as if he would somehow be able to understand her true motive that way. Eventually, he waved her in before poking his head out of the front door to have a look around. She guessed cooperating with the police wasn't the most popular of choices in this particular area.

Jessica walked through to a kitchen that was so clean,

she automatically assumed someone else lived there. It was only when she asked him if they were alone that he told her he lived by himself. She sat on a stool next to a table in the centre of the room that was so tall her feet couldn't touch the floor, leaving her uncomfortable and unbalanced.

Liam didn't bother to sit, pacing from one side of the kitchen to the other. 'You shouldn't be here,' he said.

'You didn't have to let me in.'

'I didn't know what you were here for. It's safer to talk indoors than it is to be seen with one of you out there.'

'Why do you think I'm here?'

Jessica didn't think he would answer but figured it was worth a try. She guessed he could probably reveal any number of things if he wanted to.

He said nothing, stopping pacing to lean against a counter top. 'I've got to go to work soon.'

'Where were you on the night Nicholas Long died?' Jessica asked.

She saw his nose twitch but his reply was almost instant. 'I was playing computer games with Scott.'

'At whose house?'

'His. I told you that.'

'What games did you play?'

Liam shook his head, breathing loudly. 'Football probably.'

'Which team did you play as?'

'I don't know, different ones. What does it matter?'

He wasn't getting flustered by the questions but was certainly struggling not to raise his voice, even though she doubted it would sound any more menacing because of how high-pitched it was.

'I spent this morning going through CCTV footage,' Jessica lied. 'It's taken us ages because there's hardly any around but considering you left together – and spent the early hours of the morning together – it's pretty strange there's footage of each of you going your separate ways.'

Liam didn't speak, drumming his fingers on the counter. Jessica resisted the urge to look towards the knife rack she had seen on the way in, even though it was closer to her than him, desperate to trust her instincts.

'I don't believe you,' he said eventually, although he didn't sound so sure.

'I can take you to the station and show you if you'd prefer?'

She knew she had him when his eyes flickered towards the back door. As quickly as they had shifted, they moved back to her. Liam's voice was shaking as he finally replied. 'It's not what you think.'

'What do I think?'

Liam's eyes continued darting from side to side. Jessica could see his grip on the counter hardening, the muscles in his shoulders rippling through his shirt.

'I didn't kill him.'

'I never said you did.'

Liam paused, not knowing if he should believe her. 'I . . . can't tell you.'

Jessica hadn't known for certain Liam's alibi had been made up but she had suspected it ever since things began to fall into place.

'Maybe you should try me?'

Liam's upper arms were beginning to shake but Jessica felt a calmness, unthreatened despite his size. 'You wouldn't understand what it's like,' he said. 'It's not easy being like this when you're supposed to be a tough guy.'

Jessica was initially confused, thinking he meant his size. When he realised she didn't get it, Liam pushed himself up from the unit, picking up a tea towel from a cupboard handle and beginning to dry up. Jessica turned to look at him but he was deliberately facing the other way.

'There's this old public toilet block on my way home,' he said. 'I walk back after work most evenings and it's at that time of night when hardly anyone is around.'

He reached to place a mug onto a shelf above him.

'And that's where you were that night?'

'Yes.'

'Does Scott know about what you do there?'

'Yes.'

'So why did he insist you were with him?'

Liam turned to face her, holding a second mug in one hand and the tea towel in the other. 'Because I asked him to. He's not going to get into trouble, is he?'

Jessica didn't know what to say. Liam not wanting his friend to get into trouble was admirable as she realised how clever Scott had been.

It was still circumstantial but with the theory that Kayleigh was pregnant with Nicholas's baby – however willing or not she had been in the process – the thought had occurred to Jessica that perhaps there was another son out there.

That hadn't given her all of the answers but because Kayleigh had never registered a child, Jessica guessed it must have been given up or left somewhere anonymously. As Izzy checked the adoption records, Jessica went through the newspaper archives with Garry, assuming one of them would find something.

She wouldn't have discovered any of that had it not been for the initial idea which led her to Kenneth. When she had seen Nicky's gums bleeding, Jessica realised it was the third time she had seen blood in the club. Nicholas had had a nosebleed – but Scott had been sucking his finger on the very first occasion she had visited the place, throwing a reddened tissue in the bin as he tried to stop the cut bleeding. As they left, his finger was still in his mouth, the blood flow refusing to stop.

Kenneth's explanation for why the bleeding could run in the family wasn't proof of anything but Jessica couldn't think past Scott being Kayleigh and Nicholas's child – even if he had an alibi for everything.

Of course, as with his mother, Scott knew that if you wanted someone to do something for you, the best way was to ensure they thought it was their own idea.

Liam had made it easy because he'd told Scott the secret about what he got up to in the public toilets after hours. Scott just had to bide his time until an evening where Nicholas was particularly drunk and then he could act, safe in the knowledge that when Liam saw what had happened the following day, he would contact him in a panic knowing he didn't have an alibi.

Scott had ensured he had a reason why he couldn't be the killer and hadn't even needed to ask.

When Jessica didn't reply, Liam repeated his question with more edge to his voice. 'He's not going to get into trouble, is he? It wasn't Scott's idea. I should be the one in trouble.'

'He won't get in trouble for this,' Jessica replied.

Liam didn't realise the specific meaning of what she'd said; the possibility that Scott could be involved in Nicholas's murder seemingly hadn't occurred to him.

He put the mug on the shelf and placed the tea towel on the draining board. 'I know you have no reason to believe me but it is the truth. I wouldn't have hurt Nicholas, I promise.'

Jessica started to move towards the door.

'Is that it?' Liam asked, surprised.

'Yes, but I might need to come by the club later. Are you all going to be there?'

'I suppose so, I'm opening up.'

'What time will you be there until?'

'Probably one in the morning or so.'

'Everyone? You, Scott, Nicky and the girls?'

'Yes.'

Jessica reached into her pocket and took out a business card, flipping it over and taking out a pen to write her mobile number on it. 'If any staff member leaves, let me know.'

'Nicky?'

Jessica said nothing but she could understand why he thought that. 'Anyone,' she repeated.

She walked quickly towards the front door. As her hand closed around the handle Liam spoke quietly. 'Just remember everything I told you at the club,' he said.

Jessica didn't know exactly what he meant but, as her phone began to ring, she knew it would be Cole to say the warrant had been granted.

33

Two plain-clothes officers had been sent to the club to make sure Scott was there and didn't leave as Cole, Jessica and a specialist team raided his flat. Jessica thought hanging around a strip club sounded like easy work if you could get it.

Scott had a mortgage on a flat on the edge of an estate bordering Eccles and Salford. When Cole had given her the address over the phone, Jessica winced as she knew the area well. The estate was in the shadow of a large tower block. When she had started in uniform, a large number of their call-outs were to the district. Although things were a lot better now, back then a few of her colleagues had referred to the area as 'needlepoint'. Officers had dreaded the Friday and Saturday night reports of fights or over-doses.

When they had confirmation of where Scott was, the tactical entry team got them into his property as discreetly as possible using a drill as opposed to a battering ram, since they didn't want to risk alerting anyone else if at all possible. Although it was still loud, no one appeared to notice them in the fading light. Jessica supposed that, given the area, the last thing most people wanted to do was question their neighbours about why they might be making so much noise.

Three other members of the search team entered first, with Jessica and Cole at the rear, leaving one final person to hold the door closed from the inside and at least give the impression it hadn't been forced.

The front door opened directly into a living room. As the other officers moved into the rest of the property, Jessica and Cole began in the lounge.

'I don't get why we didn't just arrest him?' Jessica whispered.

'Why are you whispering?' the chief inspector replied out loud, although not quite at full volume.

Jessica moved across to a cabinet next to the television and opened the top drawer. Inside were rows of computer games. 'Why don't we just arrest him?' she repeated.

'The super reckons that if we're wrong, it's easier to apologise for a mix-up here than it is to be sued for wrongful arrest. It's cover-your-back thinking.'

That sounded about right, though Jessica didn't reply, seeing as he might as well have said 'if *you're* wrong'.

As she closed the drawer and looked around, she thought Scott's flat was typical of someone his age. There was a large television, with various electrical items underneath, but little else in the way of decor. She tried to remember what her priorities might have been when she was in her early twenties but it seemed such a long time ago.

She left the chief inspector in the living room, walking through the closest door into what turned out to be a kitchen. Her eyes were drawn to the grubby rings on the top of the cooker. She skimmed through the cupboards, not looking for anything specifically – even if the array of dry and tinned foods was unerringly close to what she used to buy before moving in with Adam.

There were many occasions where she almost felt guilty for her upbringing, as if having two parents who cared for her was something she should apologise for. So many people used their lack of a settled family life as the reason for the actions they chose to make. She felt an urge to try to see things from another angle but Scott had done things you couldn't just say sorry for.

As Jessica wandered into a hallway, she saw one of the other officers walking towards her. Without speaking, he beckoned her into a bedroom, pointing to a shoebox that had been pulled out from under the bed.

'I think that's what you're after,' he said quietly.

Jessica sat on the floor, leaning against the bed. She could see instantly what was on top of the box. She re- membered Leviticus Bryan's words: 'He keeps impeccable records of everything; staff, accounts, who owes him money, the lot.'

She was holding a sheet of paper that had clearly come from Nicholas's filing cabinets. It was on the type of printer paper she remembered from school: perforated holes along either side, and rigid grey type.

As Jessica read, she wondered at which point Scott had figured out who his father was. He had been left outside Nicholas's casino and then taken into care but it was perhaps no wonder that when he was old enough to understand what had happened to him as a baby, he felt drawn back towards the man who owned that place.

Perhaps he recognised the way they both bled? Maybe he saw something facially?

She wondered how driven she might be to find out who she was if that was the only clue she started with.

Once Scott had discovered who his father was, he had seemingly turned his attention to finding his mother's identity.

The pages were dated from over twenty years beforehand and listed Eleanor and Kayleigh's birthdays, salaries, a list of payments and their then addresses. Someone, presumably Nicholas, had added four stars in the top right corner of Kayleigh's page.

At first, Jessica was confused by what it might be for but then the horror of the person Nicholas had been came rushing back. She wondered how many other women in his files had similar ratings next to their name.

Scott would have worked his way backwards through Nicholas's files. The final payment on Kayleigh and Eleanor's documents coincided with a few months before Scott was born. He would have seen Nicholas in action, knowing how he was with the dancers. It wouldn't have taken much to put two and two together.

Jessica glanced towards the box to see if there were any other similar papers but there was only what was in her hands. Eleanor had told her that Nicholas didn't like losing staff, so it was perhaps no surprise that she and Kayleigh were the first two possibilities Scott had been able to narrow his potential mother down to – hardly anyone else left voluntarily.

Jessica peered up to see Cole standing in the door. She

offered the papers to him, turning her attention to the other contents in the box. As he sat on the bed close to her, Jessica picked up a hairbrush and turned it over in her hands. There were still a few hairs entwined in the needles but she put it to one side, eyes drawn to the envelope underneath.

Inside were three letters which Jessica read and then handed to the chief inspector. After scanning, he seemed slightly confused but Jessica showed him the hairbrush.

'I've never heard of home DNA tests,' he said.

Given the number of television talk shows where most ended with such results being announced, it was easy to see where Scott might have got the idea from.

'Adam was offered a job in one of these places,' she said. 'There are a few around this area. You send them a mouth swab, or some blood or, I guess from this, some hair, and they'll see if there's a match for you. I have no idea how accurate they are but you would have to assume they work. Adam didn't fancy it, even though the money was good.'

Cole glanced back to the letters before replying. 'Perhaps Scott broke into Eleanor's house in the first place simply to find something of hers that could be tested? He didn't know whether Eleanor or Kayleigh was his mother.'

'I guess so. They said there was nothing missing but then so did Kayleigh. You wouldn't expect something like a brush to go missing from a break-in.'

'What about Oliver?'

Jessica sighed, thinking about the poor boy's parents.

'Only Scott will be able to tell us. Maybe he was in the wrong place at the wrong time? Perhaps Scott flew into a rage, thinking Eleanor was Oliver's mother and the boy had stolen his life? Either that, or he was simply practising. It's not easy suffocating someone but I suppose, if that's what you want to do, you're better starting with someone skinny and easy to overpower, then working your way up. Oliver's body was always the one that confused us because he had no link to Kayleigh or Nicholas. Because Scott didn't know which of the two women was his mum, he broke into Kayleigh's too. Dumping the body confused us because we thought it was connected to something it wasn't.'

The chief inspector pointed to the first printout. 'But how did he find out where they live now? This information is all out of date.'

Jessica shrugged but, judging by the way Georgia had found Adam with such ease, it wasn't too great a stretch to imagine that at least one of the women was traceable on the Internet.

'Did you read the final letter?' Jessica asked.

Cole held it up. 'That's how he knew for sure Nicholas was his father, because he got a sample tested.'

'He probably saw the way Nicholas was with all the women that worked at the club. There can't have been a shortage of things to take from his boss that could be sent off for analysis, especially with the nosebleeds. That gave the confirmation of who his father was, then he wanted to find his mother.'

'I can't imagine what it must be like to kill both of your parents,' the chief inspector said, tailing off.

Jessica turned back to the box, pulling out a browner, crustier version of the newspaper article she had read about the baby being left outside the casino. 'I guess neither of us know what it's like to grow up not knowing your parents. You must spend all your time wondering who you are.'

Cole didn't speak for a while but she could guess he was thinking something similar to her – a near-understanding of what Scott had done. He killed his parents because they hadn't wanted him. Whether he knew his mother had become pregnant as she was trying to pay back a debt was something only he could answer.

Jessica stifled thoughts of what could be inside her as she heaved herself up from the floor, handing the box to the chief inspector.

'I think it's time to go pick him up,' Cole said.

'We should probably wait until the club is closing and empty. He's got no reason to assume we know. We've got people watching him.'

Cole nodded in agreement. 'I'll need to talk to the super anyway, he might want to go in heavy but I will mention the fact there would be lots of people around if he goes in straight away.'

'I'll go in,' Jessica said. 'I think he'll probably come quietly if we do it softly.'

'What makes you think that?'

Jessica shrugged. 'I don't know, instinct.'

34

Jessica sat in the hospital's waiting room staring at the floor. Her response to Cole ran endlessly through her mind. *Instinct.*

She couldn't have been more wrong.

Not only that but Liam had told her not once but twice what might happen, at first hinting in the club and then in his flat, telling her to remember what he had said.

'. . . *He has different ideas, dangerous ideas. His dad knew what to leave at home and what to bring here . . .*'

She could feel Izzy looking at her from the seat opposite but couldn't meet her gaze. Instead she focused on a spot on the floor, following the cracks in between the tiles and trying to forget the situation she had been responsible for.

Longsight was one of the rougher areas of Manchester, where gang violence and gun crime were higher than anywhere else in the district, but even so, she had rarely seen anyone other than an officer with a gun and had spotted more officers with firearms in airports than she ever had while on duty. The official report would almost certainly say the chance of Scott pulling out a firearm was minimal but that wasn't the point – she felt guilty for not foreseeing what could have happened.

Jessica doubted there would ever be a time where she

forgot what took place in the reception area of Nicholas Long's club. Thanks to television programmes and films, you expected a gunshot to be loud but nothing could prepare you for the way the noise seemed to suck everything else out of the room. Your ears were left ringing, the shock clouding your thoughts to such a degree that you weren't sure if what you saw was real.

The fact the gun had gone off only sunk in when Jessica saw the blood splattering across the bar and wall. Flecks landed on her face, making her shiver with shock.

By the time she had reached to her cheek to wipe it away, everything was over as officers stormed through one door, Liam and Nicky rushing through the other. She could see their lips moving, accusing eyes staring towards her, but nothing seemed to make sense as the echoes of the gunshot bounced around her head.

Jessica blinked back to the present as she heard the nearby doors clunking open. She glanced up hoping to see one face but instead it was Cole who walked through. He had long since lost his tie, and his shirt buttons were half-undone, patches of grey hair spidering through. His face already told the story but he spoke the words anyway.

'He's dead.'

Jessica looked up to catch Izzy's eye but she was staring at the chief inspector.

'They say he was gone by the time he got here,' Cole added. Jessica stared back at the floor, even as Cole began to talk directly to her. 'It's not your fault, Jess.'

She knew he would say that but it didn't matter what anyone else told her, she blamed herself.

'What's going to happen now?' Izzy asked as the chief inspector sat on a seat two away from Jessica.

'There'll be the usual inquiry,' he said. 'Nicky Long will be in serious trouble because of the weapons on his premises. He's already in custody but not saying much.'

Aside from a couple of people chatting quietly in the far corner of the room, there was a hush as Jessica refused to look up from the floor. It was only when she heard Izzy giggle that she realised there were footsteps nearby. She glanced up, not knowing what to expect, but couldn't stop herself from laughing at the sight which greeted her. She even thought she heard a gentle snigger escape from the chief inspector.

When it was clear no one else was going to say anything, Jessica figured she might as well take it upon herself.

'That's an extreme way of covering a bald patch,' she snorted.

Rowlands stood in the aisle with a bandage wrapped around his head, his arm in a sling. There was a large red graze across his chin and one of his eyes had blackened. 'Thanks for your sympathy. You too,' he added, nodding towards Izzy, who was holding her hand in front of her mouth to stop herself laughing.

'What have you done to yourself?' Cole asked sensibly.

'I've broken my arm in two places and the doctor says I've got concussion. Is Scott . . . ?'

The chief inspector nodded. 'Dead before he arrived.'

Izzy was looking at Rowlands. 'I'm still not entirely sure what happened,' she said.

He nodded towards Jessica, saying she had the answer.

Although she wasn't keen on constantly recanting how she had messed up, Jessica figured it was a story she would be telling frequently over the coming weeks to various high-up people.

Rowlands sat next to Izzy with a wince Jessica was convinced he was putting on.

She took a deep breath. 'I thought Scott would come quietly because he had nothing to gain by not doing so. There was nowhere for him to go. What no one realised was that Nicky had brought guns into the club and there was a shotgun under the counter. As Dave stepped in to arrest Scott, he yanked it out and pulled the trigger.'

Izzy looked at the man next to her, who Jessica noticed was sporting a pained expression. She wondered how long he would be able to get sympathy for it. 'It happened really quickly but it seemed to explode in his hands. There was this enormous bang and within a blink it was over. Scott was sort of blasted backwards into the fridges. Blood went everywhere.'

'Ballistics have the gun and will look at what's left of it,' Cole said. 'One of the guys on site said something about it possibly happening if guns aren't cleaned but I wouldn't know enough to say.'

'So what happened to you?' Izzy asked, nodding towards Dave.

Rowlands looked at Jessica, rolling his eyes. 'Go on . . .'

Jessica wasn't particularly in the mood for joking around but she couldn't look at the bandage around his head without smiling.

'When the gun went off, there was an enormous noise but I was further away and it wasn't pointing at me. Dave stumbled backwards and fell over a table. At first I thought he'd been shot because of the way he went down. It was only afterwards I realised he'd jumped because of the bang.'

Rowlands threw his hands in the air. 'He was pointing a gun at me, I thought I'd been shot!'

Although he had a point, it didn't stop Izzy giggling. 'Aww, did the big bang make poor Davey Wavey fall over,' she teased.

'How did you break your arm?' Jessica asked.

The constable looked away, wanting to downplay things. 'It was trapped between me and the table as I fell.'

Jessica met Izzy's eyes and knew they were both thinking the same thing. The constable said it first. 'So basically, you broke your arm because you're a bit of a fatty?'

Rowlands looked at Cole, annoyance on his face. 'This is workplace bullying.'

The chief inspector nodded before breaking into a grin. 'Noted, although as you are on injury leave and this isn't our workplace, I'm not sure I can take any action . . .'

Jessica was stifling a laugh but Izzy didn't hold back, cackling so loudly the receptionist on the far side of the room shushed them.

'Can we go for a walk?' Jessica said quietly, standing and looking at Rowlands.

Izzy and the chief inspector took the hint and didn't

move, although Cole told her she would have to give a proper statement when she'd had some sleep. She knew that would only be the start. Scott would now never be able to respond to their unanswered questions. She wondered what she would be able to tell Oliver's parents for closure.

Rowlands stood gingerly, with Izzy smacking his backside and telling him to stop faking it. Jessica led him through a set of double doors, following the signs towards the cafe. Inside there were half-a-dozen people sitting around tables. Although it was the early hours, Jessica could smell bacon as they approached the counter.

'What do you want?' she asked.

'Are you buying?'

'Yep, you can have whatever you want up to a maximum of four English pounds and fifty pence.'

The weary-looking server filled two bread rolls with bacon and although the bread was slightly stale and the meat overcooked, it was as good as anything Jessica could remember eating.

She sat opposite Rowlands but neither spoke as they ate. When she had finished, Jessica pushed back in her chair, watching Dave closely. It was impossible not to smile given the state of his bandage.

'What?' he said, licking his fingers.

'That's ridiculous.'

Dave nodded, although he looked tired and his expression was serious. 'What are we going to do?'

Jessica didn't know how to phrase things, so instead

spoke without thinking. 'I love you too, just not like that. We've been mates for ages, we've done all sorts together but I don't see you in that way.'

'I know.'

'I'm in love with Adam.'

'I know.'

'But we can still be mates and have fun working together.'

'We can't go back to the way we were though, can we? I can't un-say something.'

Jessica picked at a rogue piece of meat between her teeth. 'I'm sure we'll live, there's no way I'm going to be able to look at that bandage and not take the piss.'

Rowlands didn't reply and Jessica realised she had gone too far. 'You'll be able to talk to someone,' she added more softly.

'I will if you will. He pointed the gun at you too.'

Jessica didn't reply, standing and offering her arm to help him to his feet. 'Come on, it's bedtime.'

Rowlands smiled, heaving himself up. 'You know what's happening this weekend, don't you?'

'No.'

'Hugo and Caroline are off camping. I think *she* thinks he knows what he's doing. He'll do what he always does and wing it. The last I heard, he'd bought this pop-up tent from a charity shop for three quid.'

As they began walking towards the exit, Jessica laughed. 'I think she's had a fascination with him ever since he drew her on that napkin at her wedding. I lived with Caroline for almost ten years and if there's one thing she's not suited to, it's outdoor life. Let alone in a tent that cost under a fiver.'

'I'll tell you his side of the story if you share hers?'

Jessica held the door open for him, linking her hand through his good arm as they walked.

'You're on, DC Rowlands.'

35

Jessica sat opposite Cole peering around the walls of his office. The framed certificates and commendations were the same as ever but something felt different. The chief inspector put his desk phone down and apologised before fixing her with a gaze she could only describe as fatherly. She wasn't sure if she liked it.

'It wasn't your fault,' he said gently.

'It was.'

He leant back in his seat and put his hands behind his head, speaking firmly. 'I hate to be the one to tell you this but things at this station don't actually revolve around you. Regardless of what your opinions were, if I didn't agree, I wouldn't have suggested anything to the superintendent. If he didn't agree, it would have occurred differently.'

'What's going to happen?' Jessica asked.

'We've got a few results back from the gun. They can't be sure because it exploded but our people reckon it was old and hadn't been looked after properly. They say it's incredibly rare but, if you don't keep them clean, the bullet or cartridge can become blocked in the barrel. The pressure still has to go somewhere, so it explodes. A piece of the barrel went through Scott's skull, another just below his heart. You and Dave are lucky none of it came your way.'

'What else?'

'We've confirmed that Nicholas was Scott's father and Kayleigh his mother.'

'What about Oliver?'

The chief inspector shook his head sadly. 'We'll never know. He was probably in the wrong place at the wrong time.'

Jessica said nothing, although the silence seemed apt. There was no way she was going to let anyone else have the job of having to tell the teenager's parents what had happened.

'My wife and I are getting a divorce,' the chief inspector said suddenly, his words quiet and deliberate. 'We've told the kids but there's a lot to sort out. She's going to have the house, with the children staying there, but then we don't quite have the money for me to get anything too comfortable. It's so complicated but I don't want to do anything that will make it harder for them.'

Jessica let his words sink in before replying. 'I'm sure you've done it for the right reasons.'

'It was my idea in the end.'

Jessica didn't know what to say although she suspected he was telling her simply because he had no one else to talk to.

Before she could come up with something sympathetic, the chief inspector sat up more formally. 'I've been talking to the chief superintendent this morning and we'd like you to take Jason's job as inspector now he's officially told us he isn't returning. We'll have to do things through the right channels, obviously, but it will all be for appearances. The job's yours if you want it'.

As Jessica remained silent, he added: 'You don't have to tell us straight away'.

'It was only a few days ago I messed up and nearly got Dave killed.'

'I already said that wasn't your fault but if it wasn't for you, we would never have reached this point. We would simply have three unsolved killings on our files.'

Jessica didn't want to argue. 'I didn't even apply,' she said.

Cole shrugged dismissively. 'Who else is there?' After a pause, he added: 'It's a reasonable amount of extra money and fewer weekends.'

Neither of those factors influenced Jessica. 'Can I let you know?' she asked. 'I've got two things I need to do first.'

Despite being on injury leave, Dave joined Jessica and Izzy in the pub around the corner from the station. His every movement was punctuated with an 'ooh' or an 'aah' but Izzy was having none of it.

'You do know you weren't actually shot, don't you?' she said.

'I still broke my arm.'

'Yes, but only because you eat too many pies. Stop whingeing and come back to work.'

Jessica sat quietly, thinking through the best way to

phrase things. The other constables realised she wasn't joining in, a clear sign something was up.

'Are you okay?' Izzy asked.

Jessica picked up her pint of lemonade, holding it in front of her face as a shield.

'I'm not married,' she said quietly. 'I should have told you before.'

Izzy and Dave glanced at each other, confused.

'But you did go to Vegas?' Izzy said.

Jessica nodded, remembering. 'We went there wanting to get married and we sort of did. We were checking out of the hotel at the end when a police officer stopped us and said they had arrested the chapel owner because his licence had run out. Everything happened: the ceremony, the holiday, our wedding night . . . but it was taken away because he wasn't legally allowed to marry us. The officer said they'd arrested the guy – apparently it's a scam that has been building out there, they take your money and by the time you know anything's wrong, your holiday is over. He said they'd help us find somewhere to get it done legally but we had to go. We'd already exchanged rings and got used to it. We're married in every way other than the one that matters – legally.'

For a moment, neither of the constables spoke. Eventually Dave broke the silence. 'What are you going to do?'

Jessica knew they would have an understanding from now on. Things might not be exactly as they were before but they were both adults – and she still wanted to be his friend. She could feel Izzy watching her, asking silently what she was going to do about the other thing.

'We'll probably talk about it tonight,' Jessica added, answering both of their questions. 'But first we've got something else to sort out.'

Jessica put the stick from the pregnancy test on the coffee table and sat next to Adam on the sofa. He snaked a protective arm around her.

'Did you wee on that?' he asked.

'What else would I have done with it?'

'I was just wondering who's going to clean the pee-stain off the table.'

Jessica nestled her head on his shoulder, forcing him to hold her tightly. She could feel his heart beating quickly through his clothes.

'So you finally told them what really happened in America,' Adam said.

'It took me long enough. I suppose I liked the idea that everyone thought I was married.'

'What do you want to do about it? Shall we try again?'

Jessica wrapped her arms around him tightly, squeezing until he grunted. She didn't answer, not knowing what she wanted. Jessica counted every beat of his heart, wondering how many times it was going to pulse before the three minutes were up. Eventually, he tapped her gently on the shoulder, saying it was time.

Jessica released him but could feel her own heart pounding as she reached forward and picked up the stick, deliberately holding the indicator bar downwards.

'Well?' Adam asked.

'Well what?'

'What does it say?'

'What do you want it to say?'

Adam grinned. 'I'm not sure the world's ready for another mini-you.'

Jessica smiled back. 'But . . . ?'

'. . . But, it would be pretty fun inflicting another you on everyone.'

Jessica took a deep breath and could feel her hand trembling. She knew her life could change based on what was on the other side of the stick. A lifetime of being scared of children had suddenly been replaced by a surprising feeling of being comfortable with one of her own.

She pressed her thumb across the result and turned it over. 'Are you ready?'

Adam grinned. 'For you? Always.'

Afterword

If you've not finished the book then you should probably go back to wherever you were, because there are spoilers ahead.

I always say that, because I'm one of those people who flick to the end first. I don't know what's wrong with me: it's like a disease.

Anyway, here's a conversation:

Me (talking to my wife): 'You know this book I'm writing? I kind of feel that to make it as authentic as possible I'm going to have to do a little more close-up research than usual.'

My wife: 'Okay . . .'

Me: 'Large parts are set in a strip club, so I think I'm going to have to spend six or seven months undercover. I'll probably need to visit two or three times a week just to make sure I get the feel of it right.'

My wife: 'Er . . .'

Hands up – how many people have ever had the above conversation?

No, me neither, but I'm sure it would have been interesting.

The idea for *Thicker than Water* came from various smaller ideas. A few years ago, I had a very minor operation on my leg to remove a piece of grit or something that had become caught under the skin and created a lump. It was simple enough – in–out, go home and watch the telly. Except that it didn't stop bleeding for three days.

With that, I started looking for reasons why it wouldn't stop and stumbled across von Willebrand disease. On the third day, my cut healed itself and I've never had anything like that since but something about the condition stuck with me.

Another aspect of the story is something I should now confess to. When I was at school, a kid I knew showed me how to get through a closed fire escape in much the same way as I describe in this book. Our classroom used to be locked at lunchtimes but we would sneak in, move a few things around, sketch symbols on the board, and then leave. The key is to be subtle: small changes, nothing big. Because the room was locked, no one ever figured out how it happened, with theories of ghosts and poltergeists abounding. Twenty-odd years later and it's time to hold my hand up. It was me and the other person who will remain nameless. Sorry. It was funny at the time though.

There are, as ever, a bunch of people to thank for getting the book to you. My agent, Nicola, of course. I've seen her little office with its wonderful view of a brick wall and a roof. There's a car park if you squint. It's what dreams are made of but she whiles away there, haranguing people to make sure I can continue to write these things and that they get into your hands in as good a state as possible.

Then there is the Macmillan crew: Trisha, Natasha, Andy, Jodie, Sandra, Susan, Tom and a few others I've hopefully not forgotten. Imagine having me email you every day to ask what's going on with this or that, or to nitpick about stuff. That's what they have to put up with.

Lastly, as I've said before, thanks to my wife. No Louise = no Jessica. Book 7 is set on a Caribbean island[*] so I'm off for my six months' research. See you soon.

Kerry Wilkinson

---
[*] It's not really.

Readers' Questions & Answers

Bearing in mind your west country roots, do you think Jessica will ever venture to the south-west?

– Duncan Partridge, Yeovil

I'm not sure that Jessica's driving could handle the narrow, winding roads! In all seriousness, I think she has enough places to explore closer to Manchester for a fair while yet.

Have you got used to seeing your name in print on your books yet and how does that feel?

– Fiona Douglas, Wallasey

I handle a lot of these things with a shrug and, for the most part, people I know find it stranger than I do. I worked in journalism for a decade before writing fiction, so I'm used to bylines. By the time something comes out, it can be years since I finished writing it, so I'm usually concentrating on whatever my next project is.

Did you interview any police officers to help with the creation of the police work featured in the Jessica Daniel series?

– Dahviad Tierney, Ireland

Yes, but not just police officers because so many of the stories involve other departments and organisations. A lot of the research is informal but I try to write about people rather than institutions. That means that I'm usually looking for a way to write around the paperwork and officiousness. I'll usually have pages of notes for research and then try to use as little of it as possible, while still making the story broadly realistic.

If you could choose a cast for a film or TV series to adapt your Jessica Daniel books, who would you want to play the main characters?
– Andy King, Nairn & Kate Brown, Basingstoke

There are two actresses who resemble Jessica as I see her. Rebecca Hall (who has been in *Red Riding*, *The Town*, *The Awakening* and *Iron Man 3*) and Oona Chaplin (who was in *Game of Thrones* and *Dates*).

Are you ever going to spin-off any of the characters into something else?
– Sarah Smith, Hampshire

I've always liked the idea of having a world around Jessica by which she's influenced and that she has an influence upon. I have a stand alone crime story called *Down Among the Dead Men*, which looks at what happens between two warring crime bosses in Manchester. It's within Jessica's world and the ramifications of that is something that will be touched upon in later Jessica books. That should be out in 2014.

Andrew, the private investigator from *Playing with Fire*, will definitely be back in his own series too. When I first plotted that story, he was a lot less likeable in the initial notes but he ended up sticking with me.

You're not going to stop writing Jessica books, are you?

   – *Fiona Rodgers, The Algarve, Portugal*

I'll keep writing her for as long as I have ideas of what she might be up to in her life. Rest assured, that will be for a fair few books yet – although it's also nice to work on other things.

Where do you do your writing?

   – *Sam Hudson, Trafford*

Largely on my sofa at home but I'm pretty good at switching off and getting on with it. I've written on trains, planes, my parents' garden, hotel rooms, on holiday – anywhere and everywhere, really.

Would you get on with Jessica?

   – *Lizzie Robertson, Ontario, Canada*

This question threw me a little but . . . probably not. Not at first anyway. I'm generally quite quiet unless I know people, plus she's something of an acquired taste. Give it a few beers and I'm sure we'd be getting on famously.

What made you want to write?

   – *Blake McDonald, Dorset*

I was at Robin Hood's Bay in Yorkshire with my wife and we were listening to Ricky Gervais on the radio. It dawned on me that he is one of the most famous comedians/writers/actors in the world – but nobody knew who he was until he turned forty. I always liked Simon Pegg and Edgar Wright for doing their own thing with *Spaced* and *Shaun of the Dead*. Nobody offered them the careers they have now; they each sat down and wrote a TV series. I had not long turned thirty and figured I'd try to make something happen for myself.

I'd been doing the same job for a few years and wanted to try something different. If you want to do something in life then, unless you marry a royal or have an MP for a parent, you'll probably have to make it happen for yourself. I'm not afraid of failing so I thought I'd give it a try. If writing novels hadn't have come off, I would've found something else to have a go at.

What did you want to be when you were young?

– Lily Gray, Newcastle-upon-Tyne

Something sporty, with the only problem being that I was – at best – only *OK* at most sports. I finished fourth in some 400m county race in Somerset, despite leading on the final bend. I was mediocre at football and it was only really cricket I had any degree of ability at – if you can call it that. I did once score a century at Fulwood & Broughton CC, which is about as good as it got.

With a distinct lack of talent, I figured the next best thing was to try to become a sports journalist, which is what I spent ten years doing after university.

What is your favourite film?

– Shaun Wright, Blackburn

Back to the Future. When my parents first got a video player – a top-loader – my mum recorded it off the TV, cleverly cutting out the adverts. I watched that tape to death and have seen the film so many times. It has the perfect balance of comedy, action and drama – plus it's not afraid to invent its own rules.

It tells you how time travel works and you just accept it. I generally think with science fiction that the more you explain the technology, the weaker your story. If your characters are strong enough, readers and viewers will forgive you most things.

Do you share any personality traits or interests with Jessica?
– Trisha Jackson, Pan Macmillan

I think we both look for humour in most situations, even those that are darker. It's something journalists and public workers such as police officers and paramedics have to have because of all the things you see and do. She says a lot of things that I might only think but keep to myself. When I first started writing her, I was hesitant about letting too much of that out but now everything goes in.